"A luscious novel that opens new doors and brings new obsessions to the Gothic and romantic mythology of the vampire: queer sensibility, the secret Polari language, sectarian violence, the Moon and the Tarot, images as precious as Symbolist paintings. It leaves you with a strange nostalgia and a scent of what has been lost."

Mariana Enriquez, author of *Our Share of Night*

"Utterly astounding, beautiful, and audacious."

Ally Wilkes, Bram Stoker award®-nominated author of *All the White Spaces* and *Where the Dead Wait*

"A haunting, surreal examination of monstrousness and fate, this remarkable queer horror novel is evocative and powerfully chilling."

Eric LaRocca, author of *At Dark, I Become Loathsome*

"A restless meditation on vampirism through the competing lenses of the moon-fixed dreamer and the mad scientist."

Noah Medlock, author of *A Botanical Daughter*

"This exquisite novel is sure to haunt readers long after they have finished the final page."

Johanna van Veen, author of *My Darling Dreadf...*

"A unique voice and vision. Morstabilini puts a fresh spin on vampire mythos and the Gothic genre and delivers something unforgettable with this novel."

A. C. Wise, author of *The Ghost Sequences*

"*A Blood as Bright as the Moon* is such a charismatic book, vivid and audacious, and I love its hopeful heart."

Aliya Whiteley, Shirley Jackson and Clarke award-nominated author of *The Beauty*

"A breath of fresh air to the vampire genre!"

Tobi Ogundiran, award-winning author of the Guardian of the Gods duology

"A bold new entry into the vampire genre. I've never read a novel that so deftly merges brutality and hope in each and every line."

Erin E. Adams, author of *Jackal*

"Sharp with intricate danger. An imaginative Gothic by way of Catriona Ward and a horrific theatrical fairy tale."

Hailey Piper, Bram Stoker award®-winning author of *Queen of Teeth* and *All the Hearts You Eat*

BLOOD AS BRIGHT AS THE MOON

ANDREA MORSTABILINI

TITAN BOOKS

A Blood as Bright as the Moon
Print edition ISBN: 9781803369754
E-book edition ISBN: 9781803369761

Published by Titan Books
A division of Titan Publishing Group Ltd
144 Southwark Street, London SE1 0UP
www.titanbooks.com

First edition: September 2025
10 9 8 7 6 5 4 3 2 1

This is a work of fiction. All of the characters, organizations, and events
portrayed in this novel are either products of the author's imagination or
are used fictitiously. Any resemblance to actual persons, living or dead
(except for satirical purposes), is entirely coincidental.

© Andrea Morstabilini 2025

Andrea Morstabilini asserts the moral right
to be identified as the author of this work.

No part of this publication may be reproduced, stored in a retrieval
system, or transmitted, in any form or by any means without the prior
written permission of the publisher, nor be otherwise circulated in any
form of binding or cover other than that in which it is published and
without a similar condition being imposed on the subsequent purchaser.

A CIP catalogue record for this title is available from the British Library.

EU RP (for authorities only)
eucomply OÜ, Pärnu mnt. 139b-14, 11317 Tallinn, Estonia
hello@eucompliancepartner.com, +3375690241

Set in Adobe Garamond Pro by Richard Mason.

Printed and bound by CPI (UK) Ltd, Croydon, CR0 4YY.

TO BARTOSZ, WHO IS HOME

The purity of the unclouded moon
Has flung its arrowy shaft upon the floor.
Seven centuries have passed and it is pure,
The blood of innocence has left no stain.

W. B. Yeats, *Blood and the Moon*, III, vv. 1–4

… cleave to no faith when faith brings blood.

Arthur Miller, *The Crucible*

For God's sake let us sit upon the ground
And tell sad stories of the death of kings…

William Shakespeare, *Richard II*, III, ii, 155–156

I

A SOLITUDE OF CASTLES

THE GLOBE

WE LIVED IN Frankenstein, which is ironic, I guess. When I say this, I don't mean that we lived in the village—we wouldn't have lasted long. We lived in the castle atop the hill, a small mossy ruin without a roof. Its arched windows framed enough empty, egg-white sky to convince everyone that the castle was deserted, a crumbling vestige of old times, where only colonies of bats dwelt, and the occasional ghost.

That was true enough.

The village itself was not much, just a road cutting through a narrow valley, with small clumps of cream-coloured houses on either side of it, climbing the slopes of the hills with the obduracy of goats. Their slanted roofs nestled together against the woods, which in that part of the Rhine region are deep and dark and patient.

There was a repair shop by a bend in the road, and a train station with two trains passing through each day, one that went to Mannheim, and the other which ran in the opposite direction, towards Kaiserslautern. A *gasthaus* stood by the tracks, with a black knight painted on its side wall. A shallow brook snaked behind it. A little further off, past the brook, an austere, angular church loomed over the eastern part of the village. Purple briers flanked the stone steps climbing to the portal, where graceful black letters carved above the entrance announced, "How lovely is thy dwelling, O Lord," and gave the year of the church's foundation: 1871. On the left, a gravel pathway led to the graveyard, which for most of the year was more densely populated than the town it served.

In Frankenstein it didn't take long to know the faces of everyone, and I had become an expert at recognising the traits of distant relatives coming to visit for Easter, a nose in the shape of a gargoyle, a pair of legs curving outward at the knee, a beard the colour of foamy stout. It was my responsibility. As we owed our continued existence to the secrecy of it, streets had to be patrolled, town borders policed, the train station surveilled. Since my vision was keen, and my nose for trouble honed by a lifelong inclination to suspect the worst, watch duty always fell to me. In fact, I volunteered for it.

I had a reason; and the reason was the last house in Frankenstein.

It was—perhaps it still is—painted bright blue, with a steep gable roof from which a single dormer window poked out. It sat away from the rest of the village, closer to the forest than to the nearest neighbour. It had no fence, but two lanky pencil pines growing in front of the entrance gave it a modicum of privacy. At the back, where the dormer window was, the forest's larches— black in the summer but golden now that October had yellowed each needle with a seamstress's patience—scratched at the wall.

No one knew I visited this house every night when I was

4

out keeping watch. Not Regina back at the castle, who'd have thrown me out had she suspected; nor my dear friend Agata, to whom I confessed everything—except this.

I climbed the tree closest to the dormer window, my black Chesterfield melting away into the shadows. My nails dug in the wet bark until I reached a bough polished with long nights of waiting. The wood knew my spine well.

The light was on in the study, though the room was empty. Upon the large oak desk, ancient of build and oriental of fashion, a half-drunk glass of wine stood beside an old Adler typewriter. It had no paper in it, but a large, leather-bound book was propped against the keys. I recognised it. *A Treatise on the Diseases of the Nervous System*, by James Ross, M.D., LL.D., Fellow of the Royal College of Physicians, London.

I liked the woodcuts in it, the precise lithographs, and often-times—when I was sure the family was away in Ingolstadt—I had snuck inside to look at its pictures of brains in various states of malfunctioning, wondering just where it was, that mine was wrong. I never found an answer.

The October air was mellow, damp with the possibility of rain, and the window had been cracked open, which is how I heard him before I saw him. His footsteps along the corridor were slow; sleepy perhaps, yet still purposeful. He was not an idle man. Finally, he appeared.

Martin Hunger.

Husband of a wan Frenchwoman with the endangered sophistication of a Sumatran cochoa, father of a ten-year-old son who liked to read mystery novels, and a seven-year-old daughter who liked to pick mushrooms in the woods, Martin Hunger was professor of physiology at the University of Ingolstadt, a surgeon of the brain with a reputation for flawless execution, and a world-renowned expert on congenital diseases of the mind. The blue house at the end of Frankenstein had belonged to his great-grandfather on his mother's side, and the family always came back in the summer, sometimes in the winter too, if small restorations were in order. This time he had come alone.

He was wearing a checkered dressing gown. It was too small for his square chest, greying but still lined with muscles—too small, and too short. His wife's. I could picture him soaking in the immaculate bathtub, a ghostly steam rising from the warm water, his weary eyes closed, until an urgent idea had pierced through his doziness like a ray of moonshine from a shuttered blind. He'd risen from the tub, water splashing everywhere from his sudden jolt, grabbed the first thing he could find, wrapped it around himself. The dressing gown clung to his wet shoulders, and I could see wet footprints shining on the wooden boards.

Martin's hair was already thinning on the peak of his wholly German hair, but around the ears it still shone with filaments of red gold. He was in his forties, though the wrinkles around his eyes, always squinting, made him look older. He put on his glasses, sat down, and craned forwards upon Ross's *Treatise*.

A slight hump of the back, accentuated by years spent with his nose inside medical atlases, pulled the dressing gown away, and from the shadows outside I saw his neck, the taut skin pulsing, the bluish bas-relief of the vein running close to the surface before it disappeared below the collarbone. The cross he always wore was dull with use and age, save for Christ's angular knees, which shone like glassy doorknobs.

My arms ached with want.

There would be a creak as they'd push open the window frame, but Martin wouldn't hear it. His concentration braved children's crying, telephones ringing, radios blaring—what was a creak in a night such as this, when a sharp wind blew from the west, rattling the old house? Fused with the shadows of the trees whispering outside, my own shadow would slink in unnoticed, creep towards his back, raise up to meet the soft dip between shoulder and neck.

It would have been easy; too easy, almost. My arms and shadow knew better. They knew what I had to ask Martin, and that was not the way to get his attention.

How, then? I couldn't rap at the windowpane, or scratch at the wood until he saw me. He'd think a hungry soul had risen from the grave to torment him, my sight would stop his heart. I looked like a revenant.

No rouge could disguise my sallow cheeks. No powder could attenuate my bony features, or do something for the black hollows under my eyes. No brush had bristles strong enough to untangle the prickly blackthorn of my hair. I would have to wear a mask not to scare Martin to death, and while I often thought about asking the Baron for one—he had hundreds of them—the truth is that I was frightened to put my question to Martin. As long as it lived only in my mind, I could fashion the answer I wanted. Asking it would make it real, which meant I'd have to live with the real answer.

So I kept to the dark, and watched on, spying Martin's face for something I had no name for, and the fine layer of skin above his carotid for something I knew all the names of—in all languages. It was an agony, but a hopeful one.

Martin read from the *Treatise* for a while, then he jumped up, rushed to the bookshelf on the opposite side of the study. He was closer now. Through the open window, he smelled of fresh cotton, of soap. He got on the tips of his toes and dragged down a large volume bound in maroon cloth, which looked like it weighed more than his daughter. He dropped it on top of the *Treatise*, started browsing it. The belt of his dressing gown had given, and now it hung loose around his waist. Thick blond hairs curled below his navel. A drop of water crawled down his ankle.

Again, I felt the urge to slip inside, to sneak from shadow to shadow, find his neck, kiss it, bite it. But he would never answer me then.

I let myself fall to the ground. A weasel rummaging through the leaves yelped and scuttered away from me, darting towards the forest. I ran after it. The gaunt elms on that side of the valley rose from the mist like so many desolate phantoms lingering on a battlefield. A pale eagle-owl flew in front of me, the tip of its wing brushing against my cheek.

I only slowed down when I reached the trail leading up to our castle, because the path was steep, my breath short with more than the run. It was just as well. I didn't want Regina to see me flushed, didn't want her asking questions. I pulled on the roots of a fallen horse chestnut half-sunk in the muddy side of the hill to hoist myself up the final curve.

Somehow tall and squat at the same time, all red rock dripping with dark creepers, Castle Frankenstein leaned against a large stone shoulder, itself red in colour. The stone was so bulky that the road to the castle had to draw a wide bow around it, and what lay beyond was blocked from view. When I approached the gate from this side, I always feared an ambush. That night I walked into one.

There was a snow globe sitting in front of the gate.

The glass was cracked, the snow swirled no more.

Inside, a miniature white castle shone pink at the light of the moon.

THE GARRET

THERE IS A castle on the moon.

This is what Regina taught me, after she found me in a draughty garret near the church of St Nicholas in Deptford, where I had been living—hiding, rather—after I left home, in the south of Europe. I looked up from my misery, and there she was.

Long red hair that framed her face as a bride's veil, the right eye pointing outward as if looking out for threats, Regina had the arresting presence of a fiery *sirin* on an old Russian print. The night she found me, though, her face was soft, like a mother's. She crouched down in front of me, her black frock rustling about her feet as if a flutter of moths was trapped between its folds.

She told me she had been watching me for days. Watching, as I made my way through the streets of the city, shimmering with rain, the halos around the lamp-posts as distant as other suns, far-away and forsaken. Watching, as I prowled the dimly lit alleyways of Southwark, stalking the public houses for the intoxicated sailors, stonecutters and actors who stumbled out of them.

Watching, as I dragged them giggling in the dark; and later on, as they crawled back into the light, while I stayed behind, praying for an oblivion that did not end with the crowing cock.

I was praying to the wrong god, she told me, and punctured her upturned palm with a hatpin.

The blood dripping down her fingers was more akin to water than blood, even though what it resembled the most, in the way it behaved, was liquid mercury.

It was not red.

It was silvery pink, the colour of a waning moon.

The same colour as mine.

"When did you know?" she asked, getting back up and looking around the small room. Her lips pursed. The smell was foul.

I was seven. I was hiding in a cupboard with a school friend, in the pitch black of our youthful eagerness, playing at touching each other, until I tried to kiss him like I had seen them doing in the movies, and he punched me on the nose and ran away and left me there, bleeding that strange thin blood which was not like the blood I had seen on his knees when he scraped them.

Then I knew I was different. And soon I discovered my brain worked differently, too.

I liked graves, not playgrounds. Merry-go-rounds made me sick, I had no taste for heroism. I feared my happiness was poisonous, it could spoil everything I felt happy for, and everyone I felt happy with. Balance was precarious, the world a book of signs I was good at reading—they all spelt doom.

If you've ever seen a spider trying to trap a hornet in its web, you know what it's like to inhabit my mind. I'm the hornet, *and* the spider trapping it.

Soon after the realisation that I was different, there came another one: I could not stay home. Home was a place of rolling grass dappled by a perpetual summer sun that made it impossible to hide; a place of sidelong glances following you down the streets like flies, the buzz of tongues just as persistent. Tongues talking, tongues tittle-tattling, tongues tipping off my mother about my every move. Sometimes, I caught her looking at me as one looks at tea leaves at the bottom of a cup, telling the fortune written in them. She tried to predict my future in the way I moved my arms, cocked my head, rose on my toes. What she saw must have filled her with shame, because her soothsaying always left her shaking her head, her eyes veiled over. I started to think she'd have preferred me dead, because that way she could control what would become of me—worms, and the lustre of bones.

So I left, and never returned; my heart broken, but still mine.

I sobbed and Regina was on her knees again. She told me she could save me.

I didn't know I wanted to be saved, but I did, and I followed her aboard the Night Ferry to Paris. From there, we made our way to Frankfurt and then Mannheim, until we reached Frankenstein. As we travelled, she told me the story of the castle on the moon, and the King who lived in it.

The King had a name. Ludwig II of the House of Wittelsbach, King of Bavaria.

Some called him the Swan King because Lohengrin—whom he loved—was the Swan Knight. For Regina, though, he was the King on the Moon, or simply the King.

He was born on the same day as his grandfather, the old king, at the very same hour, a momentous occurrence. The year: 1845, year of crows and violins, ships adrift amidst the ice.

The King grew up to be a quiet, thoughtful child, prone to morosity, who liked listening to his mother as she read parables from the Bible, building models of the Holy Sepulchre, and dressing up as a nun.

He also liked to sleep during the day and stay awake at night, because once he had found a dying cygnet in a bush, and he had pierced his skin on a rose's thorn trying to save him. Then he had seen that his blood was pink with white-bluish flecks in it, just like ours, and had grown convinced that the moon had mothered him, that at birth she had placed a stone from her heart inside his tiny ribcage.

She whispered to him at night, when he got up from his bed and tiptoed to the window to look at her, high upon the blue mountains. There would come a time, she'd say, when she would call to him, and he would come home—the home of emperors and builders of wonders, knights of the Cross and the Cup. Of Lohengrin, son of Parzival. Home was Montsalvat, where the Grail was hidden. Take a sip, and you will be saved forever.

As the Night Ferry crossed the Strait of Dover, Regina told me that the King hated the wretched age he was forced to live in. A bloodless age, without mystery and magic, without honour. When everything else failed him—family, love, state—he turned to building castles, just as, when still a little child, he had built models of the Sepulchre.

In a way, his castles were graves. Linderhof, Herrenchiemsee, Neuschwanstein—all crypts he haunted, forlorn, fleeing the pomp and circumstance of the capital, searching for a moment of grace on mountain lakes and misty forests. He liked to race with his coach through the trees at night. He was mad, everyone said.

He wasn't, and no one knew that, unbeknownst even to his most trusted advisors, he was building his final castle. The castle on the moon.

"I can take you there," Regina had said as we entered Frankenstein.

THE CARDS

"Where did you find it?" Agata said, looking into the snow globe. She was holding it as one might a toad, or something that bites.

It was well past midnight and we were in her room, a small guardroom in the only remaining tower of Castle Frankenstein, just below mine. She called it her fainting room on account of the dozen *méridiennes* and ottomans crammed inside, and often joked that you couldn't trip without falling onto a cushion. The other pieces of furniture were an old armoire and a dressing table, its surface dripping with wax from the candles Agata had placed on it over the years, the new ones often sticking out from the old, deformed stubs. In the oval mirror in front of which she was now sitting, the flames had the mischievous appearance of little red sprites floating around her head.

As the windows of our rooms—unlike in the rest of the castle—were boarded up with wooden planks, there was no danger of someone from the outside noticing the candles, though this made for very stuffy air. Sometimes, when we were feeling giddy, and Regina was away on some business, we'd unscrew one of the planks, to allow a fresh breath of night to gush in. It was risky, but we'd had our fair share of kids on a dare or drunkards lost in the woods stumbling at our door, and we had our ways of dealing with the intruders, tricking them away. A witch's whisper in the shadows of the courtyard, a wisp of light leading unsteady legs to sleep in a ditch.

That night Regina stayed in, and the window was sealed shut.

Agata moved the snow globe closer to the candles, pressed her nose to the model to study it. I was afraid her ruff would catch fire.

"It was in front of the gate when I came back," I said.

"It's Neuschwanstein," she said.

I knew. I could not fail to recognise King Ludwig's white palace, its red gatehouse, the rectangular tower, the soaring pinnacles. The model was sculpted with precision, every detail, no matter how small, rendered with a miniaturist's care, from the stepped gable above the gatehouse to the triumphant Saint George stabbing the dragon in the throat, frescoed on the palace's entrance.

"Do you think—"

I stopped.

Agata turned to look at me. Her face was pinched after so many weeks of confinement, with a green, impish tinge to it. Her black, trumpet-sleeved dress emphasised the pallor, bringing to mind pictures of deathbeds and blood-stained handkerchiefs. The cheekbones, always a prominent feature of her lineaments, now stood out like snowy outcroppings from a mountaintop, and so did the long, bony Spanish nose.

Out of boredom, she had styled her curls—naturally blond,

14

but dyed in a darker shade some months prior, and now dull like ancient, burnished brass—into a high pouffe. Inside she had hidden a handful of teardrop pearls inherited from a grandmother or a great-aunt, one could never be sure when her family was involved as she was always scarce with details, a scarlet guilt creeping up from her neck every time she talked about them. At the candles' light, the pearls beamed like a wolf's eyes behind a boxwood.

"What?" she said, her fingers tightening around the globe's base.

"Do you think someone left it for us?"

A crystal flake still stuck to one of Neuschwanstein's turrets. Agata sat the snow globe down on the dressing table, contemplating it as though the palace's door might fling open and the King march out in full uniform.

"It is a common enough trinket," she said. "The King's famous in this part of Germany too, even if we're far from his castles. And Christmas is near. Perhaps a little child dropped it?"

I didn't say that there was no reason why a child should have a Neuschwanstein snow globe in his or her pocket, at the top of our hill, on a rainy October day.

"Perhaps," I said instead.

Agata seemed content with this answer, and went back to putting carmine on her lips—the operation I had interrupted when I came in with news of my finding. She looked at me through the mirror.

"Do you want a reading?" she said.

We moved some ottomans around, got down on the floor. Agata's rumpled gown swelled up around her waist like a ripe, blackening persimmon. She gave me the deck.

It was a little habit of ours, adopted many years before and cultivated during the long, bleak Frankenstein winters. Agata always seemed soothed by the rustling of the deck, and I'd come to rely on the acuity of her readings, especially at times when I myself was feeling rather purblind. Ever since Regina had consigned her to her room for breaking the most fundamental rule of our order—never disrespect the King—Agata read my cards every night.

☙

IT HAD HAPPENED a sweet night in late August, a few days after the celebration for the King's birthday.

I was in my room drawing up a map of our valley—an endeavour which occupied the best part of my waking hours, when I was not on watch duty—when Agata burst in, throwing herself at my knees and clutching my arm. The map was to be a gift for the King, when he received us, and I hastened to salvage the corner she had trampled on.

"Oh, my dear Ambrose!" she said. "William loves me, and I love him, and I want to play until the sun comes up. Come!"

William was the young mason she had taken a shine to, a robust youth with hair so blond on his head and arms, it looked almost white. He lived by the train station, in a small cottage with a riotous mass of ivy growing on its front wall. If you squinted, it looked like a strange leafy anchor hung above his door, dropped there from some cosmic schooner adrift between the stars.

I tried to calm her down. I offered her tea from my stove, and a couple of cushions to make herself comfortable while it brewed, but she listened to no reason. She was so flushed she tore the starched ruff from her neck. I could see where William had bitten her.

"No, no, no," she insisted. "We won't sit around like a couple of crones, drinking tea and wasting time away. Come, Regina will never find out—she's not here."

"How do you know?"

"I saw her in the village. Heading out of it. She was making sure no one was following, but I saw her. William's house is just off the main road, on the way to Diemerstein, and I was looking through the curtains while he was in the tub. Perhaps she's out having fun, too."

Somehow, I doubted it. It was more likely that Regina was fetching a vital component for her experiments, something big and expensive that only the big, expensive shops of Kaiserslautern carried in stock. She had her ways to circumvent the opening hours.

"And the Baron?" I asked. Regina might be out, but her lackey always stuck around.

"Ambrose!"

Agata was getting impatient, her energy, frustrated by my cowardice, turning sour. She flashed her teeth in disgust. "We can't live our lives like this! We are still young, you and I. Come, I'll play something you haven't heard in a long time."

In the end, I could not resist her.

I wanted to prove her right, be young with her.

We snuck across the courtyard and down into the undercroft that served as our great hall. It was there that we celebrated the King's birthday on the twenty-fifth of August, along with the few other commanded feasts our calendar called for—the third of May, to commemorate the Audience that changed the King's life forever, and thus ours too; the thirteenth of June, to honour His ascension, when we poured our pink blood into a cup and set it ablaze, so that the vapours might reach Him; and the twenty-first of December, to mark the longest night of the year.

The hall was spare, with a sturdy walnut table in the centre and four wainscot chairs around it. Their backs were carved with scenes of swans and swords. The ceiling above the north-western wall was partially collapsed, and a faint moonlight was seeping through, escorted by ribbons of mist. The cavernous fireplace was just underneath the hole, and in front of it stood the Bösendorfer, black and regal in its otherworldliness as the moon made its lacquered wood translucent.

Agata sat at the piano, the entirety of her face cracked open by a smile of childlike delight. Her fingers spidered in the air, anticipating the coldness of the keys.

"Are you ready? Chopin, Étude Op. 10, No. 4, *presto con fuoco*."

A sudden fear shook my back, and I almost cried out for Agata to stop.

Chopin was forbidden inside the castle.

Chopin, and Mozart, and Beethoven, and Brahms—they were all forbidden.

Only the music of Wagner could be played on the Bösendorfer, because only the music of Wagner pleased the King, who was ready to bankrupt a realm to finance the maestro's dreams. He had built an artificial grotto in his park with a lake in it, a waterfall. An electric power station allowed him to conjure a rainbow among the stalactites, create waves in the water. Musicians concealed by the fake rocks would play *Lohengrin* for him, and this was what was expected of Agata as well.

Sometimes, when we were sure Regina was out, Agata and I would listen to Chopin or to the works of new artists whose vinyl records I picked up in town. Their rhythms were so outrageously different from what we were used to that our jittery hearts threatened to break. Our favourite was a record called

18

Funeral. The name on the sleeve, Arcade Fire, sounded like an incantation. We'd worn grooves in it. We played our contraband records on an old portable gramophone Agata had hidden inside the padding of a green velvet sofa, so positioned that one had to climb over several hassocks to reach it. We would huddle in a corner, shielding the gramophone with our bodies, and would listen to the music at a volume so low we had to hold our breath in order to hear anything.

This was another matter, though. This was blasphemy. But Agata didn't care.

She played the piece once, fiendish in the speed it required, her fingers so quick upon the keys that they seemed to warp the air around them. Then she played it again; and again; and again; each time quicker and quicker until I could hear the bones in her hands almost breaking from the tension. A transmogrification occurred before my eyes.

Agata was superb, as always, but mad with a fire I had never seen before. Her skin was so pale I could see her pink blood coursing through her veins, burning bright, and turning my friend into a blazing seraph. She played and played, unrelenting, bobbing her head as she went, throwing her hair this way and that. She stomped her feet on the ground, and howled with joy, and the rats around us retreated in fear, because they had never heard such commotion in the grimy, swishy undercroft they had reluctantly granted us access to.

The music was infectious. Soon I found myself dancing in the dust.

I clapped my hands and bats flew down from the rafters and out into the night through the hole in the ceiling. I threw open my arms and pretended I could fly too, jumping and leaping and bouncing and twirling until I saw stars—

—and Regina's white face looking at us, her eyes black with anger.

She stepped towards the centre of the hall.

When Agata saw her too her fingers froze mid-air, the music as dead in the room as the echo of laughter from centuries past.

"I don't remember… What are we celebrating tonight?"

Regina took another step towards us.

Even the rats hid from her wrath.

"Is it the first time the King heard the music of Wagner? But this is not Wagner, is it? No, I guess not," she said. Half-plunged into the darkness, she looked like a stone atlas, bearing on her shoulders all the weight of the castle above us. "No," she repeated. "No."

The next night Agata and I began our confinement. As I had been dancing, and Regina decreed that dancing was but an effect of music being played, I was sentenced to thirty days of confinement in my room, with dispensation to attend Mass each Sunday and practise whenever Regina called it.

Agata was still serving her ninety days, and going crazy with loneliness.

છ્ય

I STOPPED SHUFFLING the tarot deck and passed it back to Agata. She started laying down the cards in the strange, asymmetrical design she favoured. It looked like a cathedral's floorplan, though whatever god was celebrated in there must have been a trickster who liked its crosses askew and its naves winding.

"Did you see someone while you were in town?" she said, almost casually, as she put down the final card of her diagram.

She knew about the men I visited sometimes, in their houses

or in the woods, when I was on watch duty: a lawyer who worked in Frankfurt and came back on the weekends to be with his ailing parents; a teacher at the Kaiserslautern high school; a train conductor who often worked on the Mannheim route and was, as of late, my only constant social call. As intimacy with outsiders was, if not forbidden, at the very least frowned upon, we always had to discuss this matter with caution.

"No," I lied.

She knew about the conductor, the lawyer, the teacher. She didn't know about Martin.

Martin didn't mean sex, or companionship, or even infatuation. He meant something else. He meant treason; he meant defection.

I remember when I first heard about him, during one of my watches. A tiny, almost inconsequential bit of hearsay, someone telling someone that someone else had been cured from a supposedly incurable malady by Benedict Hunger's son, Martin.

At first, I didn't pay it any attention, until one night I found myself near the blue house and went to have a look. The family was away and I slipped in, found Martin's tomes in the study. I spent hours looking at them, trying to decipher the meaning of the inscriptions below each woodcut, searching for my affliction, the one I had discovered in the cupboard; the one that had driven me from home and to the garret where Regina had found me. Later, as I was rummaging through Martin's desk, I dug out a stack of notes from the bottom of a drawer. I was leafing absent-mindedly through them when I saw something that made me stop. It was the beginning of an article Martin was thinking of submitting, according to what he'd scribbled at the top of the first page, to the *Journal of Neurology*. The title, typed on the Adler and underlined with a red pen, was "Noctambulism and Other Phenomena of Extreme Nocturnality: A Proposal for a Cure". Only the first few sentences survived among the notes, but what I read there, promising the possibility of "a full recovery from all those darkenings of the mind which appear to stem from an imbalance of the circadian cycle", produced a startling realisation:

Perhaps I don't need Regina. Perhaps he *can help me.*

That's what Martin meant to me. He meant that I was considering a life outside the castle, a life without Regina. She called us an Order, The Order of the King on the Moon, but I'd come to feel we were more of a cult—*her* cult—and you never should tell the leader of a cult that you might have found a way out.

That's why I had to keep Martin from Agata, because she loved me dearly, and would do anything to keep me from harm. I could not endanger her so. At least, not until I was sure that what Martin had to offer was a viable alternative to Regina's plan. Then I'd take Agata with me and run away. Martin would whisk us to Ingolstadt, or even further away, it didn't matter where, as long as he could help us.

When she understood that I wasn't going to add anything else, Agata sighed. "How I miss going out—what day is it?"

"Saturday, the twenty-third of October."

She counted fast. "Thirty-six days still to go," she said, her face dropping.

Something strange happened then.

Behind her, beside the door where the candlelight never ventured, Agata had hung an old portrait of herself. She was a child in it, dressed in a red satin gown and sat on a Louis XIV armchair. They had put a tiger pup in her lap. Agata never looked at the portrait, and whenever I'd bring it up, she'd bare her teeth. "That old daub," she'd say. Even so, the few times I had suggested that perhaps she ought to throw it away if it irked her so, she had been as adamant in defending the picture—her only family heirloom—as she had been in disparaging it when I was admiring, out of curiosity more than politeness, some aspects of it. In truth, there wasn't much to admire. The painter had lacked any true inspiration, and had left almost no trace of his artistry in the execution, which was rather vulgar. However, when lying on a sofa after a night playing Russian checkers with Agata, I often thought I could discern the echo of an intention in the way the child held the cub, a purposefulness, a kind of stubborn temerity in the way her fingers stuck together, as if the painter had poured all his talent into that single detail.

That night it wasn't the hands, though.

It was the eyes.

Amidst the dusty *méridiennes*, for a brief moment, the Agata holding the tarot deck to her chest wore the same expression as the Agata holding the tiger on her lap, and from where I was sitting the two of them aligned. It was then that I saw something in the child's eyes that was not there before. A sorrow, a rage, a hunger.

All that is good has passed for me, Agata's eyes were whispering.
I've destroyed it myself, the painted ones were shouting.

"Pick a card to turn," Agata said. Her voice seemed distant, her pale face wavering in the dark like a friar's lantern in a marsh. She seemed about to fade, to disappear into the picture, her portrait self sucking her back in. I knew it was only a game the light was playing with my tiredness—it was almost dawn—but I couldn't stand still and watch her vanish.

I reached across the cards and hugged her. She smelled of powder and wax and smoke, and the tobacco she was fond of chewing, and it was her smell, more than her bony frame, that dispelled the illusion. I stole a nervous glance over her shoulder, but whatever sorcery the portrait had just woven had dissipated. It had gone back to being the coarse job of a hack more interested in the faded grandeur of Agata's family—and their gold—than in the soul of his subject.

"Do you think Regina will ever forgive me?" Agata whispered in my ear.

"I am sure of it."

"Do you think she will tell the King I disobeyed her, when we see him?"

"I am sure she won't. She knows you meant nothing by it," I said.

What I wanted to say was: why do we care about the King, and what Regina might tell him, if and when he agrees to see us? Why do we let her dictate what music we can play, what books we can read, what prayers we may say, whom we can see, and talk to, and be affectionate with? When we accepted her invitation to Frankenstein, relinquishing our old lives, did we also relinquish the right to decide where, and how, we should find happiness in our new ones? What if there is another way, and I have discovered it?

Agata broke away, sniffed. Her eyes were wet. "Pick a card to turn," she repeated.

I turned my eyes down, grateful to let the portrait disappear into the shadows on the wall. I chose the card closest to me, the lady's chapel of that bizarre cathedral.

A black swan, with a red beak. I knew this card well. It always came up in our readings, and Agata had become convinced it represented me. She smiled.

"The Father of Cups, again," she said. "Pick the second one."

I chose the transept, turned it.

"The Nine of Swords," Agata said, and flinched. She placed a finger on the card, moved it away from her. The illustration on it was disturbing. Two eyeballs plucked from their sockets, with maggots crawling above them. A forest of swords grew impenetrable along the margins, their points trained towards the centre.

"What does it mean?" I asked.

"It means you are struggling, you are trapped inside your skull and cannot see a way out. Doubt and concern are eating away at you like maggots. But—" She stopped, looked at me with a mixture of concern and suspicion. "I've never pulled this card for you before. What changed?"

On the card, the eyes were ravenous with surprise. Was that what my eyes looked like as I watched— I stopped before my mind could conjure up a picture of Martin. Skulls were veils to Agata, I could not betray myself.

I shook my head to clear it, then I noticed that the eyes on the tarot were pointing in two different directions, like Regina's. I felt them on me, seeing right through me, seeing my secret, the worry which was not *eating away* at me but *gobbling up* my insides. Soon the worry would have no more stomach to consume, it would start burrowing its way out of me; soon it would show on my face, a leprosy of lost faith. Then Regina would know about Martin, about the hope which bloomed in my heart's darkest cave, the question begging to be asked.

I shrugged. "I don't know what changed. You are supposed to tell me that."

"Pick the third card. Perhaps it will clear the Nine's meaning."

This time, I chose the card sitting the furthest from me, the portal of the cathedral. I turned it.

A nosediving owl, with a black sword in its talons.

"The Son of Swords," Agata said. "More swords. Although this is not as bad a card as the Nine. It represents a man. He's assertive and strong, but he might also be violent. And he's wise, though you don't know the real extent of his knowledge. Do you know who this card could represent?"

My wayward thoughts ran to Martin, and this time I was too slow in steering them away. Agata was looking right at me, she saw him.

"Who is he?" she asked.

I smiled to stop my face from crumpling, closed my eyes to hide the fear widening them. I offered her the picture of Martin's neck, his broad chest still wet from the shower, his muscled legs. He liked to run, often at night, after working at his desk, sweat plastering his hair to his forehead. I offered Agata the cross, the navel.

"A man in town," I said. I could feel Agata's magpie eyes searching every line on my face. She could not resist secrets, especially those brought into the open by her cards, and as she felt this one was dangerous, she wanted it even more.

"Why haven't you told me about him?" she said.

"I just spy on him. The old cat and the mouse," I said. My eyes were still closed, but she knew I was lying. I heard the ruffle of her dress as she got up from the ground, swished away from me.

"You know you can trust me," she said, her voice raw.

"I do," I said. And it was the truth, and it was a lie.

I looked at her. She had lain down on the yellow-and-purple *récamier* closer to the boarded-up window, her favourite one.

"I'm tired," she said. "We will have to finish the reading another day."

I knew it wasn't true, but I went to her and kissed her forehead. She wore a pale, spiritless smile. Anger was already leaching out of her. She smoothed the velvet lapels of my Chesterfield, which was a gift from her, a present she had given me for the first King's birthday we'd spent together at the castle. She too had run away from her home, somewhere in the Pyrenees, and had been brought to Frankenstein six or seven months before me. She was thinking about leaving until my sudden appearance one night changed her mind. We were the same age and felt an immediate kinship for each other. She was my sister, we were bound. Keeping things from her pained me.

"Will you bring me something back, the next time you go to the village?" she said.

"What do you want?"

"Just a memory will be enough," she said.

"A memory? What do you mean?"

"You will see something—a flower in a pot, a red bathing suit hung up to dry. You will see something that's full of colour, and remember it, and share your memory with me, and it will be like I saw it too. A good memory. Will you do this for me?"

"I will," I said, and thought of Martin again as I left, wondering why it was tonight, of all nights, that he had shown up in the cards.

❧

MY ROOM WAS just below the tower's roof, in a dovecote that I had scrubbed clean my first night at the castle. Regina had insisted that I choose one of the underground rooms, they were safer, but I was used to garrets and could not bear the thought of living down there. In the end she had to allow me my wish.

That was before, when she was still trying to win me over to her cause; when she needed me. It felt good to be needed. She had asked me: *What will you bring to the faith?*

The Baron brought his muscle and his scheming, and his knowledge of the stars. Agata brought music, because she had no rivals at the Bösendorfer, and she also brought money, as she came from a family of landowners whom she'd robbed before running away and Regina was clever enough to know that faith, without money to sustain it, is often called delusion. As for myself, it turned out I brought three things:

My nosiness, which made me an excellent spy.

My eagerness to please, which made me an excellent servant.

My misery, which made me the perfect believer.

She needed those things, and me. But that, as I said, was before. Before she had me in her thrall, and turned from saviour to jailor, from mother to abbess—though the difference is tenuous at the best of times. It was before I started doubting her, and the King.

I used to fantasise about the moment when I'd meet him.

On the nights I woke with my hands sweaty and unsure and felt myself slipping, I'd climb what remained of the castle's watchtower, whose parapet hung just above the large red boulder. I'd lie up there, and dream about the castle in the sky, the white keep tall with turrets, the spires twisting against the night's black belly, drilling holes in it.

The King would greet me in the bailey—and what a sight he was, his eyes as blue as a winter lake frosting over, his hair blacker than the universe's yawn. He was beautiful—not as a strong, healthy man passing you by on a street; but as a god on a winged horse, crowned by fire.

He'd walk towards me. His uniform was white, but the russet turnbacks bespoke the warmth of his embrace. A white tricorn laced with gold snuggled under his arm. The sabre by his side gleamed in the blackness like the tooth of a great prehistorical predator.

"Ambrose," he'd call to me, and off his tongue my name sounded as rare as a gemstone, and just as valuable.

Nowadays I could not conjure his face anymore, nor hear his voice. When I tried, the contours were hazy, the colours wrong, the syllables crooked. The King had never looked so far away, but this did not altogether displease me. I was not ready to leave yet.

I was again thinking of Martin when, as I opened the door to my room, I realised something was wrong.

On the wall, the map of the Frankenstein valley swayed in the gust of air rushing in from the landing, where I stood as still as a cat in front of a ghost. In the soft murk underneath my drawing desk, motes of dust danced at the sound of the wood creaking.

My few possessions were mute: the hand-mirror with a knob of immaculate moonstone; the dirk an old lover from Edinburgh had given me; my yellow, crumpled copy of *The Dangers of Smoking in Bed*; the tattered diary in which I wrote in the old cant I learned in Southwark, the only language I was sure Regina and the Baron could not read.

Everything was still—until I moved my eyes to the corner where my wings were hung.

White hands glided out of the darkness, their spar-like fingers sailing through the air towards me. A wrist followed, pale and thin, disappearing inside the sleeve of a black frock.

The tip of a nose, a forehead, a lock of red hair. Pursed lips, hollow cheeks.

Inch by inch, Regina appeared in front of me.

"What are you doing here?" I blurted out before I could stop myself.

For a fleeting, suspended instant, she seemed lost; she cast her outward-pointing eye around, as if she was not sure where she was. I had never before seen her in my room, except for the day when she had first shown it to me, dirty with foul droppings and dead mice, and said to me, "If you want it, you must clean it."

She fixed her good eye on me. "I was looking for you. Where were you?"

"I was keeping Agata company. She suffers her isolation."

"No," Regina said, the word a cold, hard pebble falling on the floor between us. "I've been looking for you since last evening. Where were you?"

I took a little step sideways, towards my desk. Towards the dirk lying there. I did not intend to use it, but if she knew about Martin, I might have to defend myself somehow.

"I was out on my round," I said. "Why? Is something the matter?"

She studied me. As though replying to my own movement, she too stepped towards the desk. "Did you see anything strange in town?"

"No," I lied. I don't know why I did it, why I didn't tell her about the snow globe. I was angry. I didn't like being questioned, and I didn't like her being in my room.

"Why?" I asked again, and again she seemed at a loss.

Even at the best of times, when she emerged from her workroom after a breakthrough in her experiments in pneumatics, Regina never smiled. Her face was turned to a perpetual stony frown by the purpose which alone occupied her mind. Her devotion to the King was utter—a devotion of hushed tones and hard work, because she did not care for the spirited zeal of mystics. She came from a line of clockmakers and bridge-builders, and as an engineer by training, she valued solidity, practicality. She lacked imagination, and I could see the strain on her features as she tried to think of how to reply.

"The Baron," she said eventually, starting towards the door.

"He saw something in the stars he didn't like. I just wanted to make sure." She turned to look at me—the mother was back. She raised a hand to stroke my cheek. "We are so close," she said. "I'll see you at Mass." She closed the door behind her.

I lit the three candle stubs drying on the candelabra that I kept on the desk.

I looked through my journals, my notes, searching for a sign that Regina had disturbed them. I moved to the wardrobe, then to the map, to check if something had been changed.

Everything seemed in its right place, except for my wings, which were hanging lopsided from their peg. I looked at their wooden frame, their joints, the black cloth making up the bulk of them. But I was being stupid, I was being paranoid—it must have been the wind moving them.

Dawn was near.

I straightened the wings, snuffed out the candles, and slipped inside my coffin to sleep.

31

THE PELICAN

A WHITE SUN rose above Castle Frankenstein, but in my coffin it was dark. The dark smelled of wood and velvet, of dust; it pressed down on me, and I breathed it in, was dissolved in it, and remade by it. I was a man and I was a citadel. I had arms and walls, eyes and doors, desire in my stomach and a fountain in my courtyard. The water in my fountain was pink like the moon overhead, like the blood that flowed beneath my skin, and I knew it tasted sweet. A white pelican flew down from the black sky and perched upon it.

Around the courtyard, rib-like archways and spines of stairs reached up to the rooms above, and a long, mirrored gallery. I contained armoires and riddles, paintings in gilt frames, lies and clocks, crested helmets. On the blue vaulted ceiling of my skull a creature, half man, half swan, flew towards something the painter had left out. Dances were held in my halls, chandeliers were lit at dusk. I wore curtains of wool woven with silk, offered them to those looking to hide a secret kiss. A grey sea-eagle nested behind my right eye.

There was a room, at the top of one of my towers, where a hard-wearing desk stood. It was filled with papers, phials and candle stubs. One candle, though, was lit. The window was open and a gust of wind drew from the rafters a glass-like gossamer tendril. A spider's web. When it brushed the candle's flame, the web went up in a blaze and the fire leapt onto the papers, the desk, the threadbare carpet upon which it had stood for centuries. From there, the fire spread.

It was in my hallways and on my balconies, it tickled the tapestries hung on my walls. It made the paint of the ceiling fresco warp, blowing bubbles on the swan-man's skin. My armoires were blackened by it, and my secrets and my mysteries and my swords. An acrid black smoke filled my rooms, and I knew I was thrashing inside my coffin, digging my nails into the wood, choking. A red glow was in my every window, as if the night were alive with the eyes of a hundred monsters.

I burned, and the pelican flew out of my smouldering ruin, and I was his beak and his wings, his purple-black eyes, and from the blue heavens I saw myself burn but didn't pay any more mind to clock and curtain. I soared into the sky.

But I was not whole.

A shard of glass had pierced my breast.

And, as I flew, blood rained from my breast down upon the earth.

And the trees drank it
and brooks and crannogs and
men and women and children and burials old and new
and ducks and dogs and crabs in the sand and
the sand and the ocean and the salt that turned pink
and the flowers in a garden outside a house by a great river—
lisianthus and amaryllis and camellia that I could see—and

I alighted on the flower beds.

And from the house, a man I did not know came out, with a proud nose and gentle eyes behind a pair of gold-rimmed round glasses that shone with the light of a bright, glorious day.

You are not here, the man said as he crouched down in front of the pelican who was me. *Not yet.* Then he saw the fine black ash on my wings, the blood trickling down my chest. *You are wounded*, he said.

And he said as well, *Let me heal you*, and held out his hand, and I woke up.

THE PARABLE

It was evening when I crawled out of my coffin and Manfred was sitting on my desk, whipping the poor pages of my journal with his tail. As soon as I emerged, he jumped into my arms.

He was heavy, big enough to serve as the mount of a forest goblin, with soft black fur all over his lissom body except for the tips of the ears, which were of an unusual grey that under certain lights looked almost green. His silver whiskers were so thin they vanished into the air.

He started purring against my neck, giving the skin there little bites until I understood he was nervous about something. He kept pawing at my chest.

I unbuttoned my shirt, gave him my nipple, and he started sucking on it.

As he sucked, he calmed somewhat. The effect of my blood which, rushing through my veins, made my heart heavy and my mind mad, but when I gave it to others it gave them peace.

"It's a miracle, omee," the man who taught me this property

had said over a pint in Deptford. He was being facetious, exaggerating for my benefit, but I was grateful. It was the first days after I had left home, and he was the first of my kind I'd met. Moon-kin, he called us. If this knowledge about my blood didn't do much to soothe my worry, at least it made clear that I was not poisonous; not to others, at least.

A weird air hung above the town, Manfred told me. Shadows behaved in erratic ways, especially those cast by the trees. The Hochspeyerbach, the brook winding through the village, hurried past the church, eager to get away. People he saw in the street had a hard stare. They looked at him with hostility, even the ones who used to be gentle, who gave him food. He had gone as far as a *gasthaus* deep in the forest between Frankenstein and Fischbach. Its *lüftlmalerei*—the murals which adorned the façade—appeared faded, simple evanescent outlines that looked like a child's rendition of a spectre. Only professional drunks visited the inn, and people from both towns who preferred to conduct their business away from the prying eyes of neighbours. The atmosphere there was always one of reckless merriment, but the night Manfred was there, every time someone opened the door to take a piss outside, he heard a mirthless laughter, more desperate than it was intoxicated.

Something was about to happen, he told me, and rock and tree and man were bracing for it—though no one knew what *it* was. They just felt it. Static crackled around the streetlights.

"Thank you," I said, and pulled my nipple from his teeth. It was red, raw, but Manfred was steadier now, his blue eyes brighter. I put him down on the table and stroked his head, his strong back, his tail. "Will you keep an eye out for me?"

He pushed his wet nose against my palm then jumped down, hurrying away to wherever he scuttled off when he was not visiting me. He was my best informer, but it was he who always found me, not the other way around.

The news was disconcerting. Nothing ever happened in Frankenstein. Life went on, unperturbed by rain or storm, far-away wars, disasters brought forth by the hands of men. It was a virtue of its smallness, but also a quality of the valley it sat in, warded off, shielded by mountains and forests. If it wasn't for the train tracks passing through, no one would find the village, but that was just as well, since no one alighted on the platform who hadn't been there before. You never saw strangers in Frankenstein. At most, someone left for another town or for the ground—it made no difference to those who stayed behind. There was beauty in the stillness, and peace in it.

But now something was happening, or *about to*.

I thought about the broken snow globe, the swords in the cards. My dream of fire and ruin, blood from the sky.

Midnight struck on the church's belfry, calling people to sleep; and us to Mass.

℘

THE CHAPEL WAS underground. The way to it was through the old well peeking up from a corner of the castle courtyard, by a willow whose hunkered shape gave it the impression of a wizened hunchback from an old fable. A rusty metal grille closed the access to the well most of the week, but on Sundays, at the stroke of midnight, the Baron opened it. He took great pride in this duty of his.

Hand in hand, Agata and I descended the stairs carved inside the well. Pale, fluorescent lichens caked the wall, dripping with damp. The distant sound of running water guided us, as it had done when we had first made our way down the steps, for our initiation ceremony. The air stank of rotten leaves and death by water. It was dense, warm.

"I have a feeling in my stomach," Agata whispered, drawing closer to me. "My dear Father of Cups, I'm scared."

I had not shared Manfred's news with her, because when I had knocked on her door, I had already found her in a state of agitation. She hadn't slept well, pursued by dreams herself. A god of visions and portents must have trampled across the courtyard while we slept. In a nightmare Agata had seen a white mouth munching on the tender flesh of a chicken; with breast and bone both gone, the mouth had burped a velvet shoe out of its throat.

"Don't worry," I said as we reached the bottom of the stairs.

"It will pass," I also said, but the truth is, the longer she spent locked up in her room, the weaker she was becoming. Often, when I went to fetch her for Mass or for practice, she seemed aloof, lost in a bygone time of her own; or she pretended to be sick, making excuses to stay inside. I never let her. I knew all too well from my days in Deptford what it meant to retreat from the world, searching for the fixity of statues. I knew the dangers of dabbling in the alchemy of memory. I could not lose Agata to the past, not when our future seemed within reach. If only I could muster the courage to speak with Martin.

The Baron was already sitting in the first pew, the tip of his right boot courting the stream which ran the length of the chapel. None of us were permitted to cross it. Beyond lay Regina's *sancta sanctorum*, a maze of caves where she officiated the mysteries of the King, the Wings, the moon. What islets and lakes the stream drew past the chapel was anyone's guess. We only knew that, at a certain point, it climbed to the surface behind the castle and past the rookery, to die in an old quarry on the other side of the hill where it formed a little pond. Three regal mute swans had made it their home under Regina's watchful eye—the swan being the King's favourite animal, and the symbol of our Order.

"You are late," the Baron said.

He was donning his usual attire, immaculate gloves and black-and-crimson cape—you would think Mass were just a brief stop on his way to the opera. The right side of his face was covered by a gold-sequined vizard. He was proud of his collection of masks and kept them in six large coffers with wrought-iron bands. We knew because, one night several years prior, Agata and I had slipped inside his room, a disused cellar several storeys beneath the great hall. We wanted to find out something about him—he was already living at the castle when Regina had brought us there, a sulky shadow mulishly refusing to let out anything about his past—but found only his masks and capes, his perfumes, the gloves; nothing that could reveal when he had arrived in Frankenstein, or who he was before.

"She is not here yet," I said as we took our place behind him.

On the other side of the stream, two braziers were burning, making the blackness red. A drapery of stalactites hanging from the ceiling had the cruel look of bloody blades after a battle.

"That is not an excuse," the Baron hissed. In the light from the braziers, his features had the sharpness of a torturer from the eighth circle of Hell. The sickly smell of his Hungarian water floated around his oily black hair.

As if on cue, from deep inside the labyrinth there came the sound of steps. The shadows beyond the stream seemed to stir, simmer, until they coalesced into a figure.

Regina sprouted forth from the darkness, her black frock indistinguishable from the pitch black of the cavern. She sank to her knees on the bank of the stream, cupped her hands, and drank. Her red hair was tied in a tight chignon, pierced through by a hairpin in the shape of a knife. She touched her fingers to her forehead and lips, then rose to face us. Her wandering eye homed in on the Baron; the other stayed with Agata and myself.

From the folds of her frock, she produced a small blue book, bound in silk. *The Life of the King.* We all had identical copies.

"Turn to chapter three," she said.

The echo inside the chapel made it seem as though there were thirty of us leafing through our books, like there must have been in the old times Regina was fond of talking about. Our Order was vast then, and every pew must have been full of people, coming from the whole of Europe to partake in our rituals. At one Festival of Lilies, a soprano had sung from the *Walküre* in front of a hundred officiants, two of them having made their dangerous way to Frankenstein from as far as New York.

Now that the Order's numbers had dwindled, Regina had scrapped the festivity from our calendars. At the beginning of my stay, soon after my initiation, I had offered to write to some of my old moon-blooded acquaintances in London—not that there were that many of them, since I most often kept to myself—but she had seethed at the suggestion. She had already chosen the only worthy one among their ranks, she told me, spitting out the last word.

"The little prince," Regina read from *The Life of the King,* "wandered among the bushes without aim or purpose, taken by flashes of colour and the gentle buzz of insects. At length he came upon a tall Gallic rose of singular beauty, the noble petals of a violet so soft it belonged more on the robe of one of Raphael's angels than in a garden. Underneath the stalk, a ruffled cygnet lay in a pool of blood, its beak smacking in desperation. A dog had bitten it. The boy blanched, his pulse quickening, his heart banging against its cage. He had to do something. He reached for the cygnet, and it was then that a thorn pierced his finger—and he knew the colour of his own blood."

Regina closed the book. In the coruscating light, her nails were as bright as rubies as she clawed the volume.

"Do you remember," she asked, "why the King was alone that day? Why he tried to save the little swan by himself?"

As always, the Baron was the first to answer. He leaned forwards, almost like he was trying to cut Agata and me off from a private conversation; but the chapel was small, the ceiling generous with its acoustics, so we heard everything.

"He shouldn't have been. His father was supposed to take him for a walk in the gardens of Nymphenburg."

"And why was the father not there with him?"

"Some official business had kept him. The book does not say what."

"How did the little prince react to the news his father couldn't join him?"

The Baron was ecstatic. Under the mask, his moustache was quivering with delight. Tonight he knew all the answers. "He was sad, because it was just a few days after his birthday, and the prince thought a walk with his father was to be his special present."

"Who are you in this parable, the child or the father?"

"The child," said the Baron.

"The child," said Agata and I, a fraction later.

"What if…" said Regina, stepping back from the stream, her face floating in the black throat of the cave. "What if I told you that you are neither?"

The Baron turned to look at us, his eyes wide and crazed, daring us to answer instead of him.

"What if I told you," said Regina, "that you are the dying cygnet?"

We stayed silent.

It was not the first time we had heard this parable, but never before had Regina likened us to the small swan dying from a dog's bite. Sometimes we were the child, lost and lonely, forgotten by our mothers and fathers, and she the thorn who made us see our true family was each other. Other times we were the father, guilty of forgetting our duties towards the King—she had insisted on this for weeks after Agata's punishment—and always she was the thorn, there to remind us of our calling.

We had never been the dying swan.

We did not know what that meant.

Agata's hand, which I was still holding, was growing cold and wet.

"The world bit you," said Regina. "It bit all of us, left us there to die, small and crippled, under a tall, beautiful rose. The world cares more about the rose than it does about us. We die, then someone comes along, scoops us away, dumps us wherever the dead things all wash up. Only the King, seeing the rose and seeing the cygnet, tried to save the small beast—and he was punished for it."

She continued to retreat into the shadows.

"Don't forget it," her faceless voice said, ringing under the vaulted darkness. "Only the King will care for you."

The Baron bowed his head; Agata sobbed and squeezed her eyes hard.

THE SWAN

BEASTS WHOSE BLOOD is cold need to keep warm and bask in the sun. We whose blood is the colour of the moon have the same need, but our ways are different. We love, mostly.

As I left the castle after Mass, I thought of another episode in the life of the King, what we referred to as the Audience, and what came afterwards.

It's night, the forest white with snow. Glazed over with crystals, pine cones reflect the starlight, and the trees shine like it's Christmas.

He's in his coach, silky black furs drawn around him. With the pommel of his cane, he raps at the roof. "Faster! Faster!" he shouts, and the coachman whips the horses, four Holsteiners with white coats. They come from the King's stable and know what's asked of them. Steam blows from their nostrils. The trees rush past so quick they are just the shadow of a fear—of crashing, of dying.

Then the trail breaks off, the trunks part like a curtain.

There's a small stone house in a silver glade. The coachman stops in front of it. "It will be just a moment," he mutters. "I just need to change a horseshoe."

The King gets out of the carriage, knocks on the door. He is thirsty, and longs for a fire to melt the ice from his boots.

It's no simple woodcutter who opens the door, though, but an old man of solid build and jaundiced complexion, with a greenish birthmark on his nose.

"Victor Klocker to serve you, Your Majesty. Please, come in: it's cold outside."

Regina always liked this part. She claimed to descend from Herr Klocker himself, though sometimes she called him her great-grandfather, and other times her grandfather. He lived outside Oberammergau, where she too was from, and where first she had learned about her legacy. The King, she told us, loved the town, and had attended many of its famous passion plays even before that fateful night. Never mind that the town was too distant from Hohenschwangau, where he stayed while away from Munich, for him to reach Herr Klocker's cabin during one of his midnight carriage runs. You don't ask myths to make sense of cartography.

When she told the tale, the cabin was grander on the inside than from the outside, full of curious clocks and trinkets, hour-glasses, sextants, shining astrolabes. I find it easier to believe it was full of pheasant and partridges, hams, potatoes, with a meaty smoke hanging below the rafters, but it doesn't matter what was inside. What matters is what the King left with, at dawn.

He had the poor coachman, almost frozen to death, fetch a large chest from Herr Klocker's cabin, and when the chest was loaded onto the coach, he kissed Herr Klocker on each cheek, and the old man dropped to his knees and kissed the King's ring.

Then the King was off, bidding goodbye with a final wave of his gloved hand.

As he was instructed to do, he waited until he was back at Hohenschwangau to open the chest. What he found inside, Regina said, made him cry. The sight of his own father's grave could not; but Herr Klocker's gift moved him to tears.

Inside was a large mechanical swan, with a silk-and-gold bridle around his beak. The swan that, in the legend of the Grail, pulled Lohengrin's boat.

"Quick," the King said to the first valet who happened by, "bring it to the Alpsee," and he ran to fetch Paul—his only friend, *aide-de-camp* Prince Paul of Thurn and Taxis—who was asleep in the room next to his.

The King threw himself onto the bed, grabbed the duvet, pulled it away. He took Paul, still sleeping, in his arms, and kissed his eyelids to open them.

"Paul, Paul, wake up. If you love me, you will don Lohengrin's armour and follow me. There is a surprise for you." But he meant for himself.

Paul loved the King, couldn't deny him anything. He got up, shrugged off his nightgown and put on the gold armour of Lohengrin.

And off they went, down from the castle and onto the lakeshore, where the mechanical swan waited only for Paul to step inside. The back of the machine opened to make room for a settee.

It must have been a true thing of beauty. The mirror-like wings, the slender neck which could bend in three different spots. The eyes of jet, the ivory beak. There was a carillon hidden under the feathers, and it played the music of Wagner. As soon as Paul boarded the swan, it was a sorcery. When the mechanical swan felt Paul's weight on it, the wings whirred, the neck craned, the feet paddled away. The mist took care of the rest; Paul *became* Lohengrin.

That night, they set off fireworks.

At that same moment, the King's soldiers were marching off to war, but he didn't care—not while the night was dark, and the fireworks bright, and Paul's face beautiful beside his own.

The tip of a fir caught fire. The villagers saw the flames from afar and called a brigade, but by the time they arrived, the King and Paul were far away, riding their black horses, laughing; Paul because he was young and his blood hot, Ludwig because that night he was no more an enigma to himself. He was just a boy in love.

THE QUARRY

I KNOCKED ON the glass. He was asleep, but he heard me. He raised his head from the pillow, saw me sitting outside the window, and rushed to let me in.

"I was not expecting you," Petrus said. He was in his briefs, standing on the pads of his feet to avoid the touch of the cold bedroom floor as much as possible.

"I was not expecting to come," I said, stopping his hand before he could turn on the light. I sat down on the bed, motioned for him to do the same. "When did you come back?"

"Three hours ago," he said, checking his wristwatch. His face shed sleep like a snake does its skin, with a rub and a shiver. Underneath, his strong features were emphasised by the day-old black stubble on his chin and under his nose. He was the son of immigrants, with heady Greek blood in him, and it gave his face a sheen, like the young rind of a sweet lime. "I was working the Berlin route today. It's late, even for you. Do you want something to drink? Wine? I brought back the one you like."

"A glass would be nice, thank you."

He lived near the church, in a small house made of brown bricks, with shutters painted mint green. His apartment faced towards the hill and our castle. I could see the awkward shape of it, a black silhouette against the indigo clouds amassing in the east. It would start to rain soon.

When he came back, he was holding an old porcelain tray with two glasses of red wine. The glasses were cheap, more plastic than glass; the wine weak, bitter on the tongue, but I had led him to believe I liked it, and could not tell him the truth now.

He knelt on the carpet at the foot of the bed, lay his head on my lap. His hair curled with the night's sweat, and I felt the soft dampness of his skull under my fingers.

I took a sip of the wine. "Tell me something you saw today."

"I saw a young woman on the train." His voice was far away, fighting off the day's tiredness. "She was travelling with her husband—at least I thought he was her husband. They had a small child with them, less than a year old, and the child kept crying. He was howling, red in the face for all he shouted to get their attention. Everyone else in the carriage was looking in their direction, but the woman and the man didn't seem to notice, until an old lady with a coat too big and long for her frame got up, approached the woman, and said to her, 'Your child is crying. Can't you do something?'"

"What did the woman reply?"

Petrus crawled upon the bed, straddled me. His mouth tasted of his sage-flavoured toothpaste, but underneath it I could still detect the beer he had drunk. "She said, 'He will stop when he is tired,' and went on to talk with the man in front of her."

He kissed me, scratching me with his stubble.

"Did he?" I asked, when his mouth moved up to my ear.

"Did he what?"

"Stop—did he stop crying?"

"Not until they left the train in Frankfurt."

In the dark, I searched for his face, found his lips, kissed them; then his chin; his neck. I sucked on it until I tasted blood.

When I was done, he pushed me down, undid the buttons of my shirt one by one. He took my nipple in his mouth. It was his turn to taste me, my moon blood making his light, aerial, just as his own was reddening mine, slowing it down—did Ludwig do the same with Paul, after he was done playing Lohengrin on the mechanical swan? Did he fill his friend with himself, did he suck at his neck and let the red, hot blood of man do its trick; silencing his fears; making peace between his thoughts, making him normal—if only for a while?

It gets lonely in a castle.

"Are you leaving?" Petrus asked me afterwards, as we were lying together in bed, his arm around my waist, his leg between mine.

"What do you mean?"

He propped himself on an elbow. "The first time you came to me. You told me you were leaving soon, but that was, what? Five, six years ago? You never went anywhere."

"I didn't. Do you want me to go?"

"No," he said. "No," he repeated. He kissed me, ran his hand over my chest. I was small compared to him, all bones and no flesh, a saggy skeleton, but he didn't seem to mind. "I don't want you to go, but I'm not going to see you again."

I opened my eyes. "Why?"

Outside, the rain started falling. Above our heads, the patter on the roof was gentle at first, then angry, then furious. Thunder made the windows, and his ribs, rattle.

"I can't tell," said Petrus. "But when I woke up and saw you outside the window, I thought, this is the last time we will see each other. Are you sure you are not leaving?"

I thought of Regina; of the King; the far-away castle, our promised land.

I thought of Agata, in her room, putting pearls in her hair.

I thought of Martin.

"I don't know," I said. "If I do, I'll make sure you're taken care of."

Petrus rolled over, opened the drawer of his nightstand, fished something out of it.

An old, rusty gun. A Mauser, black with a brown, ribbed handle. A thin barrel. It reminded me of his nose, whose bridge my hands knew so well.

"I can take care of myself," he said.

"Why do you have it?"

He looked out of the window, past the glass and the rain, past the roofs, past our castle. The sky was black now; the clouds fleeting gold outlines when lightning struck. No human sound could be heard.

"Sometimes I think shadows follow me," he said. "Like I'm being watched."

I took his head in my hands. "When did this start?"

"When I started seeing you." He wriggled free of my grip, sunk his face in my lap. "It happens only during the day, when I know it can't be you who follows me, but you don't have to worry. I can take care of myself," he repeated.

"Why didn't you tell me?"

"It's not important. Perhaps I'm just imagining it. And you're always here for so little, I didn't want to spoil our time together."

"I'm sorry," I said.

I put the Mauser down on the nightstand on my side of the bed, and held Petrus tight as he searched for my nipple again; hungry not like a child, but like a starving soldier. I gave him all I could, my blood and myself, and later that night, when Petrus had fallen back asleep and I was putting on my clothes, I looked at his face on the pillow. The square chin, the long lashes, the receding hairline.

Over the years he had given me little train models, a glass ball for a Christmas tree I never made, a letter where he told me that sometimes he was not sure I was real. He didn't have much money, but always came back from a trip with a little gift for me—no matter if sometimes weeks, even months passed between my visits, he would have something: the wine he thought I liked, some almond cookies I once said were good.

"I'm sorry," I repeated, and left through the door, because I didn't want to leave the window open. It was cold, outside.

∽

It wasn't a sound that alerted me; it wasn't a shadow. It wasn't even a feeling, a pricking of the thumb.

I turned and there she was, at the end of the street, standing under a red umbrella. She raised a hand, started in my direction. The pelting rain didn't seem to bother her, even though the hem of her frock was drenched. Her shoes must have been too. With each step they made a squelching sound, as though a toad was trapped under the soles.

"Would you like to walk back together?" Regina said, when she was close.

She offered me her arm, and I took it. I knew in that moment that she knew about Petrus, had known all along, but her face was smooth, expressionless, like the sphinx's.

We hadn't been this close in years. She smelled of lead and brass, of sawdust, of peat. The fabric of her frock was coarse, the arm underneath plump.

"Do you remember when I found you in London?" she asked.

I nodded. Why was she here, in the rain, so close to dawn?

I saw her emerging from the shadows of my room; I saw her receding in the shadows below the chapel. She lived a life of her own, locked away in her workroom for hours, days on end, coming out of it only to announce an advance, or else to inflict pain on everyone if something was amiss. She studied the life of the King, and the designs her great-grandfather had left her, perfecting them for the day when her plan would come to fruition. When she left the castle, it was just for practical errands, to buy a piece she needed.

"Do you remember the first thing you asked me about this place?"

I smiled despite myself. "Does it rain a lot over there?"

"Does it rain a lot over there. Yes. A very hands-on question." A pause. "My child of the South, with your bronze skin and black eyes. My child of the North, with your unplaceable accent and your love of formality. Are you happy that you said yes, that you followed me here, despite the rain?"

"I am." I wasn't lying.

She had given me something I thought I could no longer have: hope. Whatever I felt now towards her mission and her plan—*our* mission, *our* plan—I felt only because of the hope she had given me. In a way, by freeing me from the dark spell I was under, she had given me the tools to betray her, allowed my apostasy. Again I asked myself, have I lost faith in the King, or in her? Or is it in my deliverance that I don't believe anymore?

We crossed the town square, started up the road that climbed our hill. The rain had already turned the earth to mud, and the mud ran through roots and rocks, splattering us. It was hard to climb, but Regina was sure of foot, and whenever I stumbled she held me up, her arm strong, her legs unshakeable.

"I'm sorry," she said when we turned the first curve. A bench was by this curve, black now in the rain but usually white with the inscriptions of young lovers. Regina's voice was a rumble under the howling wind. A thunder was building in her pit.

She knows—and this time I didn't mean about Petrus.

She knows, and she's throwing me out. She's having me banished, I thought. The thought drowned me. I found I could not bear the possibility of saying goodbye to Agata, putting my few possessions in a box, walking away from the castle—walking away from the King, and the promise he represented—with the shame of a conviction drawn red upon my heart. I clutched Regina's arm.

"About what?" I said, forcing the syllables out.

"I've let you lapse," she said.

"I—"

She stopped me before I could begin. "There is no need to say anything. It is what it is, Ambrose. My sweet Ambrose, who wanted to know if it ever rains in Frankenstein." She stopped, looked at me. "It does," she said, "same as everywhere else."

We were in front of the gate.

There was a broken snow globe in front of the steps. A second one sat a few feet away, a third one further on. A fourth, a fifth. All broken. A solitude of castles brought me past the gate, past the rookery, down the left side of the hill, deep inside the forest. I knew where they were taking me.

To the swan pond inside the old quarry.

The rain had stopped, but the storm still grumbled above our heads, where the sky swelled like a witch's cauldron. Regina kept a few paces behind me, her unhurried steps making it clear that she already knew what lay ahead. Above, the trees talked with dripping water, a nightjar sang from a far-away branch. My heart was heavy with a presentiment.

There were white sheets afloat on the pond, three drowned ghosts.

But they were not sheets at all.

They were our swans, dead.

Their mute bodies drifted on the water, their wings spread, the necks bent like question marks.

"They were poisoned." Regina's voice was behind me, but it seemed to come from the other side of a nightmare. "The globes appeared after you left. When I came down here, they were already dead. And where were you, instead of keeping guard?"

I didn't—couldn't—say anything.

Small droplets of rain stuck to the swans' feathers, shiny as diamonds.

"Tell the others," Regina said. "We leave the day after tomorrow."

THE STARS

"WE ARE NOT ready yet," the Baron said. It was the first time I had heard him contradict Regina. His voice did not quiver.

We were sitting in the great hall. Three tallow candles burned in the dark at the centre of the table, the masts of an eldritch galleon riding the night waves with a death fire shining upon them.

"Someone is onto us," Regina said. "It is a sign, a declaration of war. We cannot wait for them to lay siege to the castle, to ruin everything we've worked for."

The Baron turned to me. Behind his red-lacquered mask in the shape of a Japanese devil, his eyes were shot with blood. He must have slept little, if at all. I doubted any of us had had much rest.

"You," he hissed. He had always detested me, another man to vie for Regina's attention, for the King's. He must have come from old aristocracy, the kind adroit at the finest machinations of palace protocols, because nothing seemed as natural to him as the superciliousness he displayed in my regard. It was clear he considered me his inferior.

"You," the Baron repeated. "How could you let this happen? It was your duty to keep watch, and yet—" He pounded the table with his fist. His walking cane, which rested beside him, gave a jolt. The pearl pommel trapped the candlelight on its surface. We all knew it hid a blade inside.

"I—" I said, then I looked at Agata. "We—"

"Don't drag her into this!" said the Baron. "This is your fault, and yours alone." He turned back to Regina. "You must listen to me. I've looked at the charts, the stars are not right yet. We risk—"

"We risk everything by staying here," she said. "Do you think I'm taking this decision lightly? It took me more years than I can count to perfect my grandfather's design, to make sure that our wings function the way they are supposed to, that they can sustain gale and storm. Years of experiments, scrapped prototypes, failures. It was before your time here, after everyone else deserted the Order but me! It was hard, solitary work, but I never complained, never wavered, because I knew what was at stake. And then it was you—you and your stars, your missing alignments. You told me the constellations were not right, they did not bode well for our mission, and I believed you, I waited. I was patient, because nothing is more important than this. Now I'm not patient anymore. I don't care about the stars anymore." Her voice rose, her hands balled into fists. "This might be our only chance, and I'm not going to squander it because your damned Mercury isn't where he's supposed to be!"

I've said that Regina reminded me of the sirens in the old Russian legends, her black frock substituting for the black feathering of the monster, but now she sang no more her song of sorrow and salvation. Lack of sleep and a new steely resolution had redrawn her features into those of a tuneless harpy in a Flemish woodcut, all teeth and anger. Hanging loose around her shoulders, her hair was a tangle of coral snakes ready to spring into life, to attack, to poison. I had to look away.

"The wings are ready," she went on. "They have been tested time and time again, and they work, as do the safety mechanisms I've built within. The trajectory is planned, and verified, you said so yourself."

The Baron, cowed and ashamed, was looking down at his nails, which he filed every day with a tortoiseshell file that must have cost more than all my possessions combined. There was something crazy and bloody in his eyes, a murder of broken capillaries. I could feel waves of resentment coming off him, hot, scorching. As much as we were not used to hearing him disagree with Regina, he was even less used to being disregarded in public.

"If we stay here, we expose ourselves to harm," Regina said. "And don't be mistaken; they mean harm, those who killed our swans and left us so eloquent a message."

She looked at Agata, then at me.

"The King's swans—dead and poisoned. His castles—broken. It means war."

"I—" The sound of my voice was so alien in the silence following Regina's words that I stopped. I looked at Agata. A steeliness was hardening her lineaments, the product of some deep thought struggling to crawl to the fore of her mind. "We could ask for help," I went on. "My old friends in Deptford—"

The air which shot out of Regina's nostrils was fire. "Your friends," she said, twisting the word on her tongue so that it lost all its meaning, "are a pack of heathens, outside of the King's grace. Their names won't be spoken here."

She rose, went to the far wall, where the King's *zweihänder* hung, sunk in the shadows of the undercroft. The greatsword—one of our most sacred relics—seemed to float in the darkness, ready to fall down and bite Regina's neck. But she was no hapless victim.

She raised her arm, and the darkness swallowed it; when she pulled it back, the sword followed, Regina's stalk-like fingers gripping the handle with a strength one would have been unwise to underestimate.

"We will not let anyone ruin our plan or delay us further," she said, and swung the sword once. The air keened. She looked at me over the invisible wound she had left in the fabric of space. "Say your goodbyes, make your preparations. We leave tomorrow."

"But the stars—"

Regina cut off the Baron's protestation. "I'm sorry if I gave you—all of you—the wrong impression that this was a debate. It isn't. We are going to leave tomorrow, at midnight, when the old day ends and the new starts. Be at the top of the old watchtower then, and you will leave with me; otherwise—I won't force you. If you prefer to stay here, you must know that you will do so outside my tutelage, and at your own peril. Your wings will be broken, and the way to the King will forever be closed to you. I alone know the way to him through mist and shadow," she said.

The Baron's head dropped at once, and for a moment he seemed ready to bend the knee too. He stormed off.

"I will be there," Agata said. She looked at me, read the disbelief on my face. "I will," she repeated as she rose from the table. In the candlelight, her white ruff shone like a ring of Saturn. "I won't have wasted half of my life for nothing, but I beg you," she said, and went to Regina, took her free hand in hers. "I beg you, let me leave the castle to set my things in order before we leave."

"Go," Regina said, and Agata too left the great hall.

"I am sorry," I said, after a long, empty silence.

Regina didn't say anything. With sword in hand, she could have been a sculpted effigy on a knight's sarcophagus, her face as mute.

"I'm sorry," I repeated. "I have failed you—all of you."

I was already climbing the stairs when her reply came.

"*Obscurum per obscurius*," she said.

cʒ

AFTER LAST NIGHT'S rain, the air outside was unseasonably warm. I unbuttoned the collar of my shirt, shrugged the Chesterfield off.

Stars as big as lit windows suggested a conspiracy of houses hidden behind the cool mist swirling up above, while down below—when I looked past the crumbling bailey walls—black alders with leaves as dark as garnets concealed the real village from my view. The silence was utter, I was alone.

Except I wasn't.

The Baron's voice crept around the willow's bark to reach me.

"Ambrose," he whispered. "No, don't look. Come here, listen."

I leaned against the tree. Hearing my name in his mouth— a rare occurrence—shook me out of my numbed stupor enough to feel the fear swelling in his voice.

"What do you want?"

The Baron ignored the implication of impatience. "Can you find them?" he said, his words barely audible above the lazy rustling of the willow's branches.

"Who?"

"The ones who killed the swans. The ones who want us dead."

"What difference does it make?"

"Something is amiss," the Baron said. The dead leaves lying on the ground around us creaked as he shuffled his feet, looking for signs that Regina was nearby. "She is not thinking straight. Her machines might be ready, but the stars are not. The sky maps—they are all wrong. Mercury's missing. He is hiding, but from what?"

"What do you mean? Do you know something that we don't?"

"I just told you, you idiot. Listen. Something is not right. Find them. If we can strike them before they strike us, perhaps I can convince her—"

Regina emerged from the undercroft and looked at me.

"I would've imagined you gone already. In the village. To say your goodbyes."

"I have to say goodbye to the castle too," I lied. "It was kind to me—to us all."

She nodded, then went her way towards the rookery. Something had to be done about the swans. She wouldn't let the beaks of vultures ravage them, because that would displease the King. The swans had to be buried.

When I was sure she had left, I turned around, but the Baron was gone. I stared at the empty space behind the willow, thinking I could still see the outline of his shadow on the wall beyond, where a hairy webworm was making its slow way past a black crack in the stone. Now I really was alone.

Was the Baron right? Could I stave off our departure?

I felt hollow, as if, during the day, a cook had come to my room, scrubbed the walls of my body clean, emptying me of heart and liver, readying me for stuffing. I couldn't say on whose table I was being offered.

When I moved, it was with the stilted purpose of an

automaton. I had to do what needed to be done, regardless of what would happen.

I went to my room, collected all the money I had, the hand-mirror with the moonstone handle, the old Scottish knife, which could fetch a good value with the right dealer. I looked around for anything else that was precious, but besides a couple of rings I had bought in Camden and a little glass statuette, I had nothing.

I took everything, put it in a shoebox, and left.

છ

PETRUS WASN'T HOME when I arrived, but I know my way around a locked house—I had always refused the key he wanted to give me—and left the money and the shoebox on his bed. On the shoebox I wrote: *You were right.*

The first time I'd seen Petrus, he'd been sitting on the lone bench on the path leading up to our castle. I'd been preoccupied with some thought or other—Martin, most probably—and I'd only spotted him when it was too late to hide.

He had looked up, almost expectantly, a big grin brightening up his bleak expression. He was alone, nursing a bottle of beer beaded with condensation, and smoking a cigarette—a habit, I learned afterwards, which he only returned to when he was feeling dejected.

"Hello," he said, taking no notice of my ghastly appearance, the diaphanous skin, the dishevelled hair, the sunken eyes. "How are you doing?"

There was something so innocent, and at the same time eager, about the way he looked at me that I found myself sitting down beside him. He started talking immediately, telling me that he'd been laid off from his job, but that it was going to be okay, he hadn't liked it very much in the first place. He was thinking of applying to another one, for the role of train conductor on the local line.

He was wearing jeans frayed at the rim, and not because it was fashionable. His plain white t-shirt was so threadbare I could see through it. His sneakers looked like they'd been worn, day in and day out, for the last five or six years, their original colour long since washed away. And yet, even though I suspected he'd spent the very last of his money on that beer, he tipped the bottle in my direction. "Want some?"

I took a sip, then said, "Why do you want to be a train conductor?"

He shrugged, lit another cigarette. Only two remained in the pack. "It's a way to get out of this fucking town," he said. "See other places."

"But you'd only be passing through," I said. "You'll always come back here."

I don't know why I said this. I was miserable myself, and looking for a way out of my own prison—my mind, the castle, Frankenstein. He winced, hurt and shame drawing deep lines on his face, but he did his best to keep his smile up. He squared his shoulders and looked straight at me. "Perhaps," he said, "but you never know. Perhaps I'll meet a rich man on the train and he'll fall in love with me and take me to his house in…" He searched for a place that was as far away from Frankenstein as he could think of. "…Cologne," he settled on, and started laughing, and later on, at his apartment, when I asked him if I could taste his blood, if he wanted to taste mine, he unbuttoned my trousers and said, "Only if you have a house in Cologne."

I didn't.

I let my fingers linger on the shoebox. On the shelf above the bed there was a framed photograph. It was of Petrus, his face red after too much time in the sun, posing in front of the Hohenzollern Bridge and the Cologne Cathedral. He had one thumb up and was smiling in that goofy way of his. "See?" he'd told me when he showed it to me. The conductor job was going well, he'd saved enough for a down payment on a house, the one I was standing in right now, wondering if it was me who had kept him in Frankenstein all those years, despite what he'd told me that first night about wanting to get out. My sweet Petrus.

I wanted a memory—a good one, like Agata had said—so I took the picture, left the frame, then left the house.

℘

MANFRED WASN'T HARD to find. I knew some of his haunts, and discovered him as he was tearing into a mouse on the bank of the Hochspeyerbach behind the *gasthaus*, where the brook bent and a guelder-rose offered him plenty of shelter. I crouched down before him, and he looked at me as he continued to chew on the mouse.

"This is it," I said. "We are leaving."

He stopped eating, sniffed the air around my face.

"You know I'd bring you with me, if I could—if I was sure that I'm going, that it's going to be safe. I don't know anything. But if I go, and if everything is all right, you must know that I will come back for you. You are my friend." I offered him my finger, and he licked it. "Do you want to help me one last time?"

Manfred pushed his head against my chin.

"You told me the town was bracing for *something*. You were right. Someone killed our swans and left us a message that means we're next. It's why Regina wants to leave."

He growled, then the growl became a purr. He nuzzled my ear.

"Can you find them?" I asked, echoing the Baron's question. "The swan poisoners. We don't have much time, but if you can find them…"

If he could find them, then what?

We would kill them before they could kill us? Would I kill for a King I wasn't sure was waiting for us—a King I didn't feel worthy of, because who could, when in his crown the entire universe rested?

I didn't have an answer, though this I knew: I would kill for Agata, and for Regina, and the Baron too. We were kin, joined by something deeper than the colour of our blood—by the history we shared. Even as I was getting ready to betray them, I knew I would do anything to keep them safe from harm.

"If you can find them," I repeated, and said no more.

Manfred crawled out of the bush, trotted towards the church and the graveyard. He was friends with ghosts there, and wisps.

"I will wait for you in my room. Tomorrow," I said to his tail. "We leave at midnight."

"We're leaving," a faint voice behind me said.

I turned and saw Agata. She was wearing a black cape drawn tightly around her shoulders, but I could spy the sparkling scarlet of her dress underneath. One of her favourites. She was going to William—keeping off the main road to avoid being seen—and for him she'd put red shadow around her eyes. Her lips were red too, but her face was chalk white. Her fingers, clutching the ribbon at her neck, were trembling.

I went to her, took her hand, rubbed my knuckles on her palm until a little of her worry dissipated. "Are you sure you want to go?" I said, searching her countenance for a sign, I didn't know of what.

"My Father of Cups," she whispered. "I need to see this through. I need to know it wasn't all for naught."

"What about William?"

Her resolution, I saw, was feeble. Doubt danced on her brow, but she shook her head. "Perhaps I'll come back for him," she said, her nose turned towards the night above us.

"What if you can't? What if—"

"Then I will see him in my dreams," she said, and her voice was a singsong falling from the stars. "I'll often dream of this place, which I know so well. The Frankenstein of my dreams won't be like the real one, but our castle will be there, and this brook, and William too. I'll knock three times on his door, and even if he's dreaming of summer he'll dream of me, and we'll dance until he wakes up."

"Will that be enough?" I asked, and she looked at me and saw my fear through my skull, and my anger. She saw what I was going to do next. But she didn't say anything. She put her hand on my cheek, kissed my forehead, then she was gone, her cape swishing across the wet grass.

I stared at her until she disappeared behind the *gasthaus*, then I sighed and went to Martin.

THE QUESTION

THE LIGHT IN the study was out. I asked a favour of the wood, and pushed the window open. I slipped in.

It was a strange feeling, standing inside his study when Martin was in the house. We had never occupied the same space, shared the same air. A barrier had always stood between us: the window through which I spied on him; the garage door I pressed my ear to while he was cutting wood for the winter or getting things ready for one of the family's camping trips in the Vulkaneifel forest, where he owned a small hunting lodge. He was an enthusiastic hunter, roe deer were his favourite prey, but he often brought home woodcocks, pigeons, quails. His son didn't like game, but his daughter craved it, and he was teaching her to shoot at foxes.

I went to his bedroom, found it empty, the bed cold. I recognised the book on his nightstand, quarter leather binding with green cloth-covered boards and the title in golden letters on the spine: *Idiocy and Its Treatment by the Physiological Method*, by Edward Seguin, M.D. I had often seen it atop the pile of volumes he kept on his study desk, and had skimmed through it, even though it had no pictures of brains inside, only illustrations of feral children found in the forests of France.

I looked in the bathroom, ran my fingers on the soft fabric of his towel, still damp.

When I reached the landing, a faint snoring sound brought me to the other side of the house, to a smoking room I had never seen before from the outside—its heavy curtains were always drawn—or visited when I had snuck in.

It was as full of books as Martin's study, but the volumes here were of a different kind, books about birds and the rivers of the region, its forests. A lot of them were books on military history, and indeed the room was decorated with far more masculine taste than the rest of the house, with a pair of scimitars crossing over above the mantelpiece and the bust of an Italian *condottiero* resting on a marble socle by the window.

There were no pictures in the room, save for a rather large, discoloured print which hung in front of the fireplace. It depicted a stylised sun suspended above a table, upon which were laid out a rifle, a knife whose handle was engraved with scenes of dogs and hunting parties, and a weighing scale. The table sat in front of a mountain landscape that I was sure represented our valley, though the perspective was off, and I noticed that Castle Frankenstein was missing from the hilltop it was supposed to occupy. Between the sun and the table, a banner unfurled in the sky, bearing the words: *Stat sua cuique dies*.

I had never seen the like anywhere else in the Hungers' house, but reckoned the family had chosen this room to honour the memory of Martin's father, a taciturn man by all accounts, at ease only when rifles were involved. A love of hunting was the sole legacy he had left his son.

Martin was asleep in a dark brown leather chair, a book splayed across his chest and a half-drunk glass of Porto still in his hands, and about to roll off onto the embroidered carpet stretching across almost the entire room. The air was stuffy, heavy with sweat and the smouldering cinders in the fireplace. A wispy coil of smoke still rose from Martin's sepiolite pipe, abandoned on a small table beside a paper knife.

I sat down in the chair in front of him, careful not to make a sound because I didn't want to startle him—not too much, at least. I waited.

Perhaps a half-hour later, stirring in his sleep, Martin shifted position, opened his eyes to the room, closed them—then jolted up, fully awake and panicked. The Porto glass sailed through the air followed by a plume of wine as Martin fumbled around until his hands found the paper knife on the table.

"You won't need it," I said, trying to keep my voice steady, though his fear had infected me. My heart was pounding, but he couldn't hear it like I could his, racing, jumping.

He had unbuttoned his shirt before dozing off. The vein in his neck was thick with terror. I saw his eyes dart to the door then to the window on his left, which opened onto a small garden. But as usual the curtains were drawn; he would fumble, I would catch him. And the drop. It would amount to nothing for me, but he would risk his legs, and again, I would catch him. He had no way out.

The spasm of his neck was painful to watch.

"Don't be alarmed," I said. "Please, I don't mean you harm."

"What do you want?" Martin said. My appearance did not kill him after all, but—

Something is amiss—

The Baron's voice boomed behind my eyes. Something cold, wet, sticky dripped down my throat and I felt the urge to flee.

Martin hadn't asked me who I was.

He was afraid, but he was not surprised.

I could feel it, this lack of shock, hard and cutting as a flint. It hit me in the chest, between the ribs. Breathing became hard. I knew then that I should leave, because the Baron's voice was right, something was amiss, but I could not. I swallowed.

"I have a question that needs answering," I said. "Only you can do it."

He lowered the paper knife, lay it on his leg, the point still aimed at me, in case I should lunge at him. His chinos showed the contours of his sex, still hard with sleep, though shrinking now.

"What makes you think I know the answer?" he said.

"I've been keeping an eye on you—something of which I think you are aware," I said, a weird sadness mellowing my voice. "You didn't ask me who I am, which must mean you know. When did you first see me?"

His face turned red, he stuttered. "I didn't. See you, I mean. But I knew you were watching. I know who—*what* you are."

I sat up straighter, this small movement enough for Martin's grip on the knife to tighten. My blood was icy, alarm slowing my thoughts to a crawl. *He knows.* Every inch of my skin itched with premonition, and my confusion must have been apparent, because I saw something akin to a brief smile flash on Martin's lips. I felt insulted by it, and it was this insult that shook me out of my stupefaction. I arranged my face into a sneer.

"If you know *what* I am, then you know that your little knife will be utterly useless, if I decide to attack you?"

"I do," Martin said. He didn't release the grip, but his smile was gone, and I was feeling more in command. I crossed my legs, feigning an almost excessive indifference.

"How did you find out about me?"

Martin studied my face, wetted his lips. He was trying to gauge what trap the question concealed, to decide how much he could let on. The vein in his neck kept throbbing and I let my eyes follow it, past his collarbone, down to the first tufts of grey hair peeping through the flannel of his shirt.

See, I wanted to say, *this is a game we both can play.*

"My family," he said. "They have been in Frankenstein for many generations, same as the denizens of the castle. We know that it's not deserted, that you live up there. Sometimes, when the wind is right, we hear music coming out from under the hill. Many turn their heads away, but my grandfather used to keep a journal about all the odd things that happened around the old keep."

"I didn't think I was famous in your family."

Martin ignored my attempt at humour. "Why show yourself tonight?"

Something is amiss. Something is not right. The stars—

The Baron's voice, again.

I knew I was in peril. If Martin knew about us, if the secrecy that Regina had taught us was paramount was breached, I was putting myself and the others at great risk by staying there. For all I knew, it could have been Martin, fed up with all our queer doings, who had poisoned the swans and left us the broken castles; Martin who wanted us dead, or driven out of town for good. But it was hard to give up the hope I had nursed during my solitary nights outside his window, the hope that his medicine could fix what Regina's faith, in the end, could not. I decided to press on.

"Since you seem to know a great deal about us, the denizens of the castle, aren't you a little curious about what it is that I want to ask you? Don't you want to know why I stalked you for years, watching you as you had sex with your wife, as you put your children to bed? I watched you read, and study, and type away at your Adler. By the way, did you ever publish the article you were working on, about noctambulism? Oh, Martin. I was with you at your mother's wake."

Martin's fingers curled around the knife.

I raised a hand in the air, smiled coyly to suggest my remorse. I wanted him as confused as I was. "I'm sorry, I should not tease you after breaking into your house, without even the courtesy of introducing myself. My name," I added, pressing a palm to my chest to signal the truthfulness of what I was about to say, "is Ambrose."

Martin was a man of science, but he knew that a name is a powerful thing; that knowing someone's name gives you sway over them. It was a primordial knowledge, etched in some part of his brain I didn't have a name for, though probably he did.

He put down the paper knife, adjusted his trousers, and allowed his shoulders to rest against the back for the chair. I saw him eye the bottle of Porto, sitting on a low mahogany table in the centre of the room, but so positioned that it was closer to me than him.

Raising both my hands to show him I had no foul intentions, I got up, picked up his glass from the carpet, shook off the last old drops, and poured Martin the wine, of a deep cardinal purple where the flames dancing in the hearth made it shine.

Now came the tricky part.

I made my way around the table, approaching Martin's chair as slowly as I could. He stank of wine and wet unease.

I stopped a full two feet before reaching him and extended my arm.

When he took the glass from me, his index finger brushed against mine and the warmth of it was almost too much to resist. Desire must have flashed on my face because I saw him recoil from me as though from an adder. I retreated.

He waited until I was sitting down again before taking a quick sip of the wine, followed by a second one, longer this time, thirstier. Even with a whole room between us, I could feel the alcohol clotting his blood, mantling it.

"What do you want to ask me?" he said, setting down the glass beside the knife. They were the only two things that offered him a little safety in the situation—at least the illusion of it—and he needed them close.

I had had many years to think about this moment; about how to phrase my question, how to leave all ambiguity out. Yet all the words I had lined up in my mind failed me. I felt the urge to lie, to dress up my ugly truth. I felt the urge to flee, because—the Baron's words kept ringing in my ears—something was not right. I knew I couldn't trust Martin anymore, but he was still the only chance I could see.

The only chance *not* to leave.

"I was born of a mother and a father much like everyone else," I said after a pause, feeling a rather Dickensian incipit might endear him, "but I am different from much everyone else. I do not know why. Is it something that I suckled on in the womb? A flaw I was born with, for which no one is responsible but fate? I don't know. It's just the way it is, the way it has always been—until I was offered a chance. Someone found me, many years ago, and told me a solution was possible, not in this world, but in the next. And now—now we are to leave tomorrow. Suppose I don't want to. Suppose I want to stay here, find peace here, without flying to the moon."

I moved fast; too fast for him to see or do anything about it.

I took the paper knife in one hand and stabbed the palm of the other with it. When his corneas processed what had happened, Martin's first reaction was to dart sideways, but

72

the sight of my pink blood falling to the floor froze his lunge mid-air.

His eyes widened, and he fell back into the chair.

"Is this one of the phenomena you've studied? I told you, I saw your paper. You wrote that you have a cure, you put it in the title." It was time. The question I'd come to ask left my mouth, exploded into the world: "Can you help me?"

Martin's features were being drawn and redrawn as different emotions—fright, revulsion, amazement—battled for control of his muscles. I pushed on.

"Can I ever stop being afraid? Can I ever be happy?"

Something flashed in Martin's face then, something ugly. A triumph of some kind, a victory he had stopped hoping for until this moment. This feeling, whatever it was, shot down from his eyes, animated the rest of his body. He grabbed my wrist, pulled at me.

"I—" he said, and this close his breath reeked not of fear, but of a strange purpose.

A nameless terror choked me. It was Agata's voice I heard now.

The Son of Swords. A man. Strong, assertive. Violent. You don't know the real extent of his knowledge.

I jerked away, flew across the room, smashed through the window. A myriad of glass shards exploded inside, making the air solid—Martin let out a cry, crouched down, covered his head with his arms, from the glass, from the monster. But I was out.

The night held me, then dropped me to the ground. I started running.

Away from Martin and the things he knew that I didn't; back towards the Castle, towards Regina. Towards the King on the Moon, who, perhaps, was waiting.

THE DOPPELGÄNGER

Is it the blood, or the mind rather? Do the red cells—are they still called red cells if one's blood is not red? Are they to be called pink cells?—do the red cells, when they course through the brain, do something to the electricity flowing there, or is it the spider trapped inside our skull that has subjugated the biology of our blood?

I don't know. I wonder if Ludwig did, though he made his choice in the end.

There must be an end.

When everything turned to shit, when Paul left him to marry and he lost his crown and country to Bismarck, he went back to the silver glade in the woods near Oberammergau.

Walpurgisnacht, night of witches and betrayal. A long, black cape billowing behind his shoulders, he retraced his steps from many years before. He stood at the door, hesitated, then knocked.

"Your Majesty. Please, come in: it's cold outside."

Herr Klocker's greenish birthmark had grown since last the

King had seen him—it now covered almost half the old man's face—but he didn't pay attention to that. He had a plea to issue; and his friend listened.

Three days and three nights passed, and still the King did not leave the house. No one knows what they talked about during this time, the book doesn't say, and Regina could never be convinced to give away the secret her great-grandfather had sworn her to.

We only know that a month later, two large chests arrived at Hohenschwangau, with a note, written in Herr Klocker's meticulous hand, proclaiming the contents to be among the old inventor's finest works yet, if not indeed the very best.

The King ordered the smallest of the two chests brought to his private chapel, then asked to be left alone. He opened the second chest, and from it a second King crawled out with a yawn and a stretch, like a brown bear waking after a long winter slumber.

It was like looking in a mirror. The automaton resembled Ludwig down to the last comedo on his long, commanding nose. It was even dressed like the true King: the same silk waistcoat, as blue as his eyes; the white, ruffled shirt; the waxed cavalry boots.

The King took a step back, gazing at his doppelgänger with a profound melancholy, though mixed with the same amazement he had felt when looking at Paul, sailing on the Alpsee upon the mechanical swan. He raised a hand, stroked the machine's cheek—his own.

"I'm sorry," he said.

"I know," said the automaton.

From that day on, whenever the King had to appear in public, at some function of state, or even at the theatre, when he could not arrange for a private show to be staged at the Residenz, it was not him who went out to shake hands, or to applaud, or to give a speech before Parliament. It was the automaton, who, it must be said, performed these tasks with remarkable bravura, mimicking the King's tics with such convincing power that not even those closer to the King ever doubted a thing. How could they?

In time, the King started resorting to the automaton more and more, taking it out of its chest every single day, winding its secret mechanism until a song started gurgling in its throat: *Hojotoho! Heiaha!*

"I'm sorry," he told the automaton every day.

And every day the automaton replied: "I know."

Shielded from reality by his brother of steel and brass gear-wheels, the King retreated to a world wholly his own, a nocturnal province of music and poetry, peaks and woods, the castles he was building. There were rough beards scratching his lips, and snow glistening white in his black hair after a midnight race through the trees at the breakneck pace he was fond of, because it made it seem like he could fly. Sometimes, in the dark, he heard the moon calling to him, like she had promised she would.

The automaton, meanwhile, was getting quite fat on account of the many state dinners he had to attend. His poor metal innards were not made for ale and pastries, and it was because of some malfunction of his metal stomach that his porcelain teeth started to rot and fall out. The King wondered sometimes, when he noticed a new tooth missing, if he should not send it back to Herr Klocker for a do-over, but in truth he was happy that the machine was getting disfigured, not because he hated it—on the contrary he loved it like a real brother—but because now that it was fat and ugly, everyone would forget about King Ludwig of the House of Wittelsbach, and leave him alone.

Near the end, he drank and danced and fucked in the deserted halls of his mountain palace with whomever wanted to be kind with him that night. He listened to Wagner, he played his Bösendorfer, he sang. He ran under the moon, howled at the stars, and not even the automaton could protect him from all that, because he was seen, spied upon.

And soon they started talking.

Mad, they said. *Unfit for the throne.*

☙

THE SENTENCE IS pronounced, all that is left is to carry it out.

The King, the real one, is at the top of Neuschwanstein's tallest tower when they come for him. He seldom gets out, these days.

Gudden, the doctor who declared him mad; the conspirators, ministers and dignitaries who looked in horror at the bleeding coffers of the crown; the orderlies who have to restrain him— they've all come up the mountain to arrest him.

In the hall, a young valet with pimples on his nose keeps refusing the automaton the key to the tower, for fear that it wants to kill itself. The boy knows no other King than this one, the false one, but he loves him; doesn't want to see him dead, even though the poor machine longs only for a last look at its twin, the King his creator built it in the image of. Because it knows that it will die soon.

They knock at the castle door, polite to the end.

They can't know that the real King is asleep in the tower, they have the other one in front of them. They can't know that there are two. They take the automaton from Neuschwanstein, drive him to Berg, which is to serve as the King's prison, though now he—he, it, none of that matters anymore—is no longer King; that's an honour that belongs to his uncle Luitpold, prince of betrayers.

They disrobe him—where does the blue waistcoat end up?

They forbid him to attend Mass.

"I'm afraid it's not possible," says Doctor Gudden. "Too many emotions are bad for Your Majesty. Though, perhaps, a walk?"

"Why not."

"It rained in the afternoon, but it seems to have cleared up, just a few clouds now. Isn't the Starnberger See lovely on a June evening?"

"Here, take this umbrella, boy," the mechanical King says. "I won't need it where I'm going."

They are dead, a few hours later, in the cold waters of the lake, face down, the doctor and the automaton, his burnished heart of gold stopped by all that water, the fine-spun whorls of his brain unstirring. He was just a robot, after all.

A sudden echo rings inside the King's chamber, in the tallest tower of Neuschwanstein: *Hojo… to… ho!…* He wakes up, and knows his twin brother is dead.

The King takes out the second chest Herr Klocker gave him.

There is a pair of mechanical wings inside; a complex, intricate mechanism of pulleys and sheaves, levers and gears, with feathers of folded silk coated in beeswax. The fabric is so lustrous it glistens in the black night as the King stands on the windowsill, ready to jump.

An angel, someone will say afterwards, for he is sighted when he flies away—but only briefly, because then he is gone, beyond the dust of the stars, to his last castle, Montsalvat on the moon, where his pink-blooded court is waiting for him.

Perhaps Paul will be there, too.

THE WINGS

MANFRED DID NOT come. I waited for him, measuring the length of my room with furious paces. Every time I faced the map of the valley, I looked at it as if it might suddenly yield a treasure—a way out. But there was none.

Something is not right.

The King was there with me, in the corners. Martin too. Martin who knew about me. Martin who had looked at me like a prize and grabbed my wrist.

Something is not right.

The Baron's words had made a kingdom of my skull. There they ruled like capricious princes who changed their minds like a weathercock does direction. There was one such vane in Frankenstein, shining gold atop a humble roof, and as out of place there as I felt inside my own prickling skin.

What wasn't right?

When the moonlight shafts, sneaking in through the planks boarding up the window, caught the spider webs dangling from the rafters of my old dovecote, they shone like so many broken snow globes.

A procession of images visited me as I paced the room, hinting at something I could not divine.

Regina under her red umbrella, outside Petrus' house.

Martin asleep in the chair, the smoke of his pipe, the paper knife.

The three dead swans with their necks asking a question without answer.

Something is not right.

Where is Manfred? I whistled to make him come, but he didn't.

What was I to do?

Something is not right. The sky maps are wrong.

I took my wings from their nail, blew the dust off.

They were nothing like the King's.

Regina might have perfected her great-grandfather's design, but had woefully neglected the appearance of her models.

Instead of the feathery wings of angels and swans, ours resembled a bat's—a thumped one at that. The main frame, shaped like two upturned Ws, was built out of wood, with metal joints made of an alloy of Regina's own concoction, which gave them a dull pearly glint. The patagium, so to speak, was made of a textile material which bore a superficial resemblance to satin, despite it being much sturdier. A leather harness joined the two Ws in the middle, for donning them. Attached to it was a lever that operated the wings, folding and spreading them.

I tried them on.

They fitted my shoulders well, the harness easily finding the groove it had dug in my flesh during countless practice lessons over the years.

80

Sometimes a kid would look up, see a large shape flying above the castle and run to his parents and talk about dragons, and the parents would laugh, but repeat the story to friends, and I knew—when it was my turn to hear it from my informers—that the kid had seen one of us.

Like the leather knew where to fit, I knew what I was supposed to do.

I knew how to operate the lever; when to open the wings, when to fold them. I knew Regina. I knew Agata and the Baron. They were my family, and they were my cult, and perhaps there is no difference.

I knew this, and didn't know the rest; what waited for me if I were to stay behind.

I knew I wouldn't go back to Martin, not now that I knew that—

Something is not right.

—I didn't know what I knew, except that I had to stop running.

With my wings on my shoulders, I went to the courtyard.

❧

"I wasn't sure you'd come," Agata said, when I appeared beside her.

She was wearing white, an impossible circumstance. She had white dresses in her armoire, the finest silks of Paris, the softest Saragossa velvets, but she never wore them. White, she confessed to me once, reminded her of the day she ran from home. After she told me this, I took to picturing her in a wedding gown as she galloped through the woods of the Pyrenees—though this was just a fantasy of mine since, like much that regarded her family and her upbringing, she didn't like to talk about that day except in the vaguest of terms. "You ran away from a lack of expectations," she was fond of repeating. "I ran away from an excess of them."

The white dress she was wearing that night, with delicate black ribbons coiling on the sleeves of her jacket and on the long skirt, didn't suggest a wedding, though. It signalled a half-mourning.

"I was not sure myself," I said. "Have you said goodbye to William?"

"He's gone," she said, playing with the bands of lace that tightened the dress at her neck. "Off somewhere else where there's work, money to be earned, a girl to marry, perhaps." She looked away, at the far edge of the valley. From where we were standing, on the old watchtower's parapet, we could see everything.

"I'm sorry," I said.

"It's just as well," she said, and smiled, and touched my wings. "Look at us, Ambrose, my Father of Cups. Finally holding up a promise, one that we made a long time ago."

"Or one that was made for us."

She shook her head. She had done her dark blond hair in a fishtail braid—a sensible choice, and yet one that also made her look younger, like she was in her portrait. The defiant fingers that held the tiger cub were the same defiant fingers that now scratched at the harness making her skin itch. Her wings were dented from many falls.

"We've spent a lifetime or two thinking about this moment. About leaving, about joining the King. Don't you want to see for yourself? I'd rather know."

I didn't, but Agata took my hand, and that was that, perhaps.

I was not alone, not tonight.

Soon the Baron joined us. For the occasion, he had chosen a simple, featureless vizard of black cardboard, which—in contrast with the garish masks he liked to wear, gesso and gold leaf, gems, sequins—gave him a hieratic appearance.

He marched up to me. "Nothing?" he said.

I shrugged, and he fell in line with us, but his movements were stilted, his neck stiff. Behind the mask, his eyes were red with more than sleeplessness. A faint growl was coming from his throat, and I thought of a wolf, beaten, bloody, cornered, yet still snarling, still dangerous—more dangerous than ever, actually.

Down in the courtyard, we heard heavy footsteps marching upon the gravel. We heard the heels turning, then the steps, measured now, climbing the stone stairs that led to the parapet. We didn't turn to look. The steps grew louder behind our backs.

Regina stopped in front of us, reviewing her troops.

"We are ready," she said when she was satisfied with the inspection, then started towards the edge of the parapet.

I found myself speaking before I had a chance to realise what I was going to say. "This is it?" I blurted. "We are going to take off just like this?"

She swivelled back with such force that, for an instant, I thought she was going to tumble forwards under the pull of her own momentum. Whatever apprehension or excitement her body was feeling, her face was blank—blanker than the Baron's mask—when she looked at me.

I searched her eyes for signs of fear or bravery, eagerness or reluctance, but found them empty, not only of feeling, but also of recognition. She almost seemed to question my presence there, my very existence. The moon and the King were her blinkers, and she could not see anything but the path they showed.

I flinched under the sheer nothingness of her gaze, and the spell broke.

Her features softened in her mother-mask. She spread her

arms, and it looked like she wanted to pull us all into an embrace.

"He is waiting," she said. "And we too have waited too long for this moment. There is nothing here to miss, and no one, and nothing and no one that will miss us."

"I will miss the Bösendorfer," Agata said.

"There is no cause to miss it," said Regina, her voice sweet, her tone firm. "My great-grandfather built for the King a special piano made of hornbeam and beech, whose strings are as fine as an elf's longbow, and just as resistant. It makes a most beautiful music, which can rival the music of the celestial spheres."

She shifted her eyes to the Baron who, under her gaze, squared his shoulders, jutted out his breastbone.

"There is a room there, filled with the most ornate masks you will ever see, with cairngorms and jaspers that reflect the sparkle of the ballroom's suspended lights. There's a *fête* every night in the halls of the King. And if you tire of the balls, there is an observatory in the highest tower, with a refracting telescope made to the exact specifications of Kepler."

It was my turn.

"And the library," Regina said. "Electrical chandeliers shine down from its ribbed vault, and velvet armchairs are found in every nook. Every work of literature that ever was written is on the King's shelves, bound in punched leather: the *Inventio Fortunata* is there, and all you may ever want to learn about Cardenio, and every map that was drawn, of lands real and invented."

She paused, at a loss, then remembered that she, too, was going to need something.

"There will be peace," she said, her voice rising, "but not idleness, because the moon is a dangerous place: we won't be its only denizens, and there will be troops to train, expeditions to organise, secret caves to brave, mountains to conquer. A whole new world that we must protect—like the King protects us. Come, children, let us go."

We went.

Because there was nothing else that we could do, and because who would refuse paradise, given the chance? Was not a battle once fought over this?

We walked in silence towards the parapet.

We did not look back.

"Remember what I taught you, and stay close to me. The road is hidden. Blink and you'll be lost forever in the void," Regina said, and with that she was off, breaking into a run and leaping from the edge.

She stood still, suspended in the black sky, then fell, disappeared down below towards the grass, towards roots and rocks and broken bones.

I drew a sharp breath, but she soared from the pit screaming with a mad joy, the wings flapping about her, faster, faster, and up, up, she went, towards the moon.

It was more than any of us could resist, even I.

We ran too. We ran and jumped and felt the pull of gravity, but knew how to wait, wait for the right moment. We reached for the lever, and the wings responded.

For an instant, a beautiful, frightful instant, it seemed they wouldn't be enough; the gravity was too strong, our will too weak. Then we started to fly.

Seconds scattered away.

The castle below our feet grew smaller, the stars above our heads bigger. The tips of the spruces tickled me as I passed, and as I darted through them, a cloud of bats, disturbed by my passage, flew with me a while, then lagged behind and turned back. There were only the four of us in the sky.

85

I was delirious with laughter, and pulled on the lever to fly faster.

A filament of black cloud dispersed before my eyes, and I saw Agata.

I called to her, and she turned and smiled. "Take my hand," she said, but the wind that blew her words into my ears and new dark clouds into my eyes was blunt and strong; it was resisting me, and once again I pulled the lever.

But it broke, and I fell.

THE KNOCK

I FELL.

Flames lapped at my face, scorching, melting. I was a star burning bright, a blaze of dreams shooting through the dark heavens, charting a course of ash and fire.

But it didn't matter.

Soon I would turn into a great white pelican and fly across the night sky until I recognised the amaryllis of my dream, and the man with the kind eyes behind the round glasses would be there, reaching out to me.

Was it time yet?

I laughed as I fell and burned.

Then the safety mechanism switched on and the wings drew themselves around me.

It was cool, inside. Cool and warm at the same time.

I felt my eyelids getting heavy, watched them as they inched closer. I drowsed—

—The blows jolted me awake.

The first one was fierce, but glancing; then a hail of punches hit the cocoon, and it started turning, spinning. I shut my eyes to ward off a sudden nausea.

The blows kept coming. The wings' membrane absorbed the worst of it, but still I could feel my skin bruising, the flesh tearing, until a spasm of searing pain in my left shoulder told me the worst had happened: the wing's protective membrane had rent.

I could not open my eyes, storms raged inside of them, but my hand could move. It ran to the shard stabbing my arm, felt it. It was coarse, knotty—a broken bough.

I was falling through a forest, which could only mean—

∾

I CAME TO and I was naked; my bones at angles impossible and painful; my skin mottled blue, yellow.

The cocoon had exploded around me.

I saw shreds of wood in the grass, shards of metal. Scraps of black fabric hung from the trees around me like ribbons from a long-forgotten celebration—a funeral, perhaps.

A movement drew my eyes downwards, to the ground.

I was surrounded by wolves, their fur black in the black night, their orange eyes trained on me.

I beckoned them, and they licked the soot and the blood. They ate away the worst.

What they could not swallow was the sun, which soon rose.

I dug myself a hole between the roots of a hazel with leaves of rust.

The wolves mounted guard. I slept.

∾

THE SUN SET and I crawled out, a finger at a time, earth running off my shoulders like rain. I looked around, gained confidence with bending my knees.

The wolves brought me to a river, and in the icy water I washed off the fall, the fire, the earth. I was bristling with shivers when I got out. We crossed an old stone bridge. The wolves stayed with me for some miles, until they had to turn back, their hunting ground needing more protection than I did.

The hike through the woods was a parade of vague spectres.

A coppice of tall, bloodless birches.

An alder blackened by lightning.

A cairn of white rocks, though some were smeared red.

I came to a dark creek, waded across. Soon I met an outcropping of wooden cottages. I gave them a wide berth.

I found myself walking past a circle of black stones, through a grove of skeletal trees.

When the branches cleared, I saw it, high upon the hill. Castle Frankenstein.

Thus began my days of solitude.

❦

DESERTED BY THE people who lived in it, Castle Frankenstein was an alien planet.

I called their names in the courtyard but only wind and willow replied. In the undercroft, the rats stared at me, red eyes full of hate. The stairs in the tower didn't creak under my steps, my soul weighed less than a feather.

I searched for Agata's smell among her pillows and her cushions.

I played our gramophone as loud as it allowed, singing, shouting along until my throat hurt.

I asked her portrait to give her back to me, but there was a growl on the tiger's tongue. I ran.

My dovecote felt immense, and I small, a mote.

I found refuge in my coffin, from the castle's creaks fooling me into the memory of footsteps, strange shadows conjuring movements where there were none.

But it was more than this. The castle didn't know parlour tricks only.

Its very geography, I discovered the following nights, was reasserting itself, as if, free of us—of *them*—the castle was reclaiming with wood and stone the space it had once lost to limbs and prayers. Its corridors changed direction, its stairs stopped leading anywhere.

Still, there were also times when I could detect no hint of this sinister agency, and Castle Frankenstein only felt empty to me, inert as skin shed by a serpent; a hull of maize, brittle and crisp.

A doubly ruined ruin, and I was haunting it.

※

How DID I spend my nights?

I never went out.

Out there were snow globes leading to a grave. Out there was Martin—I still thought of him, though not often, it was too painful—watching me as I watched him, grabbing my arm, trying to pull me *somewhere*.

I thought of visiting Petrus, but he was no medium; he didn't know how to speak with the dead, and that's how I felt.

I could not draw my map—I never did finish it, but what was the point of doing that now?

I could not write my journals. Words broke on the tip of my tongue. I couldn't manage a sentence longer than those I mumbled to myself as I walked alone from empty room to empty room, along ever dustier hallways. Often I used the old tongue, to deceive myself into believing that I was still in Deptford, that Regina had yet to find me.

"Bona nochy," I greeted the bats, the gnats, the worms, my voice shrill and strident.

I broke the gate of the well, climbed down the steps, crossed the forbidden stream.

No lightning struck me.

I found Regina's workroom, the floor littered with scraps of wood and fabric, bolts, gears. The walls were plastered with large sheets of yellowing paper, full of intricate diagrams, sketches, equations scribbled in every available margin—the physics of our wings; or, better, of theirs, because mine had broken, though Regina couldn't have meant for them—

Her hands white in the darkness of my room. The wings askew on their peg—

I left her study and its smell—old sweaty bustiers, charred wicks, betrayal—and never went back.

I kept moving.

I tried to recite our prayers, but found them hollow; hollower than before.

Had the King seen into my heart, spied my doubts, punished me?

I resented him.

I resented Regina.

I resented Manfred, who had never come back.

I resented Martin, who had betrayed me, though I could not say when, or how, or why.

I resented myself.

When the prayers failed, I tried exorcisms, enchantments.

All in vain.

The truth is, I had no more magic in me: only a madness.

❧

A WOMAN'S VOICE in my head. It's my mother's. It's Regina's. It's the moon's.

You should never think that something good can happen to you, the voice says.

Fate doesn't like it.

Fate will bring you down a notch, just you watch.

You will have to give everything back.

But I have nothing more to give—only questions.

I have them in spades.

I can dig my grave with them.

❧

ASK YOURSELF A question long enough and it loses its meaning, until you no longer know what it is that you are questioning, and it is the act itself—the endless rumination, doubt upon doubt upon doubt—that becomes the subject of your every thought.

You wear away.

The mind is not so different from the body. Sometimes they fail.

It doesn't matter if it's the body that crumbles and dooms the mind, or the mind that ruins limbs and joints. The result doesn't change. At the end there is the same shapeless, wordless void.

(Regina's last word, an echo through the mist.)

There's no one to save you anymore.

That ship, as they say, has sailed.

❧

ONE NIGHT I woke and Manfred was there.

His fur was matted with blood; only one eye, the left, shone like Saint Elmo's fire in the black pit of his muzzle.

I poured warm water from the carafe into a pewter basin, searched for a clean cloth, then knelt in front of him and set out to wash his wounds. Where his other eye should have been, a festering hole gawked at me; on his right hind leg, there was a bad-looking, foul-smelling tear.

"What happened?" I asked.

He had found the breaker of castles, the swan poisoner, in a country church of grey bricks and rusty shingles, squatting in the shadow of a towering belfry. It was almost by chance, because there should not have been a church in that patch of forest, but it was my wish that he found those who wished us harm, and he did not care if I had left already—he'd find them. And find them he did, when he had all but lost hope.

There was a bolted door, but it was open.

Inside, a darkness which reeked of incense; and underneath the incense, the smell of old wood, wet stones, secrets whispered in confession.

A glimmer. The wall near the entrance was covered with silver hands and hearts, silver feet, livers and lungs, a silver womb, arranged haphazardly around a large cross, the body of Christ pasty, the paint chipped.

A voice, a man's, from the shadows.

"Take him!"

The shadows shuddered, heaved, until two huge shapes detached from the vast, dark expanse beyond the altar, where the door to the belfry must have been.

The shapes barked, bolted in pursuit: back through the door, through a clearing and past a cairn—was I there too?—up a hill, down a hill, but they were close, getting closer, their breath stung, arches of spit glistened between their jaws.

Then the world was upside down, a constellation of pain flaring up in the sky—which was, perhaps, the ground.

I cleaned Manfred's fur as best I could without too much tormenting his wounds; they were still fresh, raw and bloody where the dogs' bites had torn the flesh.

Yet he had borne himself with the dignified nobility which is only of cats and dispossessed counts. I wished I had a fragment of his composure.

I gave him my blood, and as he fed on it, his strength returning with each suck, I thought:

The voice. The man behind it.

He owes me two wings; and one eye.

❧

First came the comet.

How many days had passed since I returned to the castle? Ten? Twenty? Or was it just the one, stretching its minutes until they resembled centuries?

The comet shone red through the boards on my window.

I thought Frankenstein was on fire, I thought the villagers were coming for me—pitchforks and torches, you know.

I ran to the watchtower.

A fiery eye was blinking in the sky, turning the spruces' needles into swords, the forest into a hellish tribunal. I was being judged.

The comet—what I thought was a comet—danced in front of the moon, then broke up into three fragments that plunged down towards the earth, faster and faster, each engulfed in a sheet of flames.

I knew what it meant.

It had happened to me.

I ran out screaming, and my scream was a raging devil.

Under the wounded sky I saw doors opening, and windows; and I heard shrieks, wails; I sensed hearts jumping with fear in ivory ribcages, infants weeping because their innocence was being stripped away too soon; but nothing could stop me until I reached the clearing where the first object—the heaviest—had crashed.

The flames crackling around the husk did not scare me.

I grabbed the wings enveloping the Baron and prised them open.

A dense cloud of bluish, choking smoke belched out of the wreckage.

"Hang on," I cried, tearing the black cloth apart.

The shell was empty.

I did not halt to think. I dashed forwards through the thicket.

I recognised Regina's wings at once, their build more primitive than ours.

The wood was smouldering, the cloth sizzling.

The whole contraption came apart as soon as I touched it, opening up like a charred flower—empty, again, save for an acrid, evil-smelling vapour.

I jumped up and ran, and followed the third trail of smoke to a large brook.

The last cocoon had fallen inside, and the current had dragged it away, towards Stüterhof, but I found it a short distance off, near a fork in the brook, where the overarching roots of a resourceful oak had snagged it.

The water and the roots had done my work for me, tearing up Agata's wings.

Empty.

I crouched down, ran a blackened finger upon the scorched leather harness.

My heart was beating slow, as though readying itself to sleep. I forced myself to look around, explored both arms of the brook, and the surrounding forest too, but already I knew that I wouldn't find anyone.

I looked up at the sky, waiting for *someone* to fall from it.

Come, I whispered. *Come, Agata.*

You don't need the wings.

I'll catch you.

The sky stayed silent.

❧

AFTER THE COMET came the knock.

Did it startle me when it came, or was I already convinced of its inevitability?

It was past midnight.

The knock shook the gate and sent a tremor through the whole castle.

I was in my room, and started moving before I could understand why.

I thought I should do something, lure the danger away from us; but there wasn't an *us* anymore, and I found myself in front of the barred gate, searching for the chink in the wood that we used as a peephole.

On the other side of the gate was a priest. He was wearing a heavy overcoat, and had his frock underneath, the collar blinking white at the centre of his neck, like bone exposed by a deep cut which had bled out.

Regina's frock. Its hem wet in the rain.

The priest didn't have much hair, but the few tufts he had,

plastered by sweat and damp to his forehead, were black and curly like a doll's. His small nose—too small for such a round face—terminated in an impressive pair of hound-like nostrils, which took up almost all the space between his sagging cheeks.

When he left, I sighed and went back to my room.

❧

I WAS STANDING behind the gate when he returned.

I saw him rounding the stone boulder. He knocked again. This time, he spoke too.

"I know you are in there," the priest said. "Open the door, I want to speak with you."

Twice again he knocked, though he spoke no more, then he went away.

I stayed where I was, head bowed, hands over my ears, trying to keep his voice in there—because I knew it, somehow, but couldn't place it.

❧

THE NEXT NIGHT, I was so close to the wood his knock made my teeth tremble in their gums.

"I know you are in there," he repeated; then added: "Ambrose."

The sound of my name almost pulled a sob from my throat, but my hands were quicker and pressed down on my mouth and nose until I had trouble breathing.

"My name is Waldemar," he continued. "I just want to exchange a few words. Will you let me in?"

I didn't, even though I felt an ache in my fingers.

They were lonely, and desperate for touch, struggling to move of their own accord.

I turned my back to the gate and returned to my tower.

❦

"Ambrose," Waldemar said on the fourth night. "Open the gate. I want to help you. Take my word for it."

I knew it was a lie, but this time I knew something else.

I knew where I knew his voice from.

A dark country church, a shout from the shadows.

Take him!

It was this priest, who had left us a procession of broken castles.

It was this priest, who had poisoned the swans.

It was this priest, who had forced Regina's hand.

It was this priest, who had set his dogs on Manfred.

I raised the drawbar and tossed it aside as though it weighed less than a child's wooden sword.

I opened the gate.

Waldemar stood before me, no more than three feet apart.

He was taller than me, and heavier by the look of his shoulders, as broad as they were slouching. He was smiling, but his face was not made for it. The deep lines which furrowed his mouth seemed like shallow dents on a wax mannequin's face.

He was the first human being I had seen and smelled in I didn't know how long, and the feeling overpowered me, muscle-tearing rage for what he had done to us subsiding under the rising waves of a warmth similar to love.

I moved—perhaps to strike, perhaps to hold.

But he was quicker than me.

He drove a stake through my heart.

II

THE OPERATING THEATRE

CHARACTERS

FATHER WALDEMAR, a priest and a schemer

PROFESSOR LOWELL CABOT, an entomologist

MARTIN HUNGER, a physician and specialist of the brain

STABIUS TANNER, a lawyer with a penchant for social reform

SIR ARTHUR GRAHAM BARRY, an old man who always sleeps, hailing from London

GASPERO SPALLANZANI, a sleek cypher, hailing from Turin

MR HOWARD SHOREY, a man with the voice of a tiger, hailing from San Francisco

PROFESSOR EDWARD GAMMELL, a historian and record-keeper

A congregation of **ELEGANT MEN**

A team of **ORDERLIES**, two of them in particular

A young **MAID**

A **HEAD** behind a skylight

A **BODY** lying on a table

I

Darkness. A vast black bay.

Then a flicker. Shadows wince as one by one the lamps lining the wainscoted walls light up. The heavy brass one, hanging from the ceiling on an iron chain, comes alive last. It is shaped like an anchor, each arm holding a bulb the size of a head.

The lamps shine on a semi-circular space, occupied for the most part by four wooden platforms, rising one above the other and cut through by a dark corridor. Two bells flank the entrance. Above it, old-looking letters have been burned into the wood:

Stat sua cuique dies

It's a Latin saying, *To each his day is given*, coming from the *Aeneid*. It means that the time allotted to each individual life is limited, and it's up to the one living it to make the most of it. A rather straightforward sentiment, the likes of which abound in literature, which was nonetheless warped out of meaning by the society that adopted it as its motto: the Royal Diurnal Society. This space is theirs.

There are no windows on the walls, but there is an octagonal skylight above the highest platform, covered with a black curtain. At the centre of the room stands a table.

And on the table, there's you.

You were an *I am*, *I love*, *I fear*. You were a man called Ambrose, whose fate was often read in the cards. You had a lover who kept a gun in a drawer, a cat that lost an eye for you. You lived in a castle made of bricks and broken windows, longed for one made of singing crystal. You dreamt of doctors, of kings; hoped for salvation and happiness. None of this matters anymore.

Now you're just you.

You monster.

You fucking faggot.

That's what the men who put you here call you—if they do at all.

To them, you are just a body lying naked on a table in front of these platforms, which were built for this purpose, to allow for a clear view of you.

The table is made of rough poplar planks. It has several holes drilled into it, which allow fluids to drain away into the box of sawdust placed underneath it. An upraised metal headboard completes the contraption, which is called an operating table.

This is an operating theatre.

Ꮧ

A FIGURE APPEARS from the corridor.

It's Father Waldemar, breaker of snow globes, poisoner of swans, impaler.

He is dressed in a black frock, the sleeves rolled up on his hairy arms. He's holding a small bucket full of soapy water and a metal can with no label on it. He puts the bucket down, looks at you with the appreciative eye of a buyer inspecting a pig at the market.

Your body is thin, the face gaunt. Your pointed features are made even more noticeable by the fact that they've pulled your long black hair into a tight bun. Your ribs stick out like hungry hands. The solar plexus is run through by eight inches of wych-elm.

Father Waldemar beams at the sight of the stake, because he was the one who drove it there. He runs his finger along the length of it, then grabs it and pushes it further down, just because he can and wants to.

The pain is geometrical, a pyramid of pain. It expands, growing outwards until it entombs you. You'd scream, but you can't. A stake through the heart does that to you. It paralyses limbs and muscles, slows down all bodily functions. The electrical impulses your nerves send to the rest of your body are sterile, they can't elicit any reaction. As such, pain exists not as a physical entity but as a notion inside the nervous system, which is overpowered by it—though not enough to shut down. That would be too merciful. Instead, you are oddly present to what happens to you, though incapable of lifting a finger to prevent it. And, since your eyes won't close, you watch on.

Upon first bringing you here, Father Waldemar was so unnerved by your dull stare that he contemplated sewing your eyelids shut, before deciding against it. They—the members of the Royal Diurnal Society coming from all over the world to see you, judge you, dispose of you—might need them open. They need you at your best.

Father Waldemar shakes the can with no label and sprays

cream on your chest, your groin, under the armpits. He produces a straight razor from his frock and starts shaving the patches of skin.

The cream he's using is cheap, the blade old. It nicks, cuts. The cream soon becomes pink with blood. Waldemar's lips curl in disgust. He grabs the sponge adrift in the bucket, wipes the foam away. Underneath, your skin is red and blotchy. He starts working on the groin. He moves your shrunken sex away from the razor as he would a dead maggot. The cuts on your balls are the worst.

When he's finished, he scoops up the bucket, pours the rest of the water all over you. Water, cream and blood wash away through the holes drilled in the table. As he admires his finished job, the livid smoothness of your skin, Waldemar lets out a contented sigh.

When he leaves, empty bucket under his arm, for a long time there's only silence in the operating theatre, the faint buzz of the lamps.

The hair on your chest starts to grow again, but not much.

☙

SPACE IS DEFINED by movement; without, it becomes a negation. A negation of space is, of course, a negation of time. Seconds pass, or they could be eons.

Martin Hunger enters the operating theatre. There are deep, red lines around his eyes. The lab coat he's wearing has several blueish stains on it, a suggestion of hazardous pharmaceutical compounds experimented with in the small hours.

He scrunches up his nose. He doesn't like the smell of the theatre, fresh paint and turpentine, with something staler beneath it, like the smell of a butcher shop turned into a haberdashery. Since there is no one here that can judge him for this weakness—there's nothing the Royal Diurnal Society prizes more than displays of virility—he daubs a little menthol cream beneath his nostrils, then sets to work.

He sticks a syringe into your arm and draws a phial of blood. Pink blood, the colour of a moon in a winter sky, with streaks of silver in it. Under the light from the anchor-shaped lamp, it emits a faint luminescence. He draws three more phials.

If, as he works on you, Martin is thinking of the night you visited him in his smoking room, no trace of this recollection lights up his lineaments, which are hard-set, focused. He puts the phials inside a plastic bag, seals it. He measures your blood pressure, auscultates your heart, the lungs. He prods your armpits with steel-cold, businesslike hands, checking for lumps, swellings. He pushes a finger inside your anus, palpates the prostate.

From the corridor he fetches a metal trolley with something that looks like a telephone switchboard on it. He glues several pairs of electrodes to your temples, your neck, your chest. The black stump of the stake looks like an altar at the centre of this strange configuration.

When the last electrode is in place, an oval expanse, previously undistinguishable from the rest of the machine, lights up in the centre of it. Thin blue waves waver inside. Martin studies them, jotting down his thoughts on a yellow pad:

conscious suspended animation (c.s.a)
is the subject forming memories? ... dubious
check amygdala fx

He turns a knob on the machine, adjusts it until the waves on the screen start to swirl. He dons his stethoscope again, finds your heart again.

pulse = brainwave = absolute somatisation

Martin twiddles the knob until the waves collapse upon themselves into a worming skein of lines. He turns the knob all the other way around and the skein implodes outward, each line fragmenting into a myriad of blue dots.

His notes take on a feverish pace:

amygdala hijack
disproportionate reaction to stimuli
this confirms my theory

As a scientist, there is nothing Martin values more than the direct observation of phenomena. As a scientist, he is driven by a need to satisfy his curiosity. He toys with the machine's voltage.

This is pain like you have never known it. Galvanic, exponential.

It starts with your toes, that curl up tight.

It radiates to your legs, your buttocks. Every muscle tenses.

Martin adjusts the voltage a little higher and your back arches up, your skull bangs against the operating table.

A little higher still and your eyes roll back, your feet kick up at the air, your arms flay around like eels. You are shaking so violently you seem to float above the table.

But when Martin adjusts the voltage all the way up, to see what might happen to you—to your brain activity going haywire— what happens is that the anchor-shaped lamp flickers, then goes out, followed by every other lamp in the operating theatre.

He asked too much of the operating theatre's electrical system.

He asked too much of you.

All is darkness.

YOU ARE NOT awake in the proper sense of the word, so you can't think. And because you're also not really asleep, you can't dream. *Conscious suspended animation.* You exist in a slip of space and time between reality and imagination, remembrance and prophesy. You are a spell, suspended in the air, waiting to be broken.

When the light goes away, you have a vision. Perhaps it's something that happened to you in the past, though you suspect this is not the case. You don't remember ever visiting a museum with the Baron, but in your vision the two of you are together, moving between rooms whose walls are painted a pale periwinkle colour and crowded with portraits.

There are oil paintings in lime-wood frames, old sycamore panels plastered over and painted with hot wax, wrinkly watercolours with all the shades of red and yellow. Every portrait is different, but they have one thing in common. They are all of men.

The Baron's cloak swishes around your ankles. His mask is a simple pasteboard bauta, the stench of his Hungarian water strong around his hair, his wrists.

As you move through the rooms, he asks you if you understand what the unifying trait is these men all share—the man dressed in a silk tailcoat who dons the powdered wig of a judge, the man with Egyptian lineaments and a bristly moustache, the one as lanky as a cypress who looks like he's on his way to a funeral.

When you can't think of anything besides them being men and happening to have rather big noses—which you suspect is not the correct answer—the Baron sighs.

What the men in the portraits all have in common, he says, *is that we don't know their names. We have their portraits, which they handsomely commissioned, but somehow, at a certain point in time, their names fell through the cracks of history. There isn't enough, in the pictures, for any sleuth to crack the mystery of their identity, and so they remain nameless, their faces no different than a mask.*

He points to his own, then whispers in your ear:

It's time to sit for your portrait.

๛

You are covered with a white winding sheet. It weighs nothing, but it's heavy on you, the fabric coarse and smelly. It reeks of brined meat.

Two men emerge from the corridor.

One is Father Waldemar.

The other is Professor Lowell Cabot, the first member of the Royal Diurnal Society to arrive, from the United States no less. Others are coming from the same country, but feigning some motive or other he managed to get an earlier flight, so he could spend a little time with Waldemar. They are both what in the Society lingo are called Jamesians, after King James and his Bible, which is to say the ultra-conservative wing of the Society. They have business to discuss in private.

Cabot looks around the theatre, his pate reflecting the light from the lamps. As he inspects the wood panelling, the platforms, the motto burned into the wood—everything but the table where you're lying—he keeps fidgeting with his green bow-tie. It's held in place by a pin with a pearl head and looks like a butterfly injected with formalin.

"This is a very good place that you have here," he says.

"Yes, they have done a good job building it to my exact specifications," Waldemar says, his voice flute-like, false. "You know how I can be."

Cabot chuckles. He does. He fishes a gold savonette out of his pocket. "Still an hour to go," he says. "Would you mind if I'd use your office to go over my notes one last time?"

"Please, old friend, you are my guest," Waldemar says. "But first, if I may… Have you come prepared?"

Cabot lifts one of the flaps of his jacket. Under his armpit there peeps the sleek, shiny grip of a gun. "My pepper pot," he says, beaming.

"Wonderful. But please, don't let me keep you. You'll need freshening up."

When Cabot disappears down the corridor, Waldemar waits until he hears the *click* of his office door closing, then runs a finger down the winding sheet. Under the imperceptible pressure of his fingertip, your profile appears. The forehead, the nose, the crevasse between your lips, your chin. The finger keeps going down, until it stops at the solar plexus. It finds the stake, but doesn't push it this time.

He just wanted to make sure.

Steps come running in from the corridor. They belong to a young girl of no more than ten years. She has bright blond hair and freckled skin. In the penumbra, she shines like a wraith.

"Father Waldemar! They're here!"

Waldemar draws his frock around his ankles and hurries away, following the girl.

"It's starting," he says, almost breathless, then disappears.

એ

A PROCESSION OF orderlies marches inside the theatre. They are dressed in white shirts, trousers, shoes and hairnets.

Three of them are each carrying a high-backed chair with black velvet upholstery. They leave the chairs around the table, then file onto the first platform to the left. Another one puts a lectern by the table's feet before joining the others. The orderlies' movements are synchronised, a white ballet of medical precision.

By contrast, the men who follow them inside the operating theatre move in a sarabande of different intentions. They shake hands, pat backs and stumble upon each other as they struggle to find their place on the platforms, crowding together or fighting by themselves to secure an advantageous viewing position. On some faces, long journeys have left red marks under the eyes, a certain irritability in the muscles around their mouths, but the general atmosphere is one of gaiety. This day will be remembered in the annals of the Royal Diurnal Society as the one when they'll do away with the indecisiveness that has plagued them for the better part of their history; the day when the Society will decide if it wants to remain a learned congregation of men dedicated to scholarly studies, or if it's time they take action. The men don't know which side will prevail, but they've all come carrying their most prized possession: their votes.

Many of them are dressed in such pomp as befits this momentous occasion: silk pocket squares, cufflinks, shiny Oxford shoes, monk straps. Others sport more casual clothing, rougher fabrics, mass-produced quality, though they too tried to clean up, ironing their shirts, shaving, combing their hair. They wear too much cologne.

In the front row, Martin Hunger is the only one who hasn't given any thought to the dress code. By the look of his beard, he hasn't shaved in days. He is talking with a younger man, freckled skin and coarse red hair. His name is Stabius Tanner, a lawyer with the air of a city about him. Their physical proximity betrays a long-standing friendship, but also something deeper—a factionalism. A little further off, Cabot is regarding them with apparent distrust. It's not the only staring contest taking place, either.

These cracks in the Society's superficial unity become rifts when, announced in a booming voice by Waldemar, three distinguished gentlemen make their entrance. They all don princely black uniforms with golden epaulettes, each sporting a gold brooch on their right breast.

A thistle for the oldest of the three, a wizened, impish man whom a couple of orderlies have to help to his chair. Sir Arthur Graham Barry is his name. He sits as director of the London chapter of the Royal Diurnal Society, and as president of the Society itself, a role he ascended to when he was twenty-three years old. The longest serving president in the history of the Society.

The second man's brooch displays a crowned bull. This man, Gaspero Spallanzani, is tall and sleek of appearance, with eyes pious and murderous—the eyes of a crocodile. He was elected director of the Turin chapter three months prior, and already he is known as a master manipulator, a procurer of favours. When he saunters inside the theatre, everyone studies him, trying to gauge where in the Society's political spectrum he is going to fall. He hasn't declared an allegiance yet.

The last man to enter the operating theatre stands out because he is big and broad, and the only black man in the room. His name is Howard Shorey, and he is director of the San Francisco chapter, a position that means he is in charge of the Royal Diurnal Society's operations in the whole of the United States. This makes him powerful, more powerful than Sir Arthur, but power is a currency inside the Society only insofar as it comes with the privileges bestowed by old blood, something of which Sir Arthur is very rich and Mr Shorey very poor. His brooch displays a phoenix rising from three intertwined flames, and it represents his hope for the Society, his will to change it.

There's a shuffling of feet as the three directors take a seat on the high-backed chairs prepared for them—the oldest one slumps down to sleep as soon as the orderlies' hands leave him—and the men who are still roaming the platforms for their greetings and some last-minute haggling move to stand behind the leader they support, an all-too-literal rendition of the phrase 'fall in line'.

A whisper or two tickle the silence.

All eyes are on the table at the centre of the theatre.

All eyes are on you, they'd tear the sheet from you if they could.

It's you they came all this way to see.

Father Waldemar walks to the lectern to give his commencement speech.

☙

WALDEMAR, *his voice filling the theatre*: Gentlemen of the Royal Diurnal Society, it is the established usage of our meetings to begin with a statement of the work, and the progress made in such work, by our honourable president Sir Arthur Graham Barry. Given the uniqueness of this occasion, however, Sir Arthur has waived his right, and left me to do the honours. I hope you will forgive me if I don't elaborate on the number of new volumes added to our collections, or the articles of historical interest we have acquired. Professor Edward Gammell will include everything in his end-of-year report, of course.

A young but balding man with a C-bridge pince-nez, standing behind Mr Shorey, raises a hand with a jovial smile on his face and waves to no one in particular. No one waves back.

WALDEMAR: Indeed, our Society has made commendable progress in the last year, though none, you will concur, as momentous as this. *He reaches towards the table, tears the winding sheet from it.*

VOICES FROM THE PLATFORMS: Heads! Heads!

The men crane their necks, rise on their toes, some climb the platforms' railings. They all want a better view of the body lying naked on the table.

An applause bursts through, making the round of the platforms. Sir Arthur jolts momentarily awake to join in. Only Mr Shorey remains motionless, his silence drowned by all the clapping. The men on the platforms whistle, cheer.

Father Waldemar raises his hands to ask for quiet.

WALDEMAR: I was but a boy of thirteen when I was inducted into our Society, yet it was already clear to me, as it had been to my father, how flawed our method was. If one knows of an intruder into his own home, one should not stand by to gather information, keeping notes of the intruder's movements, compiling registers. One should arm himself, ready himself for direct confrontation. I appreciate, of course, the benefits our more erudite approach has brought us, but for many years now I've been persuaded that the time to study inert biological samples and ancient artifacts was over; that, in order to secure some real advancement, we should try to secure a live vampire specimen. *He pauses, glances at Mr Shorey.* I know that some of you had understandable reservations upon such a course of action, which was judged too brash and—

SHOREY: —repugnant. *The final "t" is harsh as a smack on Waldemar's lips.*

WALDEMAR: And repugnant—*he concedes, knows when to pick a fight*—though when a pursuit is as noble as ours, matters of taste are perhaps best left to the chatter of women. In any event, there were reservations, until some months ago when, after a long deliberation, our president Sir Arthur wrote me a letter, approving of the plan I had devised. Please, join me in congratulating him, because without him and his wisdom we wouldn't be here tonight.

A new applause breaks through the crowd, though rather feeble now. Sir Arthur snoozes through it, oblivious to the tribute being paid to him, and to everything else.

WALDEMAR: I am sure you have many questions, and there will be time—at the end of our conference—for them. For now, I would like to address the one that must be at the forefront of everyone's mind: how did I secure the specimen? It's not been easy. *He pauses, for gravity.* Of course, we've been aware of a skulk in Frankenstein for quite some time. Our field agent, Doctor Martin Hunger, has monitored the skulk's activities, chronicling the comings and goings, the wrongdoings, the missteps. You've all seen excerpts of his detailed reports in the annual *Transactions* of our Society, but there is something that Martin and I have kept from you all these years, which is to do with why today you've been summoned, of all places, to a small country church deep inside the Rhineland.

A murmur goes through the crowd. Curious glances are exchanged, especially in the direction of Martin Hunger, who keeps his head down, tries his best to ignore the prodding eyes.

WALDEMAR: A skulk of vampires is no uncommon thing, though the Frankenstein one was uncommon in every respect. First, their leader was female; second, their number was small—a mere four vampires, a far cry from the twenty-one who hid at Moggerhanger House before a band of our brothers took matters in their own hands and torched the place.

SHOREY: They did much more than torch the place, and were convicted for it.

WALDEMAR, *ignoring him*: Third, this skulk's activities seemed governed not by the food-chain logics we've observed in other vampire-human interactions, which are of the consumer-resource type, but by an idiosyncratic eschatology, a belief that their presence here must be temporary, because a higher plane of existence was prepared for them, where their destinies would be fulfilled. A delusion, of course, a mockery of true religion, since no such plane exists for the creatures. When I understood from Martin's observations that the skulk's arrangements were nearly finalised, I took an unprecedented step. I approached its leader.

There is an uproar. The men behind Mr Shorey and Spallanzani shout and shake the railings, stomp their feet on the platforms. Only the men behind Sir Arthur—Cabot among them—stay still. They are all in Waldemar's pocket.

SHOREY, *jumping up from his seat and roaring to be heard above the commotion*: This is high treason, Father! You didn't consult us—

WALDEMAR: I did! I consulted with Sir Arthur, and we both thought best not to include anyone else in our deliberation, given the delicate nature—

Sir Arthur keeps with the angels, sleeping through the ruckus still raging in the theatre.

SHOREY: This is irregular. All three directors must be consulted on such matters. Each vertex must hold for the centre to do the same. The balance… *He trails off. This is no time for esoteric expatiations. He turns to Spallanzani.* Don't you have anything to say, director?

SPALLANZANI, *slouching on his chair, is the picture of contentment*: I don't. *He cracks a smile broad enough for everyone to see a greenish gleam in the darkness of his throat—a snake hiding in a swamp.* I want to hear what the father has to say.

SHOREY: But—

SPALLANZANI: Waldemar is chancellor, Howard. You won't get me to strip him of his title and throw him out to the wolves. If he says he talked this through with Arthur, then it's good enough for me, and it should be for you too. So, just you sit down and let him finish. *As Mr Shorey drops to his seat, teeth smashing teeth, he turns to Waldemar.* Proceed, Father.

WALDEMAR, *bowing his head, cheeks flushed with satisfaction*: Thank you, Director.

SPALLANZANI, *looking pleased with himself but feigning indifference*: Thank me later, if at all. Go on, tell us what happened between you and the skulk leader.

WALDEMAR: The vampire is a duplicitous creature by its very nature, but it is also smart, and the skulk leader understood that it couldn't risk us meddling. We struck a deal. I wouldn't tamper with their departure in exchange for one of them to be left behind for our taking. I left the who and how up to the leader, also agreeing to stage a convoluted ruse—involving such baubles as snow globes whose function I didn't care to understand—to help it. I was under the impression that the leader had in fact grown restless with its own's skulk passivity, and that it was actually welcoming my proposal. If I helped instil fear of an external threat into its subjects, it reasoned, this would hasten their departure, and thus my acquiring of the specimen I coveted. Everything was arranged, and this—*he gestures towards the body on the table*—is the result, which I've put myself at great personal risk to accomplish.

SPALLANZANI: An elaborate plan, Father. I'm surprised you got Arthur to stay awake long enough to approve it.

WALDEMAR, *faltering*: All the necessary papers were signed. They're here in my study, if—

SPALLANZANI: No need to present them. *The swampy gleam is back*. I'm just pulling your leg, Father. In any case, I'm more interested in who this vampire is and what you plan to do with it, than in how it got here.

WALDEMAR, *bowing his head*: You are right, of course. *He coughs.* The specimen is male, of an outward age between thirty and forty. It came here from England, but has Mediterranean blood in its veins, Italian probably, or Spanish. *He looks at the body. His eyes almost pet it—the butcher's tenderness before he pulls the calf's heart out.* It has lived in Frankenstein for many years, during which it was observed feeding on the blood of several men, most often drunkards or delinquents it found near some *gasthaus* deep in the woods. With some of these men, the specimen entertained illicit relations of a more habitual kind, engaging in penetrative sex with them while also letting them suck on its own blood, a practice that we've seldom recorded in other local skulks. In any case, the specimen's inverted tendencies were also shown by its proclivity, in non-sexual circumstances, towards female companionship. It is not clear if it ever shared one or more of its sexual partners with the female vampire in whose company it was often observed, but it is a possibility I wouldn't rule out, such is the degeneracy of the vampire's ways.

SOME MEN ON THE PLATFORMS: Hear! Hear!

WALDEMAR: The programme I've put together for this symposium will clarify that this specimen's perversions are as much its own as its species'. It's a fault of its blood, it cannot help itself. It is a monster, damned to be a monster. It is my intention to demonstrate this point beyond any reasonable doubt. *A pause.* It's time we end the stalemate.

Over the course of its history, and up until today, the Royal Diurnal Society has elected seventeen presidents, many of them from the moderate political centre, scholars of law who advocated for a bookish, information-gathering approach, and never once questioned the two most important tenets of the Society: the need for secrecy, and the value of non-interventionism, which was deemed necessary "until sufficient evidence has been accumulated," as some of these presidents were fond of repeating. One went as far as famously quipping that, as the Royal Historical Society didn't declare wars just to have treaties to study, so too they needn't engage in direct action against the physical and moral threat of the vampire in order to better understand it.

Occasional acts of violence towards vampires—like the infamous case of Moggerhanger House, where fourteen male vampires were tortured, raped, decapitated and burnt by a band of members who broke rank and stormed the place in broad daylight; the other seven vampires in the skulk managing a narrow, last-minute escape—were often formally reprimanded, but privately cheered on, as long as it was clear both to those committing them and to those commenting on them that the acts themselves would be brushed off with the press, the police, and whoever might have been paying attention, as the undertakings of lone vigilantes going off the rails; and that the official stance of the Society would remain one of *audi, vide, tace*.

Eventually, three hundred years of listening, observing and keeping silent whittled away at the centre's support, and birthed the Jamesian faction, which advocates for war against the intruder, as Father Waldemar put it in his commencement speech. (It was the Moggerhanger House's marauders who first discovered the efficacy of wych-elm stakes, which Waldemar has put to such good use with you.) It was first as a reaction to their rhetoric that a second faction inhabiting the opposite end of the political spectrum emerged, one calling for a deep reorganisation of the Society. Not without a certain haughtiness, they refer to their group as The Bensalem, from the name of the mythical, enlightened land in Sir Francis Bacon's *New Atlantis*, though their opponents most often call them Candides, to suggest their perceived credulity. Nowadays, the two factions spend their time glowering at each other, something which has in turn facilitated a resurgence of the moderate centre.

It's among these fluctuations that Waldemar's symposium is taking place, and as they speak or listen, every man in the operating theatre is tallying up the votes in his head, keeping count of those who are swayed, noting the strengthening or weakening of alliances. For centuries the men of the Royal Diurnal Society had almost nothing to do other than squabble between themselves, and they have developed a knack for impromptu pollstering. One could argue this is their most distinguished feature.

೧

WALDEMAR: I want to thank you all for making the journey here, and on such short notice. As moving the specimen elsewhere would have been unwise, I'm grateful for your understanding—especially Sir Arthur, who made the trip from London with no concern for his own health and against the recommendations of his physician. And Mr Shorey, of course. San Francisco is a long way from Frankenstein.

SHOREY: That it is, Father. That it is. *His sandy voice hides a rumble.* If it were up to me, I would have never allowed you the liberty to execute this plan of yours. And if it were up to me, I'd put a stop to your programme right now.

WALDEMAR, *unfussed, smiles politely*: I'm confident, Mr Shorey, that at the end of our conference we will be able to put our personal grievances aside, and remember that we here, we all strive towards the same goal.

SHOREY: And what would that be?

WALDEMAR, *with a sneer*: But of course: peace.

II

AFTER A RECESS, during which Waldemar's young maid makes the rounds of the platforms offering some light refreshments to the men, the programme can start.

First up is Professor Lowell Cabot. He is used to the ivied halls of knowledge, but addressing the Royal Diurnal Society in full assembly is different from teaching a class of students. In a class, he doesn't have Waldemar's eyes on the back of his head, judging him for every stutter, for every small mistake that might lose their cause some votes.

Cabot leads the congregation in a lengthy discussion of vampire biology, notably of the male vampire, both because you are the exemplar at hand and because the Royal Diurnal Society holds the belief that, as most witches are women, most vampires are men. (Both claims are, of course, false.) Being an exclusive association open only to men, the Society—and the Jamesian faction most of all, given their emphasis on biblical sources—feels most threatened by someone who, while being similar in appearance to any one of their members, is so different from them in deportment. It's something they simply cannot accept, and just another facet of their deep-running misogyny (though many of them would deny this accusation). What is more, the homosexual behaviour they have often observed in male vampires, though not all of them, has reinforced the Jamesians' conviction that vampires are a wrong the Society must correct, as the following proceedings will show.

Professor Cabot intends to take matters a step further. A vampire, his lecture posits, is more than a different biological entity. It is a parasite. Like a louse, the vampire attacks the surface of a body, puncturing it so that its blight can then corrupt it from the inside, as a virus would. At the same time, living amongst men as it does, the vampire takes advantage of humanity's advancements in the fields of economics, medicine and technology, like some species of ants, used to exploit the work of other organisms. Lastly, as an Amazon molly mates with a partner but discards its genetic materials, so too the vampire's relationships appear only concerned with its own sexual cravings. No one knows what an Amazon molly is, but no one cares enough to ask. The seminar is already going on for far too long, and the men on the platforms are getting bored. They didn't make the trip here to learn about biology.

The good thing about having you at hand, though, is that attention picks up as soon as Cabot moves to the practical part of his lecture.

He slashes at one of your wrists with a lancet to show everyone your pink moon blood. For many men on the platforms this is their first time witnessing this condition first-hand, which Cabot calls *selenism* and blames for the vampire's nocturnal tendencies and its need to consume human blood.

He fetches an opaque glass jar from his physician's bag, full of writhing black worms, to demonstrate the effects of it. He unscrews the jar lid, dips a pair of tweezers in, and up they come holding a leech, one of its ends a round flat sucker twitching in the air. A flutter of Cabot's fingers and the leech drops onto your body, the sucker finding the tender skin near the navel. A second leech lands upon the clavicle, a third on the thigh—it slips, but it is quick with its mouth. It finds the rosy flesh near the scrotum and sticks to it.

As Cabot continues expanding on the finer points of parasitic behaviour, you feel the leeches piercing you, sucking you. Looking on, Mr Shorey has a pout of disgust on his face. Spallanzani has all but stood up from his chair, his breath wheezing on his tongue.

Soon the three leeches are dead; curled up; crinkled.

There are gasps from the audience. Cabot takes one between his fingers, exerts a little pressure. The hollowed-out body explodes in a puff of dust.

"This is what the vampire's blood does to one of the vilest creatures on Earth," Cabot says. He flicks another leech off your shoulder. "I will leave to your imagination what this poison can do to a grown man, gnawing at him from the inside, until he is a receptacle ready to receive more and more of the vampire's blood; until he is but one of them, leaving the mores of our society behind to dwell in the shadows of abnormality and deviance."

Your blood may be the phantom of blood, but you know it's not poison.

A poison wouldn't have nursed Manfred back to health, or made Petrus happy when he was sad, but Professor Cabot doesn't know it; doesn't care for the possibility that the fault may be in the leeches, not in your blood.

Your pink moon blood is made for the lips of lovers and the wounds of friends.

Your pink moon blood is made for the sailors of Southwark, the actors of The Rose.

Your pink moon blood is made for kings.

What it is not made for is leeches, whose digestive systems are ill-equipped for it, like the stomach of King Ludwig's mechanical brother was not fit for partridge pasties.

(The distant echo of a hope rings inside your head.)

Cabot moves on to the final stage of his demonstration. He motions to Waldemar, savouring this lone occasion in which he's the one directing the other.

The priest, who for all this time has stood in a shadowy corner, pushes a panel in the wall, and the wall moves, revealing a hidden door. He steps in, pulls a lever. With a loud whirring and a judder, the black curtain covering the skylight falls down.

Sun streams in.

Your reaction is immediate.

A spasm jerks your neck out of joint, cramps as visible as eddies ripple your stomach, clustering against the coasts of the ribs. Viscid, smelly sweat swells up from every pore, pooling in your armpits and in the folds of soft skin around the groin. The leech still clinging there, shaken loose by your strange convulsions, falls through a hole in the table, disappears amidst the bloody sawdust.

Your skin reddens, and as the red spreads and the convulsions become more violent, a frothy pink foam forms at the corners of your mouth.

You've bitten down on your tongue.

இ

CABOT, *mesmerised at what the sun is doing to the body*: Nocturnality has always been the vampire's hallmark, but drag a nocturnal animal out of its lair during the day, and light will disorient it, make its movements erratic. This, though—this is a nocturnality so extreme that it is not a simple inversion of the sleep-wake cycle. It's a perversion of it.

WALDEMAR, *playing the part of the inquisitive but unsophisticated student*: What do you mean to say, Professor? Are you implying that the monster shies away from the eye of God?

SHOREY: Father, I warn you—

WALDEMAR: It's a simple question, Mr Shorey. I just wish to understand.

CABOT: Selenism is not a condition the way psoriasis is. It's a leprosy of the blood.

WALDEMAR: I must ask you to be more precise. What do you mean by this?

CABOT: I mean that there is but one cure for this malady. *He pauses.* Eradication.

SHOREY, *springing up*: I will hear nothing of this dogshit spewing out of your mouth!

OTHER VOICES BEHIND HIM: Hear! Hear!

SHOREY: I warned you before, Professor. I will not tolerate a member of my chapter spreading spite and preaching purification. I won't repeat myself.

CABOT: I—

WALDEMAR, *cutting him off*: Mr Shorey, you cannot deny science!

SHOREY: Science? And what science is this? The differences in the chemical composition of the vampire's blood—

WALDEMAR: You cannot think that chemistry is the reason why—

SHOREY: —have been known to us since the beginning of our society. And is my blood not different from yours, too? I hope so, Father Waldemar. It is you who want to present this information as a novelty and use it as the base for your campaign. I won't stand for it.

WALDEMAR: My campaign? I certainly cannot aspire to the San Francisco chair! Whose seat have I set my eyes on, then? Spallanzani's?

SPALLANZANI: I can see you in Turin, Father Waldemar. You would make a great addition to the Egyptian Museum, I've seen mummies less stuffy than you.

SHOREY: Even if you manage to wake Sir Arthur, Waldemar, it's two against one. *An attorney by training, he knows the Royal Diurnal Society's rules by heart. If this were a debate on the finer points of law, no one in the room would stand a chance against him. This certainty rings in his voice.* We will never pass your proposition.

SPALLANZANI: Now there, my friend. You have your horse and your cart in the wrong order.

SHOREY, *taken aback, swaying*: You want to vote—

SPALLANZANI: I have not yet declared any voting intention, Howard. Come to think of it, I have not yet heard any proposition brought forwards—or did I miss something?

SHOREY: Everyone in this room knows what Father Waldemar wants. War.

WALDEMAR: Everyone in this room heard me no more than three hours ago declare out loud that I desire nothing but peace.

SHOREY: We see the peace you desire. *He points to the body.* A peace made of stakes and broken bodies.

WALDEMAR: Even you have to admit that what the professor just showed us is an abomination—

VOICES FROM THE PLATFORMS, *a chorus*: Hear! Hear!

Mr Shorey turns around. His corner is quiet, but more voices than he was expecting joined in. Waldemar knows this too, can feel the tide turning already.

WALDEMAR, *calmer, with scholarly attitude*: King James wrote about this in his *Daemonologie*—

SHOREY: Enough already with your King James!

WALDEMAR, *ignoring him*: 'For as the humour of melancholy in the self is black, heavy, and terrene, so are the symptoms thereof in any persons that are subject thereunto, leanness, paleness, desire of solitude, and if they come to the highest degree thereof, mere folly and mania.'

SHOREY: What has this do with anything?

WALDEMAR: King James had witchcraft on his mind, the plague of his day, but do these words not fit, like the softest deerskin glove, the vampire's behaviour? The vampire, after all, is a servant of the same power, and it too has the mark of witches—a witch's teat. But its teat is not secret.

SHOREY: What is this insane talk of witches and teats? If this is what the rest of your programme entails, I'll leave this theatre and go straight back to San Francisco.

WALDEMAR: I will let you know, Mr Shorey, that I have seen this creature feeding a familiar in the shape of a cat from its teat, and at least one of the men it fornicated with, who is now not only ready to do its bidding, but suffering from the early symptoms of its condition: the leanness, the paleness, the folly, the unnatural tendencies. *Turning to Cabot.* Professor, based on your extensive studies on the matter, is selenism an infectious condition?

CABOT: More than the Spanish influenza.

HUNGER, *finally speaking up*: This is not true!

TANNER, *putting a hand on Hunger's shoulder, whispers*: Not now.

HUNGER, *wrangling free and stepping forwards*: This isn't true. *To Waldemar.* I have examined the man you talk about, as you well know, since you ordered me to do so. *There's a fight going inside him, for his conscience.* I have found no evidence of him developing any condition.

SHOREY, *lifting a finger against Waldemar*: You lie to us, Father.

It's getting dark outside, a deep blue dusk trickling down the panes of glass.

As Mr Shorey speaks, a head appears beyond the skylight.

At first, the head is nothing but a round shadow peeping out of a corner of the window. Only when it turns to its left is it clear that it is indeed a woman's head, with long hair tied around the neck, though it's too dark to distinguish her features.

SHOREY, *oblivious like everyone else to the head's appearance, keeps on*: You gather us all here, flouting protocol and caution, send your sycophants before you to set your stage, then lie to us. This assembly won't stand for it.

WALDEMAR: I told no lie. I have seen the creature feeding this man! I have seen it offering its teat to him and having him suck on it. I have witnessed the state of inebriation in which both the creature and the man sink into as they do so. And this is the one I know about! How many more can the creature have infected with its poison?

SHOREY: And yet your doctor, whom you told to inspect this man without first consulting your directors, found no trace of contagion.

WALDEMAR, *losing his temper*: Maybe he too is in cahoots with the creature!

TANNER: How dare you accuse him of—

☙

THE BELLS BY the entrance start to ring. Tanner clamps his mouth shut.

It's two minutes past five in the afternoon. The sun has set over the operating theatre, and as the rules of the Royal Diurnal Society dictate, no word can be uttered anymore—at least not in public. In private, as it is often the case, it's easy to break this rule, to appreciate the secrecy shadows afford to those who are willing to turn a blind eye. It's how alliances are forged.

But the time for alliances is long past.

Now what feeble pacts are already in place must hold through the night, see the men of the Society through whatever waits for them at the end of this assembly.

In silence, the men file down the corridor. Since it is impossible to wake Sir Arthur, two orderlies grab his chair and lift it, marching out of the theatre. Waldemar is the last to leave.

One by one the lamps flick off until the only visible light in the theatre comes from you, your body giving off the warmth it absorbed by the sun as faint pink luminescence. It is almost soothing.

ဢ

A GROAN COMES from the pitch-black corridor after some time, and two orderlies come in, dragging a rusty handcart filled with cleaning products.

The first man is lean, red on the neck and the cheeks. Red pimples draw a constellation on his equine face. The second is fat and balding, with a sickly sheen to his skin. They set about cleaning the operating theatre, the smell of ammonia and bleach making them dizzy. They aren't doing a thorough job, and soon they are finished.

The tall man is already marching the handcart out of the

secret door hidden in the wall when his companion stops him.

"Wait a moment. Which one do you think it is?"

"What is?" The tall man's voice is raspy, lazy.

"The witch's teat," says the fat man, his flabby tongue sponging up all the sweat that cleaning the theatre has left around his mouth. "The left or the right one?"

"I wouldn't know. Come on."

"If he's even half as wicked as the father says he is, his heart must be rotten black, so it must be from the heart nipple that he squeezes out his juice. What do you think?"

"I think you are right," says the tall man. He's impatient.

"You know what," the fat man says, "I'll try both."

A nasty sneer splits his face open. He starts with your right nipple. He pinches it. He squeezes it hard. He twists it as one would a spigot.

"Nothing comes out," he says, his face all scrunched up by the effort.

He twists the nipple the other way around, then presses down on it.

"Nothing," he repeats, and reaches for your left nipple, stopping at the very last second before grabbing it. He looks at his companion, who is staring down the corridor, for fear Waldemar might catch them.

"What do you reckon spills out of his teat? Milk like a woman, or blood, or—"

"Or what?" says the tall man, without turning.

"I don't know. Something fouler."

"That may be. Leave it, then, let's go."

"It'll just take a moment."

The fat man grabs your left nipple and presses it so hard you feel the soft texture of it tearing under his fingers. The pain flashes, sears. He doesn't relent. He squeezes and squeezes, turning his wrist this way and that before letting out a frustrated whine and trying both nipples at the same time, rubbing them, squashing them, until he throws his hands up.

"Fucking monster," he says. "Let's go."

His hands linger a little longer on your body. He tries squeezing your left nipple one last time—nothing happens.

"Fucking monster," he says again.

The two men exit the theatre, closing the secret door behind them.

III

Left alone, you drift away. The operating theatre collapses in on itself. A sorcery of memory and madness warps the wood out of shape, folds it around you. It's a coffin, and it's a boat, and you find yourself back on the Night Ferry on your way to Frankenstein. The sea is black, the sky purple. The moon shows her bitter smile. Regina is with you. She asks you how you ended up in the garret where she found you. You tell her about your mother.

How she knew you were different. How she was ashamed of you.

There was a phrase she always had you repeat, when she led you in your prayers, trying to cure you by drilling into you that you were wrong. It went like this: *You have sinned by breathing and by your heart beating, through your fault, your fault, your most grievous fault.*

The Regina that you remember had comforting words for you, reassured you that no one at the King's court would make you feel unwanted; but the Regina that is with you now says: "Your mother was right."

The night sky above you curves downwards, plunges into the sea, flattens the ferry. You are in a cavernous black space. An anchor-shaped lamp shines in the dark. Its right fluke is piercing a black swan's neck.

The Father of Cups (Agata's voice, faint).

You cannot see Regina-who-is-not-Regina anymore, but you can hear her voice: "Look at what you've done," she says.

You want to protest, say you are innocent, but there's no time: you have to do something, you cannot leave the swan up there for everyone to see, otherwise everyone will know what you have done, even though you didn't do anything.

Through your fault, your fault, your most grievous fault (your own voice).

There's a table under the anchor-shaped lamp, and you climb it, stand on the tips of your toes, but your hands cannot reach the limp blackish legs of the swan. You must jump. You touch feathers, soft and moist, and something gives—

—a shower of blood drenches you.

It keeps on falling from the ceiling, this viscous blood which is black in the shadows, the swan's blood and more, every drop of blood ever spilled on earth, it feels like, but somehow it doesn't occur to you to move aside, to take cover.

You stand there and let it soak you, make you new, wash away who you were and paint you a mask that you will never take off, lest someone recognise you.

It's time to sit for your portrait (the Baron's voice now).

Every lamp in the theatre—you are in a theatre, all red velvet and gilt furnishings—turns on, their light so bright after the dark that you shut your eyes.

You're on the stage, alone, but the parterre is filled with men in black tailcoats and white piqué vests. Some hold Ziegenhainers made of cornel, others dangle golden pocket watches from their gloved hands. All of them wear rubber masks shaped like a dog's head.

"Why did you kill it?" they ask at the same time, with the same voice.

I didn't, you shout. *I would never!*

"You are covered in its blood," they say.

I was trying to take it down. I didn't want to leave it up there.

"Why, if it wasn't you who killed it?"

Because I pitied it, you say.

They laugh, and their laughs, distorted by the rubber masks, sound like a yapping.

"A killer feeling pity," they say. "Now we have heard it all."

I am not a killer! I did not kill it!

"Then who did?" they ask.

How am I to know? It was already dead when I saw it.

"Very convenient," they say, and exchange glances between them.

There are chuckles and faint giggles from the back of the theatre, where the men in the dog masks are pressed close together in tight packs.

I am telling you the truth, you say, turning your back to them, trying to wipe the blood off your face. Your feet are slick with it, they slip on the stage floor. *Why won't you believe me?* you say.

Only one man speaks now, wearing the mask of a repugnant pug. He is playing with his stick, letting you spy the blade hidden inside the cornel.

"People covered in blood are not known for their trustworthiness," the pug-man says. "Show me a cat with a hen's blood on his paws, and I will show you who ate the hen."

Everyone laughs at this, and while they are laughing, they

lunge at you, jumping up onto the stage and laughing and woofing and grabbing you, kicking you, punching you.

They call you monster and imp, faggot, abomination.

They call you disgrace, because you are a disgrace to them.

They pin you down and rain their sticks down on you and come at you with fists and feet and knees and teeth, they twist your wrists, pry open the arms you're using to shield yourself from their blows, find what they are looking for. They bark, excited and mad, and the pug-man bites down on your nipple and you let out a cry of pain—a cry so loud that the lamps shatter and the theatre is plunged into total darkness.

A long time passes, or perhaps no time at all.

You know the feeling. It is not your first time fearing you are going crazy from fear and pain. You know how time has a way of stilling itself, coalescing into a block of igneous rock that sits on your chest, a basalt of time crushing—not by brute force but by dull persistence—the brittle bones guarding your heart.

A sound of footsteps breaks the illusion of stillness.

You recognise them; the cadence, the clangour of the heels, the rattling of the sword by his side.

When he emerges from the shadows, the King is as you always imagined him.

Young and dashing, his black curls reaching up like aerial roots hungry for light. He has donned his white uniform for this occasion—for you. How you like this uniform. The white, the gold, the turncoats in their deep dark red, the tricorn. His moustache draws an elegant line above his upper lip. He looks at you, and you are naked, but you don't feel the urge to cover yourself: he is your King, you belong to him wholly.

(Used to. *Before*.)

The King stops two feet away from you. You have never been

this close to him and there's a tightness in all your muscles. You drop to your knees, but he ignores you. It's as if you are not in the same room as him.

(You aren't. This isn't a room.)

The King unbuttons his shirt, pushes aside the lace ruffles. His chest, when he bares it, is smooth, lined with bones and muscles. (Like Martin's chest when you spied on him through the window, remember?) He has a hatpin in his gloved hand, runs the point through his rust-coloured nipple. A single drop of blood forms there.

Not red, but pink.

You open your mouth.

Were this one of your old visions, when you used to lie on the stones of the parapet and let your soul soar through the skies, the King would throw open his arms, let you suck at his teat. This King, however, does not.

"You've abandoned me," he says, then turns on his heels, retreats into the shadows.

The hatpin still dangles from his bloody nipple, but not a single drop of blood falls to floor. You'd have licked that.

Your calves turn to stone, you cannot move your legs. You cannot get up and run after him, so you send your voice down the corridor.

Sire! Don't leave me here, save me!

A voice rises up from the dark in response to your plea.

It's the King's, but also someone else's.

Several someones. Martin's, the Baron's, Regina's.

"We left you behind for a reason," the voice-which-is-many-voices says. "You have always been—"

—*wrong*, you complete the sentence for them.

A heavy weariness is upon you. Perhaps you can close your

eyes for a little while, and dream—because this is not a dream, just time and chance playing dice on your belly—yes, dream of something else, moving between dreams as one does between storeys in a glass lift.

You will stop when you see something you like, or someone you love.

You will stop when you are happy.

If you can remember what happiness feels like.

IV

THE SECOND DAY of the Royal Diurnal Society's assembly starts at noon, the morning having been devoted to smaller conferences between the different factions, to plan ahead. Waldemar and his Jamesians and Mr Shorey and the Bensalem are still entrenched in their respective positions, though after the first session the scales seem to tilt in Waldemar's favour. Spallanzani's intentions are still enigmatic, but everyone understands at once, as soon as Martin Hunger steps onto the theatre's floor, that he's going to break rank and turn his back on the conservative faction he was sworn to. Betrayal is written in black bags under his eyes. Father Waldemar appears serene, he's exchanging jokes with Cabot.

When he nears the table, Martin looks at you.

His red, weary eyes are impossible to read.

&

HUNGER, *facing the platforms*: I— *He falters, looks at Tanner. Sweat is beading his brow.* Good morning. I would like to thank you— Yes, thank you all for joining us in Frankenstein. *Again he looks at Tanner, who's nodding encouragingly.* Many of you have known me all my life, and know that I am only interested in the truth. What I am going to tell you today corresponds as closely as possible to the truth as I've ascertained it through the tests I've performed on the subject. I believe I have discovered the reason why the vampire behaves as it does, shunning daylight and consuming human blood. The cause is not selenism—*he nods towards Cabot, then looks at Waldemar*—and it's not witchcraft.

SPALLANZANI: Then what, Herr Doktor?

HUNGER: Fear. I believe that for the vampire's kin, fear is not a fleeting emotion, like it is for warm-blooded healthy men, but an abnormal, permanent condition.

SPALLANZANI, *impatient*: I'm assuming you wouldn't waste our time if you didn't have proof for this theory of yours. So, get on with it.

HUNGER: This used to be a theory, Director, when I had nothing but the occasional corpse to make my analyses on; when I was guided by intuition rather than by observation; when, in short, I was forced to forego the scientific method to become a sort of medical archaeologist—which is why I've supported Father Waldemar's call for a more forceful approach. Procuring a live vampire for my experiments was the only way to confirm or disprove my theory. Now that I've conducted several tests on the subject, I know that I was right all along. When I first observed the vampire's amygdala—

VOICES FROM THE PLATFORMS: What did he say? What was that?

SHOREY, *looking kindly at Hunger though his voice is low, a tiger's throaty roar*: You will have to treat us as children, Doctor, and assume we don't know the first thing about anatomy.

GAMMELL: Which in my case is true. *He's standing just behind Mr Shorey, almost cowering behind him.* I remain keen on archaeology.

At the back of the theatre, someone laughs. Gammell's cheeks turn red.

HUNGER, *grim of face*: Let's just say that the amygdala is a mass of grey matter situated deep inside the brain. It is responsible for our memories, but its main function is to mediate our emotions, fear most of all. My readings are clear, my findings beyond doubt. We are not dealing with an as of yet undocumented type of haemophilia, and we are not dealing with the devil's doing. We are dealing with a dysfunction of the brain, which appears to be at its most severe during daylight, though it doesn't fully subside, even at night. Blood ingestion too is an effect of this dysfunction, serving as a rudimental coping mechanism.

Heavy silence meets the revelation. There's a shuffling of feet on the platforms.

SPALLANZANI, *leaning forwards in his chair*: If these creatures are so afraid, Herr Doktor, why do they prey on men? Why don't they cower in the shadows, instead of hiding in them to ambush their victims?

VOICES FOR THE PLATFORMS: Hear! Hear!

*The voices come mostly from the platforms behind
Spallanzani, but more men join in.*

HUNGER: A scared cat can curl up under a bed, but it
can also arch its back, draw its claws. It can hiss, it
can attack. I'm sure Professor Cabot can confirm this,
having spent his career studying the animal kingdom.

*Cabot shushes the men whispering around him. He pats
himself on the chest, as boxers after a spar sometimes
do—or policemen, when they make sure their guns are
still where they're supposed to. He meets Waldemar's
eyes, winks.*

CABOT: I have no trouble confirming this, Doctor.

HUNGER: There's more. I think the vampire's behaviour is as
much congenital as it is ingrained by our response to it.
Like alcoholic fathers neglecting their sons and forcing
them into the wild, as with the case of the Hessian feral
children, we drove vampires deeper and deeper into
the night, until they could see no way out of it. We can
correct this situation.

SHOREY: Correct it?

HUNGER: With surgery. *He pauses.* I can cure them.

*Any sense of cohesion the men might have felt is blasted
away. The cracks of factionalism are fault lines driving
continents apart.*

There is shouting, and pushing, and threatening. It takes the

*concerted efforts of both Mr Shorey and Spallanzani to quell
the commotion.*

SPALLANZANI, *panting from the effort of keeping his men in
check, turns to Hunger*: You almost brought the whole
place down, Herr Doktor. Tell me. Why would we want
to cure the vampires?

The glass of the skylight shakes with a distant thunder.

It starts to rain.

A voice rises from the platforms.

TANNER: Why wouldn't we? *He reaches the end of the
platform, jumps down.* I have been a member of this
society since I was thirteen years old, same as my
father before me, same as pretty much everyone else in
this room. I have seen directors come and go, but one
thing never changed, no matter who was in charge. We
thought of the vampires as irredeemable adversaries, and
what has this approach brought us? This man can change
everything.

SPALLANZANI: You are delusional.

TANNER: That may be. Or maybe that's what everyone
thought when the feral boy found in the woods of
Aveyron was brought to Paris, and the doctors decided
not to jail him, or kill him, but to educate him, to
demonstrate that each mind has the same potential
for knowledge and compassion. Is this not the same
sentiment we should demonstrate today?

SPALLANZANI: We all know this story, Stabius. The child

who didn't know how to drink without dipping his chin in water, who tore at his new clothes because he preferred to be naked like a beast. An endearing story. *His eyes are pits.* But wasn't the experiment you're mentioning, the feral boy and the Society of Observers of Man, a failure? *He turns to Hunger without giving Tanner a chance to reply.* Herr Doktor, a question for you. This surgery you have devised, can it fail?

HUNGER: Every surgical procedure can fail, but—

SPALLANZANI: My second question, then, would be: would we know that it has failed, or would there be no way for us to learn the difference between a success or a fiasco save for direct experience?

HUNGER: It is too early to tell. I believe—

SPALLANZANI: Belief, Herr Doktor, is not something we can base a decision upon. *He turns towards the assembly.* These two men, these champions of the meek, would have you believe that we are wrong in treating the vampire as an enemy. They are fond of the feral children's example, but a feral child can't infect those who try to educate him. *Looking back at Hunger.* What would happen if we welcomed back a vampire you think you've cured, only for it to start spreading its disease again?

HUNGER: Infectivity is not yet proven. On the contrary—

SPALLANZANI: Judging from one man you examined. One man. Can you absolutely rule out that the disease is transmittable? *He stares on—Hunger lowers his head.* I see. And despite you not being able to offer any reassurance as to the effectiveness of the surgery you propose, you want us to take on such a risk?

TANNER: What is your point?

SPALLANZANI: My point is that gullibility is a terrible reason to die.

A second thunder echoes in the theatre. In the padded silence that follows, the rain patters on the roof like a drumroll.

TANNER, *turning to Mr Shorey*: You must agree with us.

Mr Shorey's eyes are closed. His inner struggle pulls his face in directions so different that he seems to be donning a rubber mask. Years of planning have come to this.

SHOREY, *with deliberate slowness*: I don't. This is not how you propose a truce to your enemy. This is not how you bring about peace. *A ripple goes through the men, but he is quick. He raises his hand and—as though this movement is so forceful that his whole body must follow it, lest his arm breaks apart—he rises too. The wave of shock freezes in the air, dissolves.* Waldemar's hellfire is a tool no different than your lancet, Hunger. I cannot approve of your solution. It's a deal where the vampires have to make all the concessions, and we none. Another imbalance, though this time camouflaged not as hostility but as cohabitation. This false acceptance would only breed self-loathing and sedition.

TANNER: What then?

SHOREY: I propose a conference. We will choose a neutral place, and there we will convene at sundown, a delegation made up of the most skilled political negotiators of our Society and their representatives. We will sit around a table, and there will be no getting up until an agreement is reached between the two of us, the men and the vampires.

A distant rumble makes the skylight rattle. The sky beyond is the colour of an old, washed-out bone. Inside the theatre, an instant of suspension is broken by a laugh, cold and heartless. It comes from Spallanzani's throat.

SPALLANZANI: You are all mad. You talk of a cure, of rehabilitation. You talk of peace. When did this happen? When we turned soft as putty, and just as dumb? *He looks at Waldemar.* You, Father, are starting to sound like the most sensible person in this Society, a beacon of reasonableness—but you're wrong too. Look at us! There's more than forty of us here, and one of him. One. And yet we only feel comfortable standing around this table because a stake runs through his heart, paralysing him. Why is that? Because he may seem all skin and bones, a poor broken thing, but we know that he's strong, dangerous with his tongue if we let him speak, and with his teeth if we let him near. *To Hunger.* Herr Doktor, I have a last question for you. This surgery you're proposing, would it do something to his strength, his endurance, the quickness of his limbs?

HUNGER, *exchanging a quick glance with Tanner*: I don't—

SPALLANZANI: I see. No need to answer. If that's the case, I change my mind. I am all in favour of this surgery.

Let's cull the beast out of them. Cut the balls from a stallion, and what you get is an outstanding packhorse.

TANNER: That is not the point—

SPALLANZANI: I know. You want to put a bonnet on the packhorse's head and teach it how to sip tea, which is an even dumber thing than what our friend here—*he points at Mr Shorey*—is proposing.

Mr Shorey starts towards Spallanzani—

GAMMELL: Wait!

Professor Gammell seems as taken aback by the sound of his own voice as every other person in the operating theatre.

GAMMELL, *stammering*: What if Caesar had listened to Brutus? How different the course of the Republic, had this happened. Or the course of Germany, had Ludwig not been declared mad and deposed only to die the following day. The Kaiserreich may have never risen! And look at the Holy Alliance birthed after the fall of Napoleon. Was it not a complete travesty orchestrated by a single man mad for power?

WALDEMAR, *knowing that Gammell is talking about him, and almost resisting the need to curtsey*: Brothers! It seems that today we go from lesson to lesson, from medicine to psychology to history, of all things!

A cluster of laughs on the furthest platform.

The bells above the entrance start to ring.

CABOT: We are lucky, the clock saves us!

WALDEMAR, *clapping his hands*: It's time for recess!

❧

Waggling his arms like a sheep dog would its tail, Waldemar ushers the men downstairs. He directs two orderlies to grab Sir Arthur and drag him down. He is about to follow, but doesn't resist the temptation of a last look at the battlefield.

Professor Gammell, a 'firster' whose father was not a member of the Society, so out of his depth in this assembly. Tanner, the idealist lawyer who's pinned his career inside the Society on another's. How they flock now to their leaders, hoping to regroup; how they huddle, whispering strategies in each other's ears.

Gammell and Mr Shorey, the diplomats hoping for peace.

Tanner and Hunger, the social reformers.

In the middle, shaking his head, Spallanzani. The cypher.

Waldemar thinks he's close to figuring out the director. There are whispers. It's said, when no one else can hear, that he is wicked, a collector of perversions; that he dabbles in occultism in that elegant city of his, which hides a black, black heart. Someone has suggested that his interest in vampires goes way beyond the purview of the Society. *If that is so…* Waldemar thinks, and doesn't finish the thought. He starts counting.

Vote upon vote upon vote, he runs the numbers in his head. Victory is at his fingertips. The Royal Diurnal Society—the inconclusive, navel-gazing Royal Diurnal Society which cannot decide what it's going to be, sipping bourbon and poring over old archives, or loading a shotgun—will bow to him.

He exits, and soon the others follow.

Martin leaves last, his shoulders slouched, his steps slow, and after he's gone nothing stirs in the theatre.

Except for the woman's head beyond the skylight, the hair

wet with rain and plastered to her face like a mask. It peeps from behind the glass, hovers there, then disappears, leaving only the dark sky to look down on you.

❧

THE SKY FALLS down, shrouds you—a winding sheet as vast as the firmament, as heavy. It pushes you down through the operating table, and you find yourself in a tight space, compressed. Like a tomb, though the proportions are wrong. Your knees are up against your chest, your head squeezed between your legs. It feels like you're moving—like someone is lifting the box you're in. Then you're thrown to the ground, the box shaking with the impact, and you think you remember this feeling.

You're wrong. You're not inside the wings' cocoon when they broke and you fell.

You are inside a chest, and when the lid is raised you recognise Herr Klocker's greenish face in front of you, and behind his shoulder a young girl with red hair and a wandering eye—Regina, before she was your Regina.

She is smiling. You've never seen her smile. You've seen her pucker and scowl; you've seen her face become a thunder, a boulder; but you've never before seen her smile. A sardonic chuckle was the most she could manage. Was she smiling, too, when she landed on the moon without you?

"What are you going to do with him, Grandpa?" she says.

"He is broken," Herr Klocker says. "He doesn't work anymore. Perhaps he never did. Some models are just like that—defective. His heart and his brain keep malfunctioning, so I'm going to take them out and swap them."

He starts working on you. Soon you have a pink Y widening on your chest. He changes his lancet for a sternal saw to break through your ribcage, then it's the lancet again to cut the tissues holding your heart in place.

It's supposed to hurt—more than the stake—but it doesn't.

Your heart comes out easily.

Herr Klocker puts it in a pewter basin, then wipes his hands and fishes a cranial drill from his bag.

A perfect circle of bone drops off your head.

Underneath, your brain is pulsing with a panicked frenzy. Herr Klocker starts scraping at it with a tapering piece of black metal, a hook of pure gold at one end. He works with it along the perimeter of your open skull, until the brain plops into his hands.

This too he throws into the basin.

"We are almost done," he says.

You are almost nothing.

First, they took away your name; then, your soul. Reduced you from an *I* to an *it*.

Now they are taking away the last thing you can call yours, the last thing that is you. You dreamt of this, of Martin putting you to sleep, Martin sawing off your skull, Martin taking your brain out to study it under the light of his lamp, finding what was wrong with it, repairing it, then waking you up and saying to you: *You'll be fine, you'll be happy*.

You were stupid.

Herr Klocker peeks at Regina's face. She is mesmerised by the sight of your empty cranium.

"This is an act of kindness," he says.

No, this is not.

"I'll swap his heart and his brain for clocks of gold and copper, and he will be delivered from the pain which dogged him all his life," he says.

No, you won't.

"This is what he wanted," he says.

No, it isn't.

You want to shout:

PUT MY HEART BACK!

PUT MY BRAIN BACK!

PUT ME BACK INSIDE MYSELF!

But you don't even remember your name.

There is no more self in you.

"He will be happy," Herr Klocker says. "A clock knows no fear, no heartbreak, no guilt. And look, how beautiful they are, the clocks I've built for him."

The first clock is shaped like a marble arch under which sits the bronze sculpture of a black swan, his eyes made of amethyst and his beak of sculpted coral. The clock itself sits atop the arch. It's round and white, with a circlet of gold keeping it in place. The hands are long and resemble feathers.

The second clock is in the shape of a tower, ebony and brass, with mother-of-pearl half-columns. The mechanism is invisible, it must be locked inside.

Herr Klocker puts the arch-clock inside your chest and the tower-clock inside your head, then sews you shut, his stitches small and perfect; they would make a royal seamstress run away in shame. When he's done, he looks at Regina.

"Are you sad for him?" he asks.

"Not really," she says.

Herr Klocker puts a pipe between his teeth, lights a match. When a faint hackle of smoke raises from the pipe, he throws the match into the basin.

Your heart and your brain go up in flames. You dreamt about this once, a long time ago.

You don't turn into a pelican, you don't fly away. You're stuck here.

All is dark around you now.

Mercury's hiding… but from what? (The Baron's voice.)

It rains in Frankenstein. Same as everywhere else. (Regina.)

Look at us, my Father of Cups. (Agata.) *Finally holding up a promise.*

After garret and castle, wings and comet, after broken globes and broken swans, after poison and stake, you're the nothing that's left behind when the fire dies. Chemistry will do its job. In time even gold can rot, and the most perfect of clocks stop.

An icy wind blows in the dark, a mist rises. There are shadows in the mist—

—are they gravestones?

You are in a cemetery. You are ash, strewn on the grass where a pyre has burned.

A face appears above you. A man's face. It's smooth, as if it doesn't know a razor's bite. He has a narrow nose, wears a pair of round glasses. You have seen him before, in a garden of gentians.

(You will see him again after.)

(Time has no meaning with a clock behind your eyes.)

The man switches on an electric torch.

At its light, he runs his fingers through the ash you left behind after the blaze.

It's pink like your blood, but he seems happy with it.

"You'll grow back," he says.

When he turns off the torch, you sleep—soundly, for once.

V

MARTIN HUNGER DOESN'T come back. Without him, Tanner looks smaller, a schoolboy in a grown-up suit, playing pretend. The other men are excited, because as they feasted downstairs—Waldemar had the church's pews moved aside to make room for tables—the realisation dawned on them that an end is in sight; after so many decades, the quarrelling will come to an end. The Royal Diurnal Society will vote.

Like a dancer from the cabaret, Waldemar has changed for the final act. A ferraiolo of black watered silk hangs from his shoulders. Just below the straps tying it at the neck, a golden cross set with garnets and rock crystals sways with his every breath. He takes to the stage.

"Brothers, I fear we have reached a stalemate," he says, insincerity making his voice slippery. "I have seen pink blood and heard of miraculous medical procedures. I've listened to talk of peace and gelding. I say: let's clear matters once and for all."

He gestures towards the orderlies. Two of them file off their platform, grab you by the arms and hoist you off the table. You are limp in their hands, your neck bent down, the knees wobbly. The stake splitting you is thick with crusts of dried blood.

Mr Shorey is on his feet, arms outstretched as though he's afraid the orderlies might drop you. "What is this, Waldemar?"

"Let's call it an experiment."

"I won't let you harm—"

"I don't plan to damage the specimen. Quite the contrary, in fact." Waldemar pauses, lets the silence stretch. "I want to wake it up."

The waves of fear coming off the men on the platforms are sudden, hot. They try their best not to show it—to mask their distress as puzzlement at the appropriateness of this twist—but one doesn't need Hunger's contraption to register the horror gripping the theatre. Only the stone-faced orderlies in their white scrubs seem immune to it.

"Have you gone mad?" says Mr Shorey. He's trembling. He sits down.

"I have everything under control, Director. My mental faculties most of all," Waldemar says. He scans the alarmed faces staring down at him as if searching for someone in particular, but it's a ploy—he has chosen already. It was easy after Hunger left. "Perhaps—ah, yes, Tanner. Our defender of the unlucky ones. Would you care to help me with this experiment? Unless you want to follow your friend, who, I see, has forsaken—"

Tanner shoves aside the men on the platform, marches up to Waldemar. He's fuming, exasperation at what happened during the first half of the meeting mixed with resentment—against Mr Shorey, who didn't support them; at Martin, who left him; at Waldemar, playing him. "What do you want me to do?"

"If you allow me…" Waldemar unbuttons the collar of Tanner's shirt, then fishes a hatpin from the folds of his frock and brushes it against Tanner's skin, where the jugular vein rises to the surface.

A perfect bubble of blood blows up on the wound.

Tanner doesn't say anything. He doesn't even flinch, or so much as wince.

Without looking away from him, Waldemar says: "Remove the stake."

A third orderly comes forwards, with a dull, dented pair of carpenter's pincers in his hands.

A small fraction of the stake juts forwards from your chest, but the orderly's hands are skilled, the head of the pincers used to the task. There's a gurgling sound as he pulls out the stake and fresh blood gushes forth, an unruly burst of opaque, mercurial liquid, splashing on the floor.

Tanner's first instinct, his anger now bleached by horror, is to draw back, recoil, but Waldemar is already pushing him forwards—towards you.

At first, nothing happens.

Your arms are still limp, your legs lame.

Then your neck snaps upwards.

You see several things at once.

You see the man in front of you with a pair of bloody pincers.

You see the operating theatre closing down around you, and you see a black man with his palms upturned, an old man sleeping, a young man gawking, and all the other men, standing upon the wooden platforms, all of them staring at you.

You see Waldemar. You *recognise* Waldemar.

You open your mouth and your throat is sore, but you cry out in betrayal and in pain, and outside the thunder claps and inside the glass shakes and the men standing under it gasp, and you struggle to free your arms and claw the air with your nails, hoping they will find flesh, and then the man with pincers steps aside and you see a man with a pearl of blood shining on his neck, and the blood is red and it must be warm and sweet, and hunger eats up all your other emotions until the scream you're screaming is only famished and you're so hungry your teeth start biting your own lips and your sex is hard between your legs, and—

"Release him," Waldemar says.

—you are free and you stumble as your feet wobble on the floor, but your arms know the way and there are shouts, and your fingers are already digging into the man's shoulders and your eyes are shot with blood and your mouth is open and your teeth are long and he is looking at the warped mask that is your face and he is in a state of such primordial terror that he releases his bladder and releases his sphincter and something breaks in his mind, and something breaks in yours too—

the broken bones and
the broken globes and
the broken necks and
the broken promises and
the broken hopes and
the broken hearts
and everything is broken

—and your mouth is on his neck and he's so afraid he doesn't even try to defend himself and in this moment you don't care if you hurt him, and you remember Waldemar shaving you and Martin drawing your blood and the American professor dropping leeches on you and the sun scorching you and the orderly pinching you and you remember that *the live specimen is male* and *the subject has a dysfunction* and you remember that you are the specimen and you are the dysfunction, and you remember feeling your heart and your brain being pulled out of you even though it never really happened, and you remember Regina and her red umbrella and you remember the Baron and Agata and the wings and the King and the moon and the fall and your mad lonely nights at the castle and you remember Waldemar knocking, and you remember the taste of blood, and you bite the man's neck and—

Waldemar runs a second stake through your heart.

Your body falls forwards into Tanner's arms and you both crash down to the floor.

A new rush of blood spurting from your wound washes over the boards. Under your weight, Tanner is weeping. His body is intact, you managed only to graze the skin before Waldemar brought you down, but fear played a trick on his brain, the trick you know so well, the hornet and the spider—it's a sticky web inside.

The storm is raging above the operating theatre, all thunder and gale now.

Waldemar steps over your bodies. "This is the beast they want to reason with," he says, an eerie calm making his vowels spacious. "The beast they want to see cured. But though you try to tame it, a panther with spotted skin is a killer. As you hold out a hand to pet the panther's head, there's already a rumble in its belly."

He grabs you by the hair, drags you to the front of the theatre, pulling you up so that everyone can see the stake cleaving your chest in half.

"The monster has eight inches of wood running through its heart, and yet, were I to pull it out, once again you would see it rising and searching for blood. There is no cure for this, no redemption, and certainly no peace between us and its kin. Do you think that after three years of siege the Romans stopped to offer peace to the Carthaginians? They burned the city and cursed the ground it stood upon!"

Waldemar drops your body to the ground. Everyone can hear the sound your nose makes when it breaks against the floor. He puts a foot on the back of your neck, pushes your face down. The rain comes down harder still. The wind wafting in through the skylight brings the stench of finality with it—rotten leaves, black earth, squiggling worms.

All colour has drained from the world.

❧

A prolonged silence—if it can be called that, with the sound of the rain and the distant thunder filling the theatre— follows. It is broken by the unlikeliest of sources. The firster, daring to speak against the Chancellor.

GAMMELL, *his voice firm now*: You live in the delusion, Father, that this is a war to be waged with iron and fire, but fire and iron must have no place in the mind of the modern man.

WALDEMAR: Modernity can't be an excuse for turning men into sissies.

SHOREY, *jumping up*: You will not call me a sissy, Waldemar, if you want to leave this theatre on your own two feet.

WALDEMAR: Such courage, now, Mr Shorey, such show of balls. But where was all this bravado when the monster was about to rip poor Tanner's throat?

GAMMELL: Did you ever think that he behaved in the way he did because of how you treated him? You drove a stake through his heart, starved him—

CABOT, *shouting*: Starved him? *He starts towards Gammell, pushing aside those who stand in his way.* What did you expect us to do? Lead a procession of young men to it so that it could chew them up?

VOICES BOOMING FROM THE PLATFORMS: Hear! Hear!

Many such shouts echo in the theatre—so many that Mr Shorey turns to look at the men in his corner, those supposed to have his back no matter what. He catches their mouths still moving.

GAMMELL: I'm just saying that if you'd shown him some respect—

It's not a voice that cuts him off, this time. It's Cabot's Remington Zig-Zag, its handle crashing against Gammell's head. The blow is hard enough to send him over the rail.

On the floor, a trickle of blood spilling from the gash just above the nape, Gammell groans.

Mr Shorey turns again to his men. He looks at them and they don't look back at him.

SHOREY: Will you do nothing? Will you just stand there?

The men stand there. They do nothing.

SHOREY, *ashen, spits on the floor near his seat*: Never in my entire life have I known such a company of cowards. *He turns to Waldemar.* There will come a day, Father, when you will pay for this. Not with your life, because I have no use for such a rotten life, nor with your soul, because you traded it in a long time ago. You will pay with your name.

WALDEMAR: My name? I will take another, make no mistake, and still the men in this theatre will recognise me. It's you they don't know anymore. Even your underlings have turned their backs on you, and it's you who's to blame. A conference. Peace. *He snorts.* You are a madman and a traitor. You've forsaken our ways for your love of the beast. I strip you of your title!

THE MEN BEHIND SPALLANZANI: Hear! Hear!

THE MEN BEHIND SIR ARTHUR: Hear! Hear!

THE MEN BEHIND SHOREY: Hear! Hear!

WALDEMAR: The representatives of the Royal Diurnal Society have spoken. Your delusions have no place among us. Go now, Mr Shorey. Take your friend with you and go.

SHOREY: You will pay.

WALDEMAR: You too, if you stay here. I'm being generous, because the punishment for treason is the gallows. Go, Shorey. Exit from this theatre—and from history.

GAMMELL, *with a groan*: Howard—

MR SHOREY: It's on you, Waldemar. *He points at the naked body lying on the floor.* You will pay for all you've done to this man. And you will pay for what you've done to this Society. You will pay.

WALDEMAR: Go.

Mr Shorey lifts Gammell up, puts an arm around his waist and holds him. They start down the corridor. The shadows close around them.

WALDEMAR LOOKS AT the men in the theatre. They are all his now.

"All my years I, too, have been searching for a cure," he says. "Not for the vampire, because the vampire *is* the disease—it's us who are ailing. I looked for guidance, and again found it in King James. We can heal, 'by sharply pursuing every one of these instruments of Satan, whose punishment to the death will be a salutary sacrifice for the patient'. Our solution, spelt out for us centuries ago."

No voice rises in contradiction. With Mr Shorey betrayed by the Bensalem and exiled, Martin Hunger off who knows where, and Tanner reduced to a slobbering heap on the floor of the operating theatre, the Jamesian faction commands a majority. Before today, no political commentator privy to the machinations of the Royal Diurnal Society could have foreseen such an overwhelming result, with two thirds of its members now deployed on one side. Father Waldemar risked everything with his plan—his position inside the Society, his clout, his reputation, his life perhaps.

It paid off.

He looks down at you. The splayed legs, the crumpled arms, the broken nose oozing blood. He kicks you over. The stake is a black hole in the white plain of your skin. His heel digs it so much further in that the tip pierces you through, comes out of your back.

Pain is no longer a pyramid. It's a galaxy, you explode inside of it.

Father Waldemar is ambitious. A two-thirds majority is not enough for him. He wants his victory to be total. He looks at Spallanzani, still seated on his chair with the simmering excitement of a child in the queue for a carousel, impatient but aware that all his eagerness cannot make the line go faster.

"Are you with me, Director?" Waldemar says.

Spallanzani points his chin at you. "What do you intend to do with it?"

"We will keep this one, extracting from it all the secrets of its species. We will cut off the source of its curse, its witch's teat, like the men from the Iron Age did with the males of its kind, slicing off their nipples before plunging them into a bog, where the peat made their skin bronze, preserving it for us to see the deep, precise cut. They knew that a vampire, though it appears to be a man, uses its nipples as a woman does—a mummery of motherhood. Can you conjure up a picture more repugnant than a man feeding a child from his breast? Yet I've seen the monster. How it offers its teat to those it ensnares, inviting them to suck its blood. No more. We'll cut the teat off this one, quarry its teeth, dissect it until we understand all its weaknesses. Then we move on to the rest."

"I demand a pound of his flesh and a phial of his blood," Spallanzani says. The lamplight, reflected and refracted upon the gemstones on his many rings, makes it seem like his hands are covered in flies.

The whispers were true, it seems. Waldemar doesn't care. He can deal with the director later.

"You can have a gallon of it, for all I care."

Waldemar shakes Spallanzani's sweaty hand, then marches to the lectern. The moment is solemn, an invisible rubber band tensing between the men of the Royal Diurnal Society. No vote of this consequence has been ever held before.

"Brothers!" Waldemar calls out. "One of your directors defected when you needed him most, but two remain seated here, ensuring the lawfulness of this vote. You have seen with your own eyes what manner of beast the vampire is. We have spent the better part of our lives trying to understand its motives, when the most terrible truth is that it has none. It is in its nature to prey upon men such as yourselves. The beast has no place amongst us, and there is but one solution: *punishment to the death*."

A pause, the last one.

"All in favour of this proposition, say 'aye'."

It starts at the back of the theatre, on the furthest platform.

It rolls down to the men in the middle rows.

It floods those closest to the stage.

A wave.

"Aye," the men say. "Aye," they all say, and even if someone doesn't say it, his silence is nothing against the bellow of the hurricane.

"Aye," they keep on saying, this final affirmation pumping so much blood into their veins that their faces are red with it.

"Aye! Aye! Aye!" they shout.

"Aye it is!" Waldemar shouts back.

Two orderlies scoop you up, place you back on the operating table. There is something of a mother's attention in the way they straighten your legs, place your arms close to your body, clean your face. They comb back your hair, tie it. They pull down your sex so that it rests shyly on the testes. They clean the smattering of blood around the stake.

When they are done, Cabot joins Waldemar beside the table. He places a long lancet in the other man's hands.

"The honour is yours."

Waldemar takes the lancet and for the briefest of instants he seems unsure what to do; then he plunges it head-first under your left nipple. He starts moving around, drawing a circle around it, and stops only when there's so much blood gushing forth that he can no longer see in which direction he's moving the blade. He hesitates for a moment, then closes his eyes and lets his hand feel its way into the flesh.

When the circle is done, it's an almost perfect O—

O is the shape you'd make with your mouth if you could, an

O so big you'd fall inside it and disappear—

A strange gurgling sound crawls out of Waldemar's throat. A laugh.

There's wild cheering from the platforms, and when the cheering grows too rowdy and the rails can no longer contain it, the men of the Royal Diurnal Society pour down, swarming the theatre to congratulate Waldemar, shake hands with him, touch the saintly hem of his ferraiolo.

As the silver-pink blood keeps flowing from the fresh wound on your breast, Cabot fills a small, ribbed jar with it, drops the sliced-off flesh inside. He presents it to Spallanzani, who takes it with the matter-of-factness of a cashier receiving money in exchange for a sale, and pockets the jar before joining the celebrations.

There are hurrays and rounds of applause, and laughing— even Sir Arthur giggles in his sleep as he dreams of butchery. The young maid in Waldemar's employ rolls in a double-decked cart filled with bottles of champagne, ale, liqueurs, and glasses, before being shooed away by the men. This is no space for a woman, not even a servant.

The men drink and hoot, shriek with excitement. They want to feel you, to finger the rim of the stake, dip their fingers into the fresh wound above your heart. Someone passes around a disposable camera so that they may snap a picturing posing with you.

You, the prize.

You, the trophy.

The ruckus inside is deafening, the storm outside unrelenting.

No one notices the sun setting, the light dimming, the two bells by the entrance ringing to signal that the day's over, the Royal Diurnal Society should disperse.

No one save for Stabius Tanner.

He is still lying on the floor, stunned, breathing rapid, shallow breaths. His eyes are open. Sometimes he blinks. He is staring at the skylight.

He sees it when the sky darkens.

He sees it when the head appears.

He sees it when the glass shatters.

⁂

SHARDS FLY EVERYWHERE.

One lodges itself in an orderly's neck. One sticks into the left eye of the man presently holding the camera, blinding him before killing him. He is still alive, though not for long, when Death falls from the ceiling with the lashing rain.

It has battered wings, this Death, and a silk dress with a starched ruff, blond hair that the rain makes almost black. She has a scythe in her hands, which are night-flowering jasmines against the coarse, splintered wood of the grips.

Death has the face of Agata, and she is furious.

The scythe's toe shines almost white—at first. Soon it is black with the blood it spills as it slices through the members of the Royal Diurnal Society.

The orderlies standing under the skylight are the first to be dispatched, the scythe opening a red grin on their scrubs. Then it's the men's turn, heads rolling with a squeal stuck between their teeth, limbs that keep on walking before they realise they no longer belong to a body and fall down like creaky reeds.

The toe is quick, it leaves fountains of blood in its wake.

The rain makes a deluge of it.

Two men, young, limber, duck under the scythe, jump over it as it descends in an arc towards their shins, then run towards the corridor. They plunge into the darkness—

—and are thrown back with bullet holes in their chests.

Petrus enters the theatre, a plume of smoke rising from his Mauser. He shoots a third man trying to slink behind his back. His fourth bullet finds Cabot's fat belly as he attempts to crawl under the operating table.

The professor oinks with pain and fear, until the next bullet shuts him up. He rolls on the floor with arms and legs in the air, his own gun still clutched in his hand.

A sixth shot narrowly misses a man's shoulder, but as it digs into the wainscoting behind, it's Agata's scythe that cleaves the body in two. Petrus throws down the Mauser, unsheathes the dagger you left him, then—

He and Agata spot Spallanzani at the same time.

He's on all fours, stomach low to the ground, trying to slither away over the dead bodies of his companions. He's moving towards the secret door in the wall.

"He's getting away!" Agata shouts. "Take him!"

Petrus starts towards the director—

A bang shatters the air.

It's louder than the thunder roaring.

It's louder than the glass breaking.

Louder than the men's dying.

It lifts Petrus up, sends him crashing against the platforms' railing. There is a hole, black, bloody, in his stomach.

As the bang's echo dies down, Spallanzani disappears behind the hidden door, but Waldemar's finger is still on the trigger as he aims Cabot's Remington at Agata.

"You whore," he says through the curtain of rain that separates them. "You left."

"Fuck you," Agata says.

She jumps to strike Waldemar with her scythe as he pulls the trigger—

From beneath the table, a shadow so small that no one saw it creeping inside the theatre leaps towards Waldemar's arm, clawing it and tearing away the fine cotton of the tunic, the skin of his forearm, the flesh of the flexor. The pain is so sudden, so violent, that Waldemar cries out and his arm jerks upwards, sending his shot through the skylight.

The storm eats the bullet.

Agata's bloody toe brushes so softly against Waldemar's jugular that at first nothing happens. Then a thin crimson line appears on his throat, like ghostly ink on a scroll. It reddens, widens, it's a gash. Waldemar's last words pour out from it.

"Whore," he says. "I'll—"

Agata beheads him with a clean slash.

Waldemar's head rolls away.

It ricochets against Cabot's ass then stops in the lap of a dead orderly, who seems to cradle it as if it were a newborn babe.

The priest's body, after it loses his head, loses the ferraiolo too. The cape slips away from the neckless shoulders, and when it touches the ground the body crumples forwards.

Father Waldemar is no more.

Manfred shoots away from the dead priest who cost him one eye and jumps onto the table. He toddles towards the headrest and starts licking your face, your cheeks, your chin. He turns to look at Agata, meowing.

She is making her way through the carnage to reach Petrus, when, stopping to look at Manfred and measure his impatience, she hears something and crouches down.

Under a pile of dismembered bodies, Tanner is still breathing.

"Can you walk?" she says and, without waiting for an answer, pulls him to his feet.

She looks at him to ascertain if he's a threat, if he's about to collapse again, but he manages to stand upright. His eyes are red and watery, his face crinkled like a child's waking after a night terror. He stinks of rank sweat and shit. He's caked in blood, who knows whose—perhaps not his own, since he seems able to control all his limbs.

Agata nods towards Petrus' body, which has fallen in a heap. He is still clutching the Scottish dirk, his mouth open like he's trying to add something to a conversation he alone can hear.

"You take him," Agata says. "And be careful. He was a brave friend, and deserves a king's burial, with golden masks and servants of Egyptian faience."

She drops the scythe, which clangs loudly in the operating theatre.

All is silent now.

She scoops you up. You are so thin, so light.

"Let's go," Agata says.

Tanner is the first to leave, carrying Petrus' body; then it's Manfred's turn. Agata goes last. She doesn't look back.

You don't either.

ও

NOTHING MOVES IN the theatre for a long while, save for the rain falling from the wound in the ceiling, but then the rain stops and time passes again, until a deep yawn comes from the only man left standing—or sitting, rather.

Sir Arthur stretches his arms, opens his eyes, looks around. He is puzzled.

"Is it over?" he asks.

III

WANDERING FIRMAMENTS

LUDWIG

ON THE LAKESHORE

I IMAGINE IT went like this.

A young moon sings murder in the sky. Dusk bestows a bloody sheen to the lake. The rain has stopped for now, and breaking coyly upon the shore, the water murmurs. The two men walking by pay no heed to what it is saying.

One man wouldn't understand even if he did.

The other doesn't need to. He already knows the end has come.

A western wind whistles through the trees hiding Castle Berg—his prison—from view. Only its tallest tower peeps through the treetops. In the glimmering light of early evening, it seems to him that a dusting of snow from his childhood still shines on the battlements. Or maybe it's just old rain. More rain is coming, a storm. It will be quick, but heavy, because it's summer, the sweet middle of June. The air is rich with promise, yet sour with the impossibility of it—at least for King Ludwig. He won't live another hour.

"What do you think it was?" he asks.

"What was, Your Majesty?" says Doctor Gudden. He's grey, plump and short, his figure cutting an almost comical contrast with the King, tall and imposing.

I would like to know whether Gudden was an honest man put in an impossible situation, trying to do his best with the hand he was dealt; or a willing participant in the caricature of justice being performed in the castle, the empty oaths, the false reassurances, the all-too-real humiliation inflicted upon the King. He used to command the vast altitude of mountains, the stars in the midnight skies when he went on his mad carriage runs; but mad indeed, they said, and now they've locked him up. There's a padlock on his door, bars on his window, a spyhole in the wall. They watch as he measures the length of his small room in frantic paces.

"Was it my love for Paul?" the King says. His white hand slips out of the glove, plays with the tip of his moustache. "Or was it my friendship with Wagner? Or the castles that I built, or my infatuation with the theatre, my contempt for military life? Was it the fact that I didn't produce an heir to the throne of Bavaria? Was it all the women I could've loved but didn't, or the woodcutters and the soldiers I could and did? Was it the chancellor, or just my uncle the prince, chomping at the bit because of the crown which was mine and not his? Was it all the money I spent? Was it just one thing that damned me, or was it the sum of all these parts that turned the love of my people into hate?"

"Your people love you very much, Your Majesty."

The King lets out a sigh that could be a sneer, or a sob. The cold air makes steam of it, pulls it up, towards the moon.

"Then why am I a prisoner in my own castle? Is this not the most important thing—that my people love me?" he says, then stops, takes Doctor Gudden by the arm. He turns towards the lake, makes the doctor turn too.

The sky is almost black with night and storm clouds, save for the moon's corner, red with purpose. A faint, milky mist is drifting on the water, masking the horizon.

"They are coming, you know," the King says. "As we speak, boats are making their way across the water, searching for me, for they knew I'd be out at this time of the evening. They glide across the smooth, silk-like surface making the sound of the nightingale, singing his song of longing. It's the male, you know, that sings at night—when he is lonely. And I'm so lonely."

A burble rises from deep inside his throat, breaks against the teeth, splinters into a silvery wave of whistles.

Doctor Gudden is scared. Deep lines dig into his forehead.

When he sees the doctor's face, pale with dread, the King lets out his booming laugh. He turns away from the lake and starts along the shore again. He is a giant of a man, his stride chivalrous, unmatchable by the poor doctor. Gudden is breathing heavily when he catches up.

It's starting to rain again.

"The boats, Your Majesty," he puffs. He keeps looking at the misty water, fearing a fleet of ghost ships is about to break through. And is that—is that a nightingale? Where is the song coming from, from the trees behind them or from the water in front of them?

"What about them?" asks the King.

A thought has furrowed his brow, casting a shadow on his eyes. He seems distracted. There's more than a bit of impatience in his voice.

Gudden doesn't know where to look anymore. If only the castle were in sight, he could make a sign, wave his arms, ask for reinforcements. "Who is coming for you?" he says, then pauses, slows down, decides on another strategy. "I'm afraid the weather is turning foul again. Perhaps Your Majesty would like to go back?"

The King keeps walking.

Two steps, and he's four yards away from the doctor. Gudden has to run again, mud splashing around his shoes. His trousers are already wet with slime. A fat drop of rain falls on his face, past his glasses, splashes right in his eye, and there it is—the nightingale again. It comes from the lake, he's sure.

"Your Majesty!" he calls, desperation creeping into his voice.

The King doesn't turn, though he slows down—enough for the doctor to reappear, after a short while, by his side. The sight of the old man panting and wheezing makes him feel sorry for his previous intemperance.

"You should open your umbrella," he suggests, then takes it from the doctor's hands, opens it for him and gives it back.

"Thank you, Your Majesty. It's a pity you left yours at the castle."

The King smiles, shakes his head. He looks up. Whatever red remained in the sky the last time he looked at the moon is gone. It runs in his blood now. The moon has given him the last warmth of sunset. A parting gift.

There's quietness in his spirit. He feels it growing inside him, like a tree, pushing a greening branch into every vein, the roots tight around his heart—not squeezing it, but shielding it. His body is a forest. Is Birnam Wood come for him at last, or is it the forest around the Alpsee, and he's going back, and will Paul be waiting for him? Who knows about such things. Damnation and salvation have occupied his thoughts so often of late that their respective meanings have become porous. Now is not the time for philosophy, anyway.

The nightingale sings again.

The King turns to Gudden.

"Do you know the story of the knight and the castle on the moon?"

AMBROSE

AT A FUNERAL

THERE IS NO castle on the moon.

No donjon white against the black expanse of never-ending night, no spire curling towards the stars. There is no postern gate for midnight trysts, no glass staircase ringing with the song the spheres sing as they turn—and no king at the top, no tricorn, no sabre promising the sharpness of his kisses.

Agata doesn't tell me this, but she doesn't need to. She doesn't like to talk about what has happened up there. She tells me three things.

That Regina died.

That the Baron is dead too.

That she left, because she knew something was not right.

Only the last night I spend in Frankenstein does she tell me something more.

⁓

AGATA'S DOOR IS ajar, I don't knock.

It's been little more than two months since the operating

theatre. Her room is now Tanner's infirmary and her dressing table sits unused against the far wall. The *méridiennes* have been pushed to the sides, the carpets rolled up and thrown behind a stack of ottomans. A bed with metal railings stands in the centre of the room, with a simple rocking chair beside it. A black folding screen by the window allows Agata a little privacy when she needs it.

She is sitting on the chair when I come in, holding Tanner's hand.

He's still not well. He's hot with a brain fever that doesn't subside, always shaking no matter how many quilts Agata piles upon him. His face is pasty, yellow around the mouth. The fear that got hold of him in Waldemar's operating theatre drains colour and life out of him, leaving him both exhausted and restless. I had thought him done for, but over the past two weeks I started spying signs of improvement. His nights are less agitated, he doesn't wake up screaming every time the church bell rings. The few times I've seen him off the bed, his feet were steadier, his steps straight. And he's getting used to my presence. I know I should feel guilty for how he feels—it's me that broke him, after all—but I don't.

Agata is patient with him. She has got into her mind that she must make him better. He is her self-administered penance for what she did in the theatre—or he used to be, back at the beginning of his recovery, when she just put icy towels on his forehead and prepared him chicken broth with stewed carrots. But one night a little while ago, when I came in to talk with her, I saw they were holding hands. They didn't see me at first, and I didn't let myself be heard. Tanner's eyes were half-closed, but there was pink in his cheeks, and he nodded faintly as Agata talked with him, telling him about the time she'd stolen a white mare from her father's stable to run away from home, all her mother's jewels stashed in a sack she'd sewn from her old petticoats. He managed a weak laugh, and that's when I knew she'd given him her blood. That's why he's getting better.

Now, when she strokes his forehead to feel if it's hot, and he opens his eyes to look at her, something passes between them. It's not a mother's love for a sick child, or an ailing pilgrim's gratitude towards the nun caring for him. It's a wife's love for a wounded soldier coming back from a far-away war, a husband she doesn't remember but is learning to love again—and he's doing the same.

When she notices me now, Agata looks up and smiles. She is tired, but there's something resembling serenity on her brow. She is wearing her apron. I seldom see her without it these days. It doesn't matter if her dress is silk, or chiffon, or velvet. Above it, she always wears her nurse's apron, stained with blood and soup and the suds from when she gives Tanner a bath.

"Is it time?" she asks. Tanner is asleep. He is still not used to our strange rhythms, though what he does during the day, when we are not around, is a mystery to me.

"Yes," I say, and add nothing because there is nothing to add. I bow my head.

She disentangles her fingers from Tanner's. He groans when she gets up, but he doesn't wake. She disappears behind the folding screen.

We have torn down all the planks boarding up the tower and a warm, gentle breeze makes the silk lampas of the screen shiver. They are embroidered with scenes of kingfishers and butterflies, their blue wings flittering. We don't care if this is not safe. Let them see us. Let them come for us. We are prepared, and the air in our rooms isn't so stuffy anymore, which is good for Tanner's health, and for ours too.

For once, Agata foregoes the apron. When she emerges, she is wearing a dress of black velvet and grey satin. It goes well with my black jacket, the black shirt, the black tie. The short, puffed sleeves of her dress leave her arms naked, as white and translucent as ivory tusks. She's put on sapphire earrings set in gold, but her hair is still tied in the comfortable ponytail she prefers these days. She touches Tanner's cheek.

"I'll be just a moment," she says when he opens his eyes.

He nods, smiles—the first proper smile I've seen on his face since the demise of the Royal Diurnal Society.

I give Agata my arm and we start towards the door, but she stops immediately.

I see her staring at her old portrait as if it's the first time she has noticed it. She dusted it to get rid of every possible source of distress for Tanner, but now she seems perplexed by its presence, unsure what such an old relic of her past is doing in her infirmary. She steps towards the picture, cocks her head to study her child self, the perfect curls, the despondent mouth. Then she takes the portrait off the wall, hurls it to the floor.

"I'll burn it later," she says. "Let's go."

I squeeze her hand as we descend the stairs because I need her solidity. My feet are still a little wobbly. I've had some healing to do, too.

In the courtyard, Manfred is waiting by the open grave. He turns to look at us when he hears our footsteps approaching, then scutters off under the willow, to watch the funeral from the shadows under the branches.

The air is fragrant with resin and wax. A thousand candles burn in the bailey.

Beside the grave I dug, Petrus' body lies in my coffin.

Over the previous weeks, Agata and I have washed him with

water and rosemary, then removed his organs, which we ground up and mixed with the soil where we've planted a bed of Gallic roses, by the well whose key we've thrown away. We have no use anymore for temples and Masses, just as I won't need my coffin any longer. We used salt to dry the body, then washed the salt away, and used balls of linen to fill up the body's cavities. As we waited for the linen to settle, I sewed a shroud from the Baron's old capes, and when I was done—that was yesterday—I laid the body in my coffin.

From a pocket in her dress, Agata draws a pair of small scissors. She cuts a lock of her hair, then passes the scissors to me so I can do the same. She braids our two locks into a wreath, and I put it around Petrus' wrist, surprised again by how light it is, like a hollowed-out wooden cylinder covered with parchment. I look one last time at his face, then put the photo I took from his apartment in the breast pocket of his jacket. I want him to have a happy memory with him, as he sails on.

We wrap the body in the shroud, lay my Scottish dirk on his chest, that it may protect him as it protected me when he yielded it.

We put the lid in place, screw it shut, then lower the coffin into the grave. We don't care for silk or satin, and by the time we've finished filling it with shovels, we are mucky with blades of grass and a spattering of mud.

I was the one who chose the verse etched upon the gravestone:

The mystery, the sign,
you must not touch.

It's from John Donne. I don't know if Petrus liked him, or if he ever read him. I find myself not knowing a lot about this man who gave his life for mine, but I do like the verse. It speaks of the wreath we've put around Petrus' wrist—of his soul, too, the promise that it may escape dissolution.

Agata and I stay there for a while, our heads bowed, our hands joined. When we break away from the tombstone, our feet act of their own mutual accord, bringing us not back to our tower—to Tanner's bedside; to my final goodbyes—but down into the undercroft, to the great hall where Regina used to call our meetings.

It's been months since either of us has been down here and the rats have reclaimed the space as their own. Even Manfred stays away, because the rats are fat and proud. Their eyes glint in the dark like the eggs of some mysterious fish in a fathomless trench. They sniff around the oak table where we used to feast, sit on the chairs where we used to sit. They've nibbled at the carvings of swans, the upholstery. The hall reeks of them, dry droppings and wet piss. But somehow they haven't gone near the Bösendorfer.

Perhaps it's because the piano stands under the hole in the ceiling where bats dwell; or perhaps the rats, too, liked it when Agata played.

She runs a hand over the smooth surface. A puff of dust blows up. She hasn't played in a long time, ever since Regina grounded her. She sits on the stool, cracks her fingers.

"What music did he like?"

I shrug. "I don't know. He used to talk about going to concerts, some German band or other, I don't know. I wasn't paying attention."

It pains me to say this. I wasn't listening, not really. Perhaps I was thinking about Martin and the help I hoped for from him; or about Regina, her plans, my wavering faith. It doesn't matter what distracted me—I wasn't listening, and now I will never know which music he liked.

"Play something that you like," I say. Then I add: "She can't hear you anymore."

I don't recognise the music that Agata plays. In the moonlit penumbra of the undercroft, her fingers jump on the keys like ghostly grasshoppers. The melody is sombre, a dirge, though a light trill sometimes breaks through the heavy black gauze of the bass clef.

I am horrified that I cannot cry. I know I should, I know I must, but I cannot.

I did not cry as I washed Petrus' body; I did not cry as we pulled his heart out. I did not cry as we lowered the coffin into the ground. And I cannot cry now that I hear Agata's music for the first time in months, though they feel like years. My throat is tight, my chest too, but my eyes are dry. I lower them in shame—

—and that's when I see the shimmer in the dark.

Regina's greatsword, the blade she claimed to have inherited from the King himself.

It's heavy when I pick it up, unwieldy. The sword of a giant. For the first time, I notice a sentence engraved on the cross-guard. *Obscurum per obscurius*, it says, and I remember when Regina said the same thing, the night she decided to leave, to leave me behind.

I let the sword fall to the ground, the clangour ricocheting against the wall. It sends the rats fleeing and the bats flying. Agata stops playing.

I'm done with riddles, I'm done with secrets.

"What happened up there?" I say, without looking up.

Perhaps it's because she knows I'm leaving tomorrow night, and no one can be sure if and when I'll be back. (I am, I won't.)

Perhaps it's because Tanner is getting better. Perhaps it's because Regina is gone and she can't punish us anymore. We can play the music we want, and dance too, if we feel like it.

I don't know what it is, but this time Agata starts talking.

"The moon was hungry," she says. "She ate us, but I had a rock hidden inside, and she threw me up."

AGATA

ON THE MOON

THERE IS NO castle on the moon.

What is there is this:

A vast, desolate plain, white as baking powder, crowned by rugged knolls. Their slopes are teeming with what one could mistake for copses of pale tree trunks, but they are towering flowstones, bristly with stalagmites. Black, yawning gaps open up between the rocks, cave mouths leading down to where a subterranean river must flow, the air abuzz with a watery whirr.

They land on a ridge, as jagged as the plates of an ancient reptile. From the top of it, they can see the valley beneath their feet, the monotone expanse of it, stretching in every direction until the white lip of the moon meets with the black endless night.

Agata starts to cry. She clutches Regina's sleeve, she pulls at it, puts her hands around the other woman's face and turns it towards hers. *We have to go back*, she says, *he*—she means me—*fell, he must have fallen, I turned and he wasn't there, something happened, we cannot leave him behind.*

Regina pushes her away, tears the wings from Agata's shoulders, throws them into the limitless vault arching above their heads.

We're not going to need them anymore, she says. *We're home.* She throws her own pair up and away; and away they fly like a newborn comet, back towards the world they just left, which is a tiny speck of blue at the end of the universe.

The Baron, too, takes off his wings, folds them carefully, sends them spinning into the night. He starts dancing on the white rocks as though they were a stage. He is not afraid of falling, he is not afraid of anything. He removes his mask. Underneath, there is just a face, not too young, not too old—a simple face, a forgettable face.

☙

THEY SET UP a camp just below the ridge.

As Regina and the Baron work on the tents, Agata yells at them, and when that doesn't work, she pleads. *Wasn't he*—she always means *me*—*loyal? Wasn't he a good servant? How can you think of leaving him alone down there while we are together up here?* she says to Regina. *You must go back, you are the only one who knows the way! Doesn't he too deserve to meet the King?*

Having said this, she turns around.

That's when she notices it. The absence.

She remembers what Regina used to tell us on the King's birthday, when we gathered around her in the great hall. How the castle on the moon was high and mighty, with turrets and spirals and pinnacles. How you could see it even from a great distance.

But she saw no castle from the top of the ridge. She climbs back up, looks around.

Where is it? Wasn't she supposed to see it already?

She was, if there was a castle. But there is none.

That's when she turns to ice. She bites her tongue. She waits.

The Baron finishes securing the camp's perimeter, and as they sit down to rest, Regina recounts once more how the King used the wings built by her grandfather to reach his court, after the death of his mechanical twin. A great feast in their honour, she says, is being prepared right now at the castle. Soon they'll be there, soon they'll dance with the King.

Soon, she keeps saying, as day after day—do days exist on the moon?—they break camp, trudge across the white plain, set up camp again. Do they travel at all? Sometimes Agata isn't sure. The landscape never changes, the reeking shadows pouring out of the cave mouths, the blinding flowstones, and that unplaceable humming from down below.

What is Agata waiting for? She doesn't know.

Her wings thrown away, she has no means to go back, but she keeps hoping that he—I—will appear. Perhaps it was a glitch; perhaps he was able to repair his wings. Perhaps he's about to land in front of her. She will tell him right away.

We were lied to, betrayed. There's nothing here. We have to go back.

Regina and the Baron start arguing, their already precarious affection, if it can be called that, crumbling away under their fear, their frustration.

They want to go north; they want to go west; they want to explore the cave mouth that reminds Agata of an adder's maw, the two broken stalactites by the entrance its bared fangs. They want to climb the southernmost knoll, to see what lies beyond, but it's going to take months; who can say, with this strange geography.

We should have kept the wings, the Baron says.

We don't need them, says Regina. *If you would just listen to me.*

Why should I? You brought us here to find a castle, but we've only found ice and rock.

I never said it was going to be easy. The road to the King is treacherous.

There is no road!

Because you cannot see it. I can. The King speaks to me.

If he speaks to you, why aren't we there yet?

They go on and on, until one day the Baron wakes them up shouting. Something red shines in his eyes when he tells them that he saw someone while keeping guard. A figure in the distance, blurred by the sorcerous glittering fog that sometimes rolls in on the moon's surface. *It was there*, he says, pointing to the north. *Then it disappeared behind that tor. Do you see it? It looks like a crypt*, he says, but doesn't meet their gaze.

A scout from the King, Regina says. *It must be.*

They decide to go ahead to investigate. They'll come back for the tents.

Come, Regina says to Agata, her red hair coiling around her neck like a Gorgon's.

Agata doesn't look at her. She fears being turned to stone.

Leave her, the Baron says. *Someone ought to stay behind and guard the camp.*

Never mind that the camp is a sorry triangle of lopsided tents, each storing only the few belongings they brought along to adorn their new rooms at the castle. Regina had described them in detail, the white stone walls, the marble fireplaces, the drapes around the beds. A copious amount of sodium had impressed a pattern of swans and swords upon them. Everything was ready for their arrival; they were announced by the syzygy—only the syzygy never happened.

The valley is flat like the palm of a hand, no curve of the

horizon to hide Regina and the Baron from her sight; but the valley is also as long and wide as a colossus' sole, and after a while the two figures in the distance are as small as black ants in a cup of sugar.

Still, the cry, when it comes, makes the ground shake.

Agata is up and running towards it before she can think of why she's doing that.

Regina is lying face down on the white earth, which is pink with her blood.

She has been stabbed in the back, three times, and once in the neck. A stiletto knife, judging by the types of wounds, which are precise, almost like paper cuts, but deeper, browner.

Her eyes are open, glazed over with a gelatinous film of pearly bewilderment, because she didn't think it would come to this. She didn't imagine the Baron capable of striking her while she was leading them to the castle that she had promised. She was their queen—*our* queen—missing only a King, but it was a lackey that ended her, a man she didn't think amounted to much, a man who felt he was betrayed one too many times.

Agata finds herself rummaging through Regina's knapsack until she finds a small pair of scissors meant to cut moonflowers, their blossoms like pale hands with anthers where the nails should be. She cuts off Regina's little finger and puts it in her pocket, then gets up, looks around.

The Baron is nowhere to be seen.

Agata is afraid, more afraid than she has been since Regina threw her wings away.

What if he wants to kill her too, Agata thinks. What if, now that he's killed Regina, he won't stop until he's the only one left on the moon, and crowns *himself* king?

She starts towards the camp, stops.

The Baron may have gone back by a different route, to surprise her there.

His shadow behind her tent. His leering teeth madder and whiter than the moon.

His stiletto shining in the dark, still sleek with Regina's blood.

Agata swerves, runs towards the white nothingness that stretches to the west.

She runs, and runs, and falls down, and sleeps, and wakes up, and runs, and changes direction, and climbs ridges—until she tumbles down a crater. It's here she sees something that stops her in her mindless run.

The bottom of the crater is not a bottom; it's just a landing.

A deep black O opens up in one of the walls, the darkness beyond seething as if someone is stirring it from down below. She smells the tang of something rotten coming from the cave mouth, and there, on the threshold, lies a pair of wings.

These wings are different from theirs, and from the King's in Regina's stories. Their frame is made of something that resembles steel, but can't be. It emits a faint green fluorescence. The feathers are round discs that seem carved out of mother-of-pearl.

Agata lies on the landing for an eternity of doubt, panic screwing her joints in place. When she realises that she's not mad, she grabs the wings. The metal is cold; she can feel its bite through the silk of her dress when she puts them on.

The model might be different, but the wings function in much the same way as her old ones, and she doesn't care who left them there on the moon, or when, or why. She spreads them, operates the lever, starts to soar.

As she flies up, she sees, not far from where she fell into the crater, a trail of footprints going towards the far edge of the valley. She spots the Baron's cane lying on the ground. One of his opera slippers sits atop a dusty mound whose surface is smooth like an alien altar. She's almost about to turn her head away, when the mound shakes. A hole widens on top of it, like a mouth yawning—it spits up the second slipper, bloody and mangled. She cries out, recognising her old dream, but knows it's too late. The Baron's gone.

Beyond the altar, there's a crag: the valley's end.

Agata flies higher, higher, until she can see what lies on the other side.

It's just another valley, as desolate as the one behind her, as white, as barren, but far wider, enormous, impossibly flat, of a flatness that is not natural but achieved by design, though whose design it was to devise a land so unbroken, so smooth, she cannot fathom. A land is not supposed to be featureless. This land knows not how to grin or grimace.

It is a slab of stone that reflects time back at itself until they both go mad.

Agata feels she will grow mad too if she keeps staring at all that whiteness, rolling before her eyes towards—what is that? A canyon, it seems; but the higher she goes, the more the valley and the canyon start to look like something else.

Like a tooth, and a gullet.

AMBROSE

PARTING WAYS

"THERE IS NO castle on the moon," I say. I'm not asking. I'm stating a truth that feels like a round, polished stone sitting in my stomach.

"I don't know," Agata says, drained from her lengthy tale. She is still sitting at the piano, her fingers still on the keys. "The moon is big, I don't—"

"No," I say. "There isn't. I know there isn't."

"Perhaps," she says. Her skirt whispers as she gets up.

"Did it really happen? Did the moon swallow the Baron whole?"

Agata rests her head upon my shoulder. "Sometimes I think it hasn't," she says, and I can hear a wan smile in her voice. I cannot tell if she's toying with me.

"Why do you think Regina lied to us about the castle on the moon?"

"Perhaps she didn't. Perhaps she really believed," Agata says.

For a while, we stand among the breathless shadows, feeling

the closeness of each other, each of us knowing that we won't be as close as this for quite some time. She doesn't want me to leave, but knows I must.

"Come," she says, when she feels the truce between us and the rats is over. "I want to read your cards one last time."

As we climb the stairs back to her room, I take her hand in mine. "I know," I say quietly. "About him."

She flushes, but says nothing.

"It is okay," I say, and she nods. I can feel something—worry, misplaced guilt?—leaving her limbs. Her steps are lighter, her shoulders straighter.

Tanner is awake when we enter the room. He looks at Agata, then at me.

"Is it—I didn't—" he says, and I can see he wants to add more but I stop him.

"We won't speak of it."

Agata goes to the bed, touches the back of her hand to his brow. "The fever's gone," she says, then she leans down and kisses him, her fingers searching for his across the bedsheets. "It's going to get better," she says when she pulls away, and I know, and he does too, that she's not just talking about his convalescence.

"I thought I could hear music before," he says. "Was it you? It was sad, but it was beautiful."

"I'm out of practice. I haven't played in a very long time."

"Will you play again? For me."

"Tomorrow," Agata says, adjusting Tanner's pillows. She tucks a damp lock of hair behind his ear. "Sleep now," she says, and he closes his red-rimmed eyes.

She picks up her tarot deck from the dressing table and links her arm in mine. We go down in silence, make our way to the castle parapet. The first warmth of the upcoming spring is shooting the larches' tips with a hint of green. We sit on the grassy rocks and, as I shuffle her deck and think of the night when we took flight from this very place, I look at the Frankenstein valley slinking its way through mountain and forest.

A distant chimney—whose house is that? I seem to have forgotten—is sending up a haze of grey smoke even though the night is temperate. The air smells of early pansies and charred wood. Something is burning somewhere, but the valley is quiet. No heart is going up in flames. It's late; or perhaps it's early. Either way, the night is about to end. The first train of the day goes whistling by. I think of Petrus, who will work the Mannheim route no more. A blackbird is singing in the distance.

I pass the deck back to Agata, watch her familiar movements as she builds her cathedral of cards.

The first one I pick makes us both laugh. We sound silly in the early-morning silence, young and free. Perhaps Agata is; of myself, I am not sure. Perhaps I've never been young, and I'm not free. Not yet.

"The Father of Cups," Agata says, stroking the black swan swimming on the tarot. "Will you ever find your river, Ambrose? Will you ever swim through clear waters, unencumbered by the thought of what was, and the fear of what might be?" She sighs. "Turn the second card, that's going to be what's in your future—your near future."

I turn the card and we exchange a knowing look.

The Son of Swords, the owl with a rapier in its talons. I remember what Agata told me about this card the first time she picked it for me. *A strong man, a violent man. And he's wise, though you don't know the real extent of his knowledge.*

I do now.

I'm coming, I think, and I hope the warning somehow

reaches him. I want him waiting for me, ready for me. Ready for what I have to say to him.

"Turn the third card. It will warn you about the state of the road ahead."

More swords await behind the next tarot. The Six of Swords, six swords in a jumble, lost at the bottom of a dark underground place. I think of Regina's *zweihänder*. *Obscurum per obscurius*. Above the swords, where the darkness ends, there's a sliver of light, a rainbow.

"The Six is one of the few good cards in the suit of Swords. The opposite of the Nine you picked last time. The Nine signalled despair, doubt, trouble. The Six points towards recovery, the possibility of it. Turn the last card."

Another black swan, wings outstretched over a begemmed goblet. Stars like jewels, pink, blue and yellow, shine on the night sky beyond.

"The Mother of Cups," Agata says. Relief blows into her voice. "It signals a feminine energy, though not necessarily a woman. It's an energy of care, an emotional connection. It's what completes the Father of Cups, what gives perspective and grounding to his cerebral intensity."

I look up from the diagram. I look at Agata.

"I will miss you," I say, and my breath rises in front of us like a little cloud, trapping distant stars in its curls. When the wind blows it away, it disperses, carrying along its wandering firmaments.

LUDWIG

ON A BRINK

THE TWO MEN walking by the lake haven't gone far. Too engrossed in the story he is telling to remember how to do two things at once, the King keeps stopping. The sodden doctor tries his best to keep him under the umbrella, but the King shoos it away every time.

"Listen here, Doctor," he says, his voice louder than the storm. This is his favourite part. "The knight turns the chariot and shoots upwards, where the air is fire and the fire burns forever. The lunar realm opens up in front of him—white, pure. It is this utter purity that tells him he's not on Earth anymore."

His pace is frantic now, and Gudden's fear flares again. It feels to him as if the King is not simply strolling along the lakeshore; it feels as if he's going somewhere, as if he's late for an appointment. The sky is black above the Starnberger See, the castle so small behind their backs that it looks like a model in a snow globe.

"Your Majesty," Gudden pants. "Please, slow down—the rain—"

"Doctor, have you ever visited a country abbey, under the shadow of whose windmill a concert of violins is about to start? You walk the nave, look at the altar, the crucifix hanging just above it. For a serendipitous instant, the elements of the transept are in perfect alignment with the choir and the presbytery, the gentle half-circle of the apse behind the altar embracing the scene as though staging it just for you. Yet, whatever symmetry you are experiencing is but a shadow of that which you can admire in Piero della Francesca's *Madonna of Brera*."

"Your Majesty, you are soaked, you will catch a cold. Please, let's turn back."

"When a storm is raging, much like the one brewing upon this lake, doesn't the thunder when it rumbles and then cracks upon a mountaintop sometimes remind you of a Valkyrie's laugh, though this last one possesses a degree of intensity and intent no natural thunder can achieve?"

Gudden is desperate. He keeps pushing the umbrella above the King's head, but the King is taller than he is, and his arm hurts. He looks behind his back, but all is mist on the shore. That damned nightingale keeps singing from the dark.

"I've often had these feelings, from which my love of theatre and fiction is born," the King says. "A fiction of life, pristine, like the moon the knight is visiting. Do you know what he finds up there?

> *... Other valley, other hill and plain,*
> *With towns and cities of their own supplied;*
> *Which mansions of such mighty size contain,*
> *Such never he before or after spied.*
> *Here spacious hold and lonely forest lay,*
> *Where nymphs for ever chased the panting prey.*

"I was a child when I first read this passage. Some nights, when the moon was high and I couldn't sleep, I crept out of bed and looked at the boxwood hedges and marble fountains of the Nymphenburg park, at the rose gardens, the murmuring cascades at the end of the canal, the Temple of Apollo, the grottos, the halls of mirrors—I looked at these wonders, and dreamed that I wasn't just outside Munich, but on the moon."

The King stops. His face, when he turns to Gudden, is ashen.

"Do you think that I was already lost, there and then? That my reign and myself were doomed because I dreamt not of battles, but of the moon?"

Taken aback by this abrupt halt, Gudden almost smashes against the King, and only by digging his heels into the mud can he keep from slamming into him. It doesn't matter that this King is a prisoner—*his* prisoner, in fact. He's still a king.

"You are not lost, Your Majesty," he says, his breath catching in his throat. "You are here to get better."

The King's mouth draws back, baring his teeth, which are brown with rot. He doesn't like them, so he seldom smiles. Now he doesn't want to; he wants to bite, to tear.

Lies, more lies. From his uncle the new regent, Gudden, the orderlies. Do they think he's stupid? Do they really believe they can fool him into believing they have his best interests at heart?

He raises a hand, the grimace deepening, darkening. The rain plasters his black curls to his forehead and, finally, he seems like the madman they want him to be. He wants to strike Gudden, but instead he spreads his fingers in the air, waves his hand as actors do at the end of a performance, then starts talking again.

"Many a sleepless night I've looked up to the moon, counted her speckles and believed each of them to be a castle I could retreat to. One overlooked a lake whose water was the colour of glossy silver, home to a family of swans as large as cat-boats. They would let me ride them across the smooth, mercury-like surface of the lake towards distant caves whose walls were encrusted with sceptred quartz. I would go there, I thought, when my mood was phlegmatic, and in quiet contemplation of these miracles I'd understand profound truths about human existence."

The King cracks a little smile at his past innocence. He remembers his mother's lap, hot with secrets, when he lay his head there. She stroked his hair and read him the lives of saints, but it was the death of knights he was thinking about, and Montsalvat and the Cup.

"When I grew into my manhood, I discovered another castle up there," he says. The memories he's saying goodbye to are bright, and so is his voice. "It sat in the middle of a forest of firs. There I'd head whenever I felt like waiting for midnight striking on the castle clock to go outside and dance around a bonfire with a thiasus of satyrs, naked and lustrous with sweat and sweet invites. My temperament sanguine today, I'd join in, and we'd dance and revel and drink and sing and fuck until the odious sun came up."

The rain is harder now, pelting Gudden's umbrella like knuckles against skin. "Your Majesty," the doctor pleads, "we should head back, it—"

"Do you know what wasn't there in the moon-castles I dreamt of?" the King says, his lower face a snarl. "You, and my uncle, and the fawns and stooges and underlings that suck the life out of every court. The spies, the poisoners, the assassins— the castellans of the moon have no use for such idiocy. They leave it all to us. To me, they left it all to me."

"Your Majesty…" says Gudden. He's whimpering, his voice on the verge of breaking.

The King throws back his head. The rain streaming across his face rushes into his open mouth. He gulps it down, falls to his knees.

"I was a fool," he says, but he's not talking to Gudden anymore. He looks at the fine, wet sand under his hands, splayed like crabs upon it. "I still am. Even now, at death's door, I think of the crown I wore on my head, but I am no king—I'm a fool. I always forget what it is that the knight on the winged horse finds on the moon, in the deep vale filled with broken treaties and vain designs:

Formed of swollen bladders here a hill did stand,
Whence he heard cries and tumults, as he thought.
These were old crowns of the Assyrian land
And Lydian—as that paladin was taught—
Grecian and Persian, all of ancient fame;
And now, alas! well-nigh without a name.

"Now I understand," the King says.

Gudden has retreated a few feet away. He's distressed, in a panic. He's counting how long it will take for assistance to come if he were to run back now, because he knows the King has something wicked—or desperate—on his mind. That talk of boats, now this talk of castles and crowns and moons. His madness is graver than they all thought.

The King smiles. He rises.

The sudden movement alerts Gudden.

"Your Majesty…" he says again, and already he holds out his hands, it's not clear if it's to keep the King away or to grab him, but the King doesn't pay attention to him.

His eyes are on the Starnberger See, on the mist swirling above the water, concealing, perhaps, the boats coming to his rescue; or perhaps just a lonely nightingale.

"*Well-nigh without a name,*" he says, as he starts walking towards the lake. He touches his temples with his fingers, almost as if adjusting a crown—or taking it off.

Then he steps into the water.

AMBROSE

IN THE SPIDER HOUSE

I HAVE TWO loose ends I need to tie, and he's one of them.

He doesn't make it easy to track him down, even though I don't think I'm the one he's running from.

I follow a trail of paper. I'm at the Alte Anatomie in Ingolstadt, treading softly under the Baroque colonnade. The old leather of his chair squeaks when I sit at his desk. I open his drawers, his folders. I have a certain expertise when it comes to deciphering his scribblings. He left behind an address book, but when I speak to them, many colleagues haven't heard from him in months, assume that he's holed up somewhere to conduct some research. He is. But where? A begrudging internist tells me that when he was working on something delicate, he used to borrow the dean's house in Gehlberg, in the Thuringian Forest. The internist doesn't want anything in return, he has his own old bone to pick with him. Gehlberg has a population of seven hundred souls. It shouldn't be difficult.

I follow a trail of lies. He's not in Gehlberg, but he was, I don't know for how long. He instructed a neighbour—a spinster who keeps a hart's head hung above her mantel, a Krampus figurine skewered on an antler—to forwards any piece of mail that might come his way to Vienna, where he would work as a visiting professor at the Pathological-Anatomical Institute for one semester. He's not there. And he isn't in Braşov, in Athens, in Florence, in Brussels. He's leading me in circles. *I see what you're doing, the game you're playing*, I concede with an amused nod after the umpteenth house I break into, only to find it untenanted. *It doesn't matter. I'm patient, I'll find you.*

I follow a trail of blood. Because he gets incautious after a while, or simply desperate. I find whispers in Venice, nightmares in Geneva. My moon-kin have stories to share. They don't know what the stories mean, but I do. I stare into a pair of eyes, glazed-over and rheumy. I pick up a scalpel from an empty room. The embers in the fireplace are still warm, and the scalpel is covered in blood. For this, too, he will have to answer. I'm close now, getting closer, and eventually I find him—in London, of all places.

It's a mistake on his part, because London is a city of many cities, a city of poets and pharaohs, admirals, prostitutes and conjurers; a city of playwrights and mediums, of spies and secret agents, each with a language of their own; a city of druids and Aztec priests, of mystics and drowned men; but if there is one thing London is not, it's a city of wimps.

I've taken up residence in a rather destitute part of town, in Albury Street, close to where I used to live a long time ago, by the Church of St Nicholas in Deptford. Everything was arranged beforehand—I still have friends in the neighbour-hood—and a man is waiting for me by the arched iron stairway that leads to the front door.

He's tall, his lips painted blue, his head shaved. A double-breasted leather great-coat hangs like a cape from his birdlike shoulders. He has three silver rings piercing his left earlobe, seven tracing the shape of the right auricle. He's wearing patent leather shoes, red as cherries.

"Bona to varda thee," he says when I approach. He shakes my hand.

The old language sounds natural in his blue mouth, but foreign to me; so many years have passed since last I heard it, let alone spoke it, save in my delirious ravings after my fall from the sky. I had used it in my diaries to keep Regina from reading them, but I had forgotten how it sounded when spoken by a friend, by a brother.

The man raises a finger to his nose.

"The cull you seek hides north," he says, "past the river, and north again, under the little owl's eye. Search for the carsey with eight legs—you will find the old flash cove in the vault," he says, then saunters off without waiting for a reply. When he turns the corner, he's whistling the refrain from 'The Briery Bush', though I'm not sure if I'm the thorn or the bleeding heart.

I bide my time. When a choleric humour takes hold of me— which is often these days, because it only takes my reflection in a mirror, the sight of the scar on my chest, to make my blood churn—I want to run to Primrose Hill, find the house the tipster described and smash down the door, but I don't.

I have missed the city. It is home for me—not in any Oliver Twist sort of way, the beginning of my life having begun elsewhere, but perhaps even more so, because I have not inherited it. I have won the city, claimed it as my own. So every night I walk, shirking away from the lifeless arteries full of bright-windowed shops. I plunge into mews and snaking alleyways. I follow the canals, pass through overgrown churchyards. I climb over the iron fence of some secret garden square to enjoy the moon's reflection in a pond almost smothered by pink water lilies.

I head north towards Tower Hamlets and its graveyard. I sit in a secluded clearing by a lonely tomb, its stone cracked and upturned; and I think about what I'm going to say to him when I see him. It's a burial rite, this quest I'm on. It's my old self I'm burying.

I go west towards Southwark and enter the cathedral, searching for the ledger stone I tripped upon many years before, when seeking refuge inside the church from a hailstorm. Edmund Shakespeare's stone, perhaps paid for by William. It's by the choir, and I crouch down, run a finger across it, feel in the coldness of the stone the heartlessness of money passed; and I think about what I'm going to do with him, because he too must pay.

Once upon a time, before Regina betrayed me, before Waldemar's stake, before the operating theatre, I could have thought his intentions good, stemming from a genuine desire to help my kin. I hoped for this. But that was another life. *Selenism*, the American professor who never returned from Frankenstein had called our condition. Our *dysfunction*.

The word tastes bitter, like dried blood.

Now I know better. I know that he doesn't want to help. He sees us as errors to correct, and he wants to be proven right. I cannot forgive him. I've witnessed the cost of his desire, the trail of destruction—of bodies, of minds—he has left behind in his quest for personal vindication. He must be punished for this, and for everything else too. For what he allowed to happen, for what he was complicit in.

It's time for me to face him.

The fifth night since my return I walk along Pall Mall, then north through Mayfair and Marylebone. There I turn east because I want to avoid the park—it would take me to him too quickly.

I squeeze myself between King's Cross and St Pancras, past the Old Church and the Hardy Tree with its crust of gravestones, then left towards Mornington Crescent and up towards Delancey Street, until I reach Regent's Park Road and the almond-coloured, three-storey house on whose façade a huge metal spider is forever stuck climbing down.

The carsey with eight legs.

I push the little wooden gate and go straight towards the wet, chipped staircase that leads to the basement. The door is open.

I don't see him, but I know he's working away in the wee hours, like he used to. I see the reflection of his lamp on the far wall of the laboratory.

Around me are dark walnut bookcases whose shelves are filled, some with books—old leather-bound volumes with their titles spelt in gilt letters on the spine, modern medical tomes whose paper covers are cracked with too many uses—some with glass jars full of brains suspended in formalin, along with a few that store more foreign exemplars: a bobtail squid the colour of lavender, a cinnabar starfish, a bisected baboon's head. A jar is crammed with preserved moles.

A strange, pungent smell lingers here, growing stronger with each step I take. I put no effort into concealing my presence while I walk between the shelves, which are arranged almost in a maze, and I hear when he stops typing on his old Adler, the only thing of value he took with him before running away from Frankenstein. From me.

I slow down, navigate the labyrinth of brains with the leisure of a tourist visiting the Grant, and prepare the smile with which I am going to greet him. I reach the opening between the last two shelves, which leads to a second, smaller room.

"Hello, Martin," I say to the barrel of the Werder rifle pointed at my face.

MARTIN

IN THE LABORATORY

MARTIN HUNGER DRAWS in a breath so sharp that it gets stuck in his throat, he chokes on it. He lowers his rifle. "It's you," he says.

Around us, every inch of wall—save for the portion occupied by a steel door—is covered in drawings, diagrams, charts and X-rays, some of them scribbled over with a red marker. It reminds me of Regina's old workroom, where she built our wings.

Martin's metal desk is a very poor affair compared to his antique one in Frankenstein, but it is large. It holds his typewriter, a small lamp with a green shade, what looks like a full set of medical encyclopaedias, several in-folio anatomy atlases, a copper retort and countless phials. Many are empty, but many more are full of a liquid that is most certainly blood—*our* blood.

There is no chair in front of the desk, but I find one in a corner of the laboratory, which Martin must use to reach the upper echelon of his drawings when he has to amend some discovery. I drag it across the floor, the metal screeching against the boards.

Martin rests his rifle against the desk. "You came," he says.

He looks older than when last I saw him, almost seven months ago. Months of mendings, months of wanderings. More still have passed if I need to count the last time we were both conscious and able to have a conversation. His beard is dishevelled, his hair dirty and longer than before, greyer. The collar of his shirt is yellow with stale sweat, the pits of his arms reek of unwashed weariness. Now that I'm sitting in front of him, I recognise the smell I noticed when I was making my way through the maze of shelves—it's him. His perspiration, yes, but there's also something else, something chemical. It comes from his hands, smudged with blueish stains around the nails. From his clothes, too. It's nasty, rank. It makes me nauseous.

He must sense I'm weighing his appearance, because he straightens his back, does his best to give shape to his mane, to smooth the wrinkles on his shirt. He checks his nails with a glance so rapid he hopes I don't catch it, but I do.

I point to the phials of blood. "I see you've been busy," I say.

"Yes—I mean, no, these are old—"

"I'm not jealous."

He manages a shaky laugh, then grows sombre again. He lowers his head. "I'm sorry, you know, I should have never—"

"Stop," I say, a metallic edge whetting my voice more than I intended.

Martin flinches, sits back. The creases around his eyes tell a story of sleepless nights. His bloodshot corneas are weary with hours spent on his atlases; on his notes; on the slab in the other room, behind the steel door.

I try to smile again, the curve of my lips mellowing my words. "Water under the bridge," I say, then gesture towards the door. "So, is that the room where it takes place?"

He tries two, three different approaches, each stumbling on his tongue, then settles for the easiest. "How do you know?" he says.

"London speaks many languages—some you know, some you recognise, some you have no idea they exist, but they do, and they travel fast. We hear, we know. As for me, I know that after you left Frankenstein you went back to Ingolstadt, shipped your family away to Argentina—fear of retaliation, I guess. After all, the Royal Diurnal Society still exists, albeit in a diminished form. They must not look too kindly on you escaping the way you did. Perhaps they even suspect that you're somehow involved. A vexing predicament."

"My family—"

"You don't have to worry, Martin. I'm not interested in them. It's you I came to see."

"What do you want?"

I ignore the question. "After Ingolstadt, you travelled east, to Prague, though you wanted everyone to believe you were in Vienna. It took me some time, but I saw through your deceit, picked up your *scent*," I say, making a show of scrunching up my nose. "Anyway, in Prague you found a small—what's the word that you used? *Skulk*. What a strange lexical choice. Then again, I've heard you use many words that make no sense. *Vampire*, for example. Is that how you see me? Or is that just you, sticking a generic label on something you don't fully understand? You of all people should know the dangers of faulty nomenclature. But once again I digress. Prague. There you found a small skulk, approached one of us in a club near Wenceslas Square, convinced him to follow you, to try out the procedure you once intended for me. Am I getting anything wrong so far?"

Martin's face is covered in a greasy film. He munches on his lips, doesn't reply.

"After Prague you moved to Venice, but you had no luck there, so you went to Zurich, and from there to a secluded Neoclassical villa on the shore of Lake Geneva—that's where things became interesting. You got to three of us, brought them to your mansion on three separate occasions. A week later you were gone, though. To Paris, in an apartment near the Salpêtrière that belongs to a colleague of yours. But you didn't stay there long, soon you left for London. And once here, oh my. There are a great many of us in the city, and you've become a sort of celebrity in our community."

I smile, show my teeth, the two that can be as long and pointy as a lar gibbon's, if I want—and I do. I'm surprised Professor Cabot didn't comment on them, didn't find them worthy of mention. I'm sure Martin does. I see him spying them; I see him blanching.

"My London mates don't know who you are—yet. You've been smart with your aliases, but you and I, Martin, we go way back. I had to come and see you. Because, you see, we don't know what results these experiments of yours have yielded."

It's a lie. We know. I know.

I keep on.

"I hear there's a questionnaire." He drugs the others before asking them his questions, forcing them to speak their minds, to surrender their free will to him, but I don't plan to lie anyway. As Martin himself said in the operating theatre, I'm only interested in the truth. "I would like to take it."

"Why?"

I shrug. I let my eyes wander among the diagrams covering the walls, then find the steel door to my left. I think of Agata— *Be careful*, she told me—and I think of Regina, who's dead now. I have her little finger in my pocket.

"Once I thought you were the only one who could help me.

I was ready to betray my friends, my family, for you. It's funny, you know. I've always prided myself on being a good spy, but I never suspected that Waldemar was following me, or that you were aware of my presence. Did I not want to know? Did I just stop caring? I can't change the past, but a part of me still wonders—was I right? Can *you* help me?"

A tiny ember of my old affection for him still burns somewhere deep inside me. If I could split myself open and find this ember, I would tear out my lungs to get at it and smother it. I focus on the pain in my chest, force out a strained smile.

"Why do I want to take the questionnaire? I want to know if I qualify."

I can see Martin is suspicious. He is scared, too. He tries to set his mouth in a comfortable tightness, but I've been alone with him before, I recognise the same worry he felt when I visited him in Frankenstein, before—well, *before*. He decides to play along. He opens a drawer, takes out a hefty stack of papers stapled together, fetches a red pen from somewhere under the mess on the desk.

"Name," he says.

"Ambrose. You know this. I gave you my name freely."

"Age."

"Let's say thirty-five. You'll allow me to leave it at that."

"Sex."

"You've had plenty of time to look at my sex. I was naked on the operating table, in case you don't remember."

Martin looks up from the paper. "Do you want to take the questionnaire or not?" he says, but I see through the ruse of his brusqueness.

"I'm sorry. Male. I'm a man. Go ahead."

We've come to the first fork in the questionnaire. Martin

flips some pages, lands in the middle. "How many times have you fed this past week?"

"If you mean how many times I've eaten, that's several. I eat, just the same as you. I like chicken cooked in beer, duck with vermouth sauce, and scrambled eggs. With beans and bacon, of course. I have, after all, lived here in London for most of my life."

"You know what I mean," he says, eyeing me over the rim of the papers.

"Yes, I know. I have not fed on blood this past week, nor the one before that. You have studied me, and several like me afterwards," I say, pointing again to the phials on his desk. "You know that our physical sustenance doesn't depend on it, it's just that we—"

"—like it," he says. "It's just that you like it."

"We need it. But not like the monsters in the penny dreadfuls do."

He puts down the stack of paper and the pen, rests his chin on his intertwined fingers. In this moment, it really feels like he is my doctor, I his unruly patient.

"You have to be honest with me, Ambrose," he says.

This is the first time he calls me by my name and something in my heart jumps. I look away.

"You need blood like the sleepwalker needs his barbiturate, I know this. I know this better now than I knew it before. But you *like* it. You like it when you feed, which is why you do it more often than simple need would require. You need it because it makes you forget, it silences the racket of thoughts you have in your brain, it puts your amygdala to sleep and you're grateful for it, but you like it. It makes you feel good and you like it. Am I right?"

"Yes," I say. It's true, I have to concede. "You are. I didn't drink blood. Go on."

Another fork lands us towards the end of the paper stack.

"Have you experienced palpitations or other irregular heart activities this past week?"

"Yes."

"Have you experienced any trembling, specifically of the hands or knees? Please, consider also very transitory symptoms."

"Yes. Several times, in fact. My hands and my arms—they hurt. I had several graves to dig recently."

"Have you—" He stumbles. Sweat trickles down his temples. "Have you experienced any headaches this past week?"

"No," I say.

"You will forgive me, but these next few questions are quite personal. I apologise for any distress they may cause you."

"Please, carry on."

"In the past week, have you experienced any discomfort in any of these areas? I am going to ask you about different areas, now. If your answer is yes, please explain whether the discomfort you experienced can be more easily categorised as burning, stabbing, or dull and persistent. Is this okay?" He pauses, reddens again.

"The perineum," he says.

"No."

"The testes."

"No."

"Your penis."

"No."

"Your nipples," he says, then catches himself. "I—"

I unbutton my shirt.

The scar Waldemar left me is an eye which doesn't stop crying. It's red and swollen, it throbs. Agata did the best she could to clean up the wound and dress it, putting herb compresses on it and changing the bandage as often as twice a day, without ever once complaining that she was taking care of two patients at the same time, but the scar keeps hurting. Sometimes I feel Waldemar's lancet still moving beneath my skin. I feel it scraping.

"Yes, I have experienced discomfort in my nipples. Burning, stabbing, persistent."

"Ambrose, I—"

"Keep going."

Martin swallows hard. It takes a lot of effort on his part to take his eyes away from my chest. "In the past week, how many times did you experience discomfort in your nipples."

"Every day."

"Which number from one to ten better describes the intensity of this discomfort, one being almost no discomfort at all and ten being the worst pain you've had to endure?"

"Seven. Some days eight, or even nine."

I don't say that some days it's ten.

"In the past week, how many times have you felt that the discomfort in your nipples had something to do with—" He stops, clears his throat. "With the lack of suitable partners to feed your blood to."

"None. It has more to do with my nipple having been cut off."

I have to admire Martin's professionalism. He soldiers on to the next question without missing a beat this time. "In the past week, how often did you think about this discomfort?"

"Quite often. Every waking minute, actually."

"Do you feel that this discomfort has tampered with your sexual activity?"

I let out a bitter laugh.

"I've had none, Martin. I've been busy searching for you, and before that—you know how difficult it is in Frankenstein to find suitable partners, especially now that your brothers have butchered Petrus, and that someone like Tanner spends his days in bed. He's a very beautiful man, but I'm afraid he may be falling for my friend Agata, and she for him. I didn't hear him complain about her witch's teat—unless you think that only male vampires have them, and female ones don't? If Cabot explained this during his lesson, I'm afraid I didn't catch it, as I was busy having my wrist slashed and being sucked on by leeches."

Martin's hands shake. He doesn't look up, but I feel his throat tightening. When I watched him from behind his window, I craved the slope of his collarbone, the vein pulsating under the day-old beard, the scrape where the cross had chafed the skin. Now I just want to wring his neck.

"Tanner is alive?" he asks, his voice shaky, strained.

"No thanks to you and the Royal Diurnal Society." I won't give him the satisfaction of saying more. "Please, go on."

He's still frightened, but he's angry now. Good. That makes two of us.

"In the past week, did your discomfort influence your sexual drive?"

"What do you mean?"

"Are you capable of having erections and maintaining them?"

"Yes, Martin, I am."

He skips to the last page of the questionnaire. "Do you feel sad?"

"Yes, I do. Most of the time. I once came to you about this."

"How sad do you feel, from one to ten, one being a fleeting sense of unhappiness and ten being a state of irreparable despair?"

"Five. Sometimes six. Seven, if I'm having a bad day."

"How do you feel about the future? Are you optimistic?"

"I don't think anyone has ever called me that."

"Do you feel like a failure?"

"No, but I fear I may one day turn out to be one."

"Do you feel guilty?"

"I was raised a Catholic, Martin. Guilt runs in my veins."

"Do you feel like you should be punished?"

"I think I've been punished plenty already."

"Do you feel like you're worse than other people, that you deserve less?"

"Only a fool wouldn't, Martin. What about you? Do you feel like you deserve less—or more than what befell the others?"

I would rip his eyes from their sockets to make him look at me, but still he stares at the page. There's that trembling again, his little finger giving away his terror. I want to ask about his discomfort. I want to tear the pages from his hands and shred them.

"Do you feel suicidal?"

"No," I say. "I don't."

"Do you feel like you look worse than you used to?"

"Besides the scar oozing in the middle of my chest? No, I don't. Why won't you look at me, Martin? Are you scared of me? Am I not replying to these questions as you thought I would? I am sorry to disappoint you."

"Did you lose weight recently?"

"Why, yes. You led me on a wild goose chase across the whole fucking continent."

"Are you worried for your health?"

A pause, which I stretch until at last Martin looks at me.

"No, after tonight I won't," I say.

He's white, drenched. I can almost feel piss pressing down on his bladder, wanting out.

"Martin," I say, then pause again. "Run."

I snatch up the rifle before he even thinks about reaching for it, snap it in two.

We are both standing now, staring at each other.

"Run," I repeat. "I know what's beyond that door. I know about the men you treated, the ice picks you drove into their brains. I know about the husks you created, the lifeless shells your leucotomies left behind."

Three men walked with Martin inside his villa on Lake Geneva, but it was not men that left it but walking corpses, wandering aimlessly through the streets of the city, trying to drown themselves in the cold green water. I helped bury two of them. In London it's the same story. He's hollowed at least twelve of my brothers. Their companions found them hiding in Brompton or Kensal Green, munching on old shrouds, tittering as they chewed. Some of them, at least. Others never came out from the steel door, those who turned out so wrong he had to destroy them.

"Run, Martin," I say. A white rage swells up, blinds me. My upper lip cannot cover my teeth anymore. "I'm being merciful, Martin. I could tear your throat, break your skull. I could tie you up and throw you to the wolves—my London brothers won't be as merciful as me, when I explain everything to them. But I won't. Because once I believed in you. So run, Martin, run and never perform your procedure again, or I'll find you, and I won't be so generous then."

He tries to keep his composure. "You don't understand, I—"

"We don't *need* your cure, Martin."

"You came to me. You asked for my help," he says.

Every muscle in his body is tense. I read his intentions on his brow, his calculations, whether he can fight me, prevail over me, kill me, strap me down on his table and plunge his pick into my frontal lobe. I remember his eyes measuring another room, another distance. But the truth has not changed.

He can't fight me, he can't outrun me. Not without drugging me first, like he did with the others. He knows this, too.

"That was before, Martin. Before Waldemar drove a stake through my heart. Before he put me on an operating table and tortured me. I was awake, Martin. It looked like I was sleeping, but I was awake the whole time. I felt the hands groping me. I felt you sticking your finger up my ass. I felt the leeches. I felt the lancet cutting through my skin. And I heard, too. I heard what Waldemar said about me, what you did. My *dysfunction*. I trusted you, Martin. But I was wrong. We don't need you. *I* don't need you—I just need you to run."

He looks around. The drawings, the phials, the copper retort, his papers, and what lies beyond the metal door, his operating room. I wonder if it's better, cleaner, safer than the one I was kept prisoner in.

"My work," he says. "My life—"

"Your life is what you'll go out of this house with, Martin."

"I—" he says. He closes his eyes. "I just wanted to help."

"Run," I repeat, and something in my voice does the trick, and Martin runs. Out of the study, out of the house with the metal spider stuck on it, out onto Regent's Park Road, out through the park and the zoo and across the canal, past fountains and cafés and empty playgrounds, until the night swallows him and he exits from this story.

I break the phials, think about opening the steel door but decide against it. There is nothing I can do beyond it. I'm sorry for my brothers whom he still keeps in there, the new, fresh ones he has tricked into his laboratory, drugged into surrendering to his scalpel, but I can't help them now.

I can only show them mercy.

I light a match, the sulphur smells acrid in the stale air of the study.

I lay it down on the questionnaire, and I think:

I never did find out how I fared, if I qualified for Martin's treatment.

The first page burns, curls up, then a little flame leaps out of it, spreads to the atlases, the encyclopaedias, runs down to the carpet, jumps up to catch the drawing of a dissected brain with Martin's notes on it. From there, it's easy.

The fire engulfs the whole room.

The charts and X-rays and electrocardiograms blaze away, what remains of the glass phials explode outwards, towards the bookcases, where a single spark sticks and burns shelf after shelf after shelf, the old leather-bound books shrinking away, the glass jars shattering, the dead animals inside free to succumb to their death, the moles and the starfish and the squid, until the fire consumes everything, the walls and the stairway and the spider above the door, the door, the windows, the roof. The whole house goes up in flames as I make my way down Great Portland Street.

AMBROSE

AT A SÉANCE

I WRITE TO Agata to tell her it's done, Martin Hunger won't trouble us and our brothers and sisters any more. She writes me back. The man with the blue lips and red patent shoes delivers her letter to me.

He doesn't come in. He stands on the stairs leading up to the flat, looking straight at me. He's wearing an old-looking damask dinner jacket, with black velvet lapels. His fingernails are painted the same blue as his lips.

"The carsey with eight legs went up in flames," he says, touching his right earlobe. "I reckon you found the omee you were charpering, you did the rights."

"I did," I say. "Thank you."

He nods. "No trouble. What was it, hambag?"

I shake my head. "No, it wasn't a matter of money."

"What then, if you don't mind my asking?"

I don't mind. Two weeks have passed and I reckon Martin is far away. They have a right to know, they who lost loved ones to his procedure.

"He's the one who milled a lot of culls around town," I say, using the old tongue to drive home my point. I touch the patch of skin between eye and nose. "Sticking an efink in their brains, turning them into shucks."

"The bolus bastard," the man with the blue lips says, showing his teeth. He has two blue beryls pierced to his incisors. He spits on the floor. "We knew about the millings, didn't know who the miller was. Did he cark it?"

"No," I say. "I let him leave."

"Why the fuck did you do that?"

"I owed him, in a way. But he won't ever repeat his experiment. He's done for. You have my word."

The man eyes me warily. "I'd have preferred him nubbed and thrown into the pit, but I'll take your word, and if it's bona, thank you for ridding us of him. I'll make sure the orderly daughters look the other way, and I will tell our pink-reaking bencoves the city's safe again."

We shake hands, we kiss each other's cheeks, and he holds me a moment longer.

"Thank you," he says, and saunters off.

I go back in and lock the door behind me. I trust my new friend, but I still don't want any surprises from the police.

Tanner is back on his feet, Agata writes in her letter. She calls him by his first name now, Stabius. I can sense her affection for him in the way she writes the capital S, the upper curve stretching above the other letters, as if to protect them. They take slow walks around the perimeter of the castle. He ate a steak, the other day, but has decided to stay with her. I was expecting it. The nights when he's feeling better, she plays the Bösendorfer for him. They've brought it up from the undercroft, put it in one of the old storerooms. It's draughty, but at least there are no rats.

She plays Chopin, Liszt, Mozart, but never Wagner; Wagner, she writes, she will never play again, and bids me to come back.

I won't reply, because I don't want to lie to her, and I cannot tell her that I'm going north. I need to tie up my other loose end.

∽

I ARRIVE IN Edinburgh by train. It's almost midnight, and the city centre shines with the golden lights of the Balmoral. Thin, milky clouds hurry above the Scott Monument's pinnacle.

I walk along Princes Street, going west towards Shandwick Place. The street is empty, save for the occasional stragglers going about their business with heads low and eyes glued to the pavement. When it starts to rain, they huff as they pass me, their backs hunched against the chilly wind coming in from the east, from the sea.

I turn right on Queensferry Street, make my way north past Melville Street, until I cross the bridge into the Dean Village, and I start walking along the Water of Leith.

The trees are close-packed, all but cutting off the rain from the stony path. The river is placid here, its black water glistening with eels and golden trout who come to the surface to eat the small breadcrumbs someone has thrown in, a little further ahead. There is no one on the path, save for the man I am looking for.

I am not looking for *him*—I don't know him, I've never met him, but he will do.

He's tall, a little older than I am, with broad shoulders and a broad chest. Everything about him seems broad, which in turn makes his leather jacket seem small. His hair is greying on the sides, and his moustache too, but the proud wave curling above his forehead is still as black as a witch's cat. He's a little ahead of me on the path, but he notices me, and notices that I am following. When he disappears, I know he's going deeper into the trees. I find him sitting on a smooth black stone, thigh-high.

"Bona nochy," I say, sitting down beside him. Now that I've started using it again, the old tongue feels good, feels mine. It earns me his immediate trust.

"Multy bona, and no lilly in sight with this rain, all cooped inside their charpering carseys on the other side of the water. It's only us on the walkway," he says, and places his big hand on my knee, awaiting almost no intimation on my part before running it up. His voice booms under the dripping branches. He nibbles at my ear.

"I'm looking for someone," I say, as his hand slides inside my pants.

"Why, this omee no good for you?"

I run my finger down his neck, then down his back. He takes his jacket off.

"I don't mean like this. I'm looking for a hogman, a second-mouther, if you know of one—there used to be many of them in the city, some time past."

He stops moving his hand, squares me up. "Why do you need such services? It is forbidden," he says.

"I know, but I've something to ask to an old friend," I say.

"A polari pipe no good for your friend?"

"Don't know of any so powerful, that's why I need the hogman. Do you know one?"

He resumes his moving.

"Yes, I do. I can have word reach him that you're looking for him, and tomorrow you'll meet in the Covenanters' Prison. Bona?"

"Bona," I said, pulling at his shirt.

He has a tattoo on his chest, just above the heart, where I have Waldemar's scar. A stag, above whose antlers shine an orange sun

226

and, almost covering it, a black moon. There is a pentacle drawn inside the moon. He sees me staring at it.

"It means I don't betray my brothers," he says, pulling me close. "Which is why I won't say anything to no one about you seeking the hogman, if you won't say anything about me knowing one. You have your reasons, I have mine."

"I won't," I say as I search for his neck.

"And bring a mask, 'cause his breath is foul, him being a second-mouther and all," he says, then goes quiet while we work on each other.

See, I say to the Martin that still lives in my mind, the one I watched from outside his study window. He bears almost no resemblance to the Martin of the operating theatre, to the Martin I've seen in London, the one I'll never meet again—which is lucky, for him.

See, I say to the old Martin as my new nameless friend presses his head between my legs, *no problem down there*.

When I leave the walkway and cross Bell's Brae Bridge, I keep hearing a crackling of flames, the old ones from my dreams and those devouring the spider house. They sing of peace, and new beginnings.

ᴄⱝ

THE NEXT NIGHT the air is wet, chill. The sky hangs heavy as I slip unnoticed past the man standing guard at the entrance of Greyfriars Kirkyard. Bobby doesn't bark, leaves me be as I make my way to the back of the cemetery. Ribbons of mist curl around the gravestones.

The tall iron gate barring the entrance to the Covenanters' Prison stands ajar. The crypts here are old, home to poltergeists who don't take a shine to those who disturb them, but the second-mouther must have reached a kind of agreement with them, because the door to one crypt is open and a faint reddish light oozes through. I don my mask and bow my head to enter.

The crypt is small, rectangular in shape. The stones are green with moss, the ceiling drips foul water on the leaf-strewn floor. There's a black coffin in the middle of the small space, drawing a diagonal line from the south-western corner to the north-eastern one. Small red candles burn all around it.

Standing tall against the far wall, which is made of skulls, there is a man of elfin build, his dull complexion taking on the sheen of kefir in the candlelight. His curls—brown, perhaps, or black; it's impossible to say in the penumbra—are tightly cropped but unruly, towering on his scalp like Nefertiti's cap crown. A golden headband shines in the middle of his forehead. His eyes are big, tilted at the wrong angles. According to our lore, all second-mouthers are born blind, but he seems to see all right.

He smiles at me when I approach.

His lips are small, compared to the rest of his features, but when they stretch they look like they are made of rubber, coming up almost to his ears.

Above the hogman, where the wall of skulls arches to kiss the ceiling, there's a marble cartouche bearing the words:

We the bones of the dead await here for yours.

The second-mouther gestures for me to take a place in front of the coffin, then kneels on the other side. He is dressed in a black turtleneck and black trousers, his feet bare. He has long yellow nails, with black lines of dirt underneath. He has soaked himself in perfume—grapefruit and mandarin—but it doesn't cover the whiff of swamp emanating from him. It makes it worse.

"Have you brought something of the one you wish to talk to?" he says.

I give him Regina's severed finger.

He studies it for a while. "It will cost you multy dinarly, omee. She is not close. She is *very* far."

"Will it still work?"

"It depends."

"On what?"

"On how much you can pay," the second-mouther says, making a gesture with his long-nailed fingers. "For this, quater chenter funt, and I'm being generous because you come," he says, stopping for a smirk, "highly recommended."

I look inside my wallet. "Tray chenter," I say, passing him three hundred pounds. "It's all I've got on me, I didn't expect to come here to be robbed."

The second-mouther smiles again. He's enjoying the banter. He counts the bills I've passed him, twice, to be sure. We are both used to all kinds of tricks when it comes to our moon-kin. "We have a deal, though I'm the one being robbed here, mind you," he says.

"What should I do?"

"Just you wait."

The second-mouther opens the coffin and steps inside, lying down until his head rests comfortably upon the silk pad. He wets his lips. "Ten minutes then you open it, all right?" he says. He puts the severed finger between his teeth and closes the lid.

I remain alone in the crypt.

I do not know what it is.

It may be the rite being officiated inside the coffin, which is no ordinary necromancy. It wrinkles more than the gauzy layer between this world and the next; it sends ripples not just through time, but through space, and matter too, an alchemy of sinew as much as of soul which most spiritualists consider impious—and it is, indeed, my first time witnessing first-hand a second-mouther performing his uncanny legerdemain.

It could also be that Greyfriars Kirkyard is no ordinary cemetery, the bodies it houses prone to disappearing from the earth, either of their own accord or because somebody snatched them. In the early nineteenth century, this vagrancy of corpses was so widespread that the undertakers had to build mortsafes around almost every new burial, lest they find it disturbed and empty the morning after.

Ghosts abound in the crypts, especially in the lairs in the Covenanters' Prisons, but it is not my first time amongst spirits, so that should not play a part in the sudden uneasiness that overcomes me. Breathing is hard, sitting impossible—but I know better than to disturb a second-mouther busy at his trade. So, I try to stay still, even though the lair's floor is growing teeth.

Perhaps it has to do with whom we're calling forth, with what I have to ask her, what I've been waiting to ask her ever since Agata pulled Waldemar's stake from my chest and held me in her arms as I hurled and bawled and howled for pain and betrayal.

Or perhaps it's none of these reasons, and it's the noise I keep hearing from outside the crypt—running footsteps, faint whisperings, a foreign-sounding voice calling:

"Come here! Come here!"

I'm tempted to heed the call, as much as I'm tempted to flee, thinking that perhaps, after all, it's better not to know, because knowing cannot change what happened.

Perhaps it's best to live in a perhaps.

It wouldn't be the first time for me.

The scar on my chest hurts.

Ten minutes pass and I open the coffin.

The second-mouther is lying still, his arms crossed above his heart, his eyes closed. When he opens them, they are white, covered with a translucent patina that belies the spirit pressing on the inside of his skull to get out. He sits up like a wound-up toy, a puzzled expression on his face. He looks around, at the coffin and the candles, the skulls dripping wetness from their empty green sockets, the door leading outside—and my face in front of it, barring his escape route. His pupils, the only black thing left in his eyes, contract as he focuses on me. I take my mask off.

"You," she says, and their intermingled breaths are poisonous.

"Welcome back, Regina," I say, fighting back tears.

The second-mouther looks down at his own body and gags. His fingers jump to his chest, nails digging in, then run down between the shoulder blades, searching for the wounds that she knows should be there, the ones that killed her.

She lets out a painful cry. "Where am I?" she says, her German accent giving this question the inflection I know so well—as if she already knows the answer.

"We are in Edinburgh," I say.

I can feel Regina's will trying to coax the second-mouther's right eye out of its axis, as hers used to. The body that now hosts them both rises, tries to step out of the coffin, but when the foot gets too close to the burning candles, she cries out in sudden, searing pain and falls back.

"I will rip his soul out when I go," she hisses, and the second-mouther smiles, because it must not be the first time he's heard such threats.

The time for niceties is over. I look straight into the face in front of me, searching for Regina behind the pearly scleras. When I find her, I don't let go.

"I know it was you who betrayed me," I say, angry with myself because my voice breaks when I say it.

She's past playing too. "Yes. It was my doing."

"Why?"

"If you know it was me, then you also know the reason why—you've always been nosy. It was the price of safe passage. The father knew too much already. I met with him when you were serving out your punishment for insulting the King. It was done quickly, it was easy."

I inch closer, careful not to trespass in the circle of candles, or she will rip my face off. The question I'm about to ask is etched on the inside of my skull. I see it, in charred black letters, every time I close my eyes.

"Was it worth it, betraying me?"

"The King was waiting," she says, almost as if it means nothing that she sent me to my death. I can see the second-mouther's hands crawling towards his neck. It is taking all his strength not to succumb to her will and strangle himself.

"There is no King, no castle on the moon," I say, my voice sharp-edged. I hope it cuts her. "And you knew it. I know you knew it. Why, then?"

For a moment, the second-mouther's muscles relax as an atypical melancholy softens Regina's words. "He told me the story when I was very little, same as he told my father before me—with me, it stuck. I saw myself in the King. When I stared for too long at his photographs, I could see cracks spreading on his face, the same cracks I felt on mine. There was so much pain there. My grandfather believed another world, another chance, was waiting; he spent his life building wings. He taught me how to. It was my legacy."

"Your legacy led us all to perdition."

She shrieks, and the second-mouther's hands jump around his throat, start to squeeze. "Perdition? I brought you to salvation, all of you! The castle—"

It's my turn to shout. "There is no castle!"

The second-mouther's lips turn black, his tongue swells. Regina looks at me, and in her gaze I see fury, and boundless love too—though I cannot say for whom. She smiles her mother's smile, and it's mad and scary.

"Wasn't it better, though, to believe there was?"

I slam my hand hard onto the second-mouther's face, throwing all my weight upon the coffin lid to shut it. I hear their screams from under it, I feel his fists pounding the padded wood, his knees knocking on it, until all goes quiet and I slide down from the coffin, thankful for the cold, wet stones against my burning face.

An hour passes, maybe more. When the coffin's lid springs open again, I'm still lying on the floor, amidst the leaves and the toppled-over candles and the splotches of smooth, cold, hard wax. I raise my eyes to meet the second-mouther's, around whose neck there can been seen ten deep, black bruises.

"What a bitch," he says.

A CORTÈGE OF SPECTRES

NOWHERE

THE SECOND-MOUTHER SITS on the coffin. He rubs his neck, steals a look at me. I'm on the floor, my back against the wall of the crypt. The candles have gone out. The skulls look down at us, wondering when they'll be left alone.

"What did you expect?" the hogman asks. The cockiness has drained out of his voice. He's weary, limp.

"I don't know."

"Do you want me to call someone else? Frequent clients get a discount."

I smile despite myself. "Be careful of what you propose," I say, closing my eyes. "I have many ghosts for you to call upon."

I think of the Baron, all alone in the belly of the moon. Sometimes the soil births a snake, and he mistakes it for a dandelion.

I think of the men who died in Waldemar's operating theatre, the men I never had a name for, the men whose faces I don't remember. I remember only their shouts.

Heads! Heads!

Hear! Hear!
Aye! Aye! Aye!

I think of Waldemar, and for a moment the idea of asking the second-mouther to call him forth is tempting, but I don't have any questions for him, and I don't care if he's in heaven, or in a hell made especially for him. I don't need a hogman to feel his presence. He's always with me, in the flesh he carved out of me, its absence.

I bring a hand up to my chest, feel the wound. This makes me think of Spallanzani, too. He's dead. I read the how in a newspaper in Venice, asked our informers there to find out the why.

"Do you know the name Franciszek Pobłocki?" I ask.

The second-mouther shakes his head. "Never heard of him. Do you want me to call on him? If he's not far, I can reach him without a keepsake."

"That won't be necessary. I already know the story."

"Tell me," he says.

Why not. I don't feel like leaving yet.

"Franciszek Pobłocki was sexton of Rozłazino. He died of consumption, I don't remember the year. His son Antoni followed soon after. When his wife Józefina and his daughter Antonina developed the same symptoms, his only remaining son, Józef, took it upon himself to correct the wrong, because he knew what that bizarre illness meant: his father was an *upiór*."

"What does that mean?"

"It means a vampire, like in the old tales," I say, but don't leave him time to ask more questions. I want to go on with my story. "One night, Józef went into the cemetery, dug up his father's grave, and cut his head from his frozen body. He collected all the drops of blood he could in a glass phial, stuck the head between Franciszek's feet, face down, then shovelled earth back onto the coffin—but he was heard, and seen, and brought before a judge, the Prussian Supreme Tribunal in Berlin. By that time, though, he had already brewed a potion with his father's blood. He drank from it, and gave it to his mother and his sister. Do you know what happened?"

The second-mouther shakes his head again.

"They got well, and lived long and prosperous lives," I say.

What I don't say is that Spallanzani acquired the potion's recipe from the Pobłocki family: rowanberry juice and bourbon and an *upiór*'s blood—my blood, in his case. He ground up my missing nipple and sprinkled it in his glass.

Police found him two weeks later, dead in a pool of shit.

You shouldn't trust the old tales. They never liked to tell the whole truth.

"This is it?" the second-mouther asks. "This is the story?"

"It is," I say, and for a while we sit in silence, but there is something else I'm curious to ask. "Is it true that you can snatch the souls of dreaming men too? That all it takes is for a man to get up in the night and forget to cover his place on the bed with a blanket, and you can snatch his soul until sunrise?"

The second-mouther gets up from the coffin. He crouches down, starts collecting his things, the candles, the little sacks of salt he had placed in the corners of the crypt without my knowing it.

"You shouldn't believe everything you hear," he says.

I know he can. I'm tempted to ask him—I can pay, I lied—to do it, to snatch Mr Shorey's soul while he sleeps so I can thank him, because, at the worst of times, he showed me kindness, and called me not a thing, an *it*, a monster; he called me a man. I owe him. I know just the place where he could hold his peace conference. If he ever manages to call one, I hope he's successful.

It's time for me to leave. When I get up, something light and shiny slips from my back pocket, falls jingling and jangling onto the floor. The second-mouther's eyes turn towards the sound like a magpie's.

"You can keep it," I say. "It's bound to have some value."

It's a mother-of-pearl disc, which I pulled from the wings Agata found on the moon. I kept it with me during my travels, wondering who built those wings, and why. Did they believe, like we did, that there was a castle on the moon, where they could be happy? Did they go there of their own volition, or were they tricked into it, like Agata and the Baron—in a way like Regina herself, who was taught to believe in a lie? I don't know how long this cycle goes back, no one does, and no one will. Perhaps whoever flew these strange wings found their way back; or perhaps they are still up there, waiting for the next arrivals.

It doesn't matter anymore.

"Consider it the una chenter missing from the hambag before," I say to the second-mouther as I turn to the door. He dives to grab it before I change my mind.

Outside the night is cold. A salty mist floats above the freezing grass. I start towards the prison gate.

I've said my goodbyes, I've asked what I needed to.

The only question that remains unanswered is not one for Regina; it's one for me.

Where do I go now that my loose ends are tied, now that I know there is no castle waiting for me on the moon?

LUDWIG

IN THE WATER

"THERE IS NO castle on the moon waiting for me," says the King, water up to his chin already. Gudden's body floats nearby.

"They will say I was mad, crazy, lonely. I was, though mostly I was just a man. They will say they killed me, that I drowned, that I murdered the doctor, that he murdered me, that it was a plot, that it was an accident. It's none of these things. It's just death, senseless and meaningless like every other death. The mist clears, or perhaps my eyes are growing accustomed to seeing through veils. I don't see any boats. Perhaps they were a dream, or perhaps it doesn't matter even if they are real, and making their way to me right now. Soon, nothingness—which is not peace, nor torment, just emptiness. I will melt in the water, a drop of me swallowed up by a fish, so I can be born again when a man eats it. I will lodge in his heart, hold my court there. Now I walk forth, a prayer on my lips.

"Don't forget me," the King says, and goes under.

AMBROSE

AT A FORK IN THE MIST

THE WHITISH MASS of the kirk rises from the mist clinging to the gravestones, its pinnacles the only elements to retain their solidity in the wee hours after midnight. It's easy to get lost.

I pass a tall obelisk, almost glassy in the half-light. It stands upon a plinth whose inscription has the arcane look of a hiero-glyphic book hand. I stoop to look at the faded letters, trying to decipher their meaning, and when I get up, the mist is murkier around me. I don't know which way I'm turned anymore. I hear a faint rustling coming from a bush somewhere behind me, so I decide to go in the opposite direction.

This is the exact moment in which the wandering firma-ment above my head shifts, drawing different constellations to portend my future. Sometimes it takes just this—turning left instead of right—for an entire life to change, because the path I take doesn't lead me to the exit; it leads me to him.

I'm skirting a row of squat crypts, their rusty gates dangling from the hinges. A faint whistle pierces the white mist rolling

239

inside one of the vaults. It makes my skin jump.

"Come here!" the disembodied voice I heard before says—only now a body emerges from the mist.

It's a man, who runs in my direction and almost crashes into me.

"Where did it go? Did you see which way it went?"

He must be in his thirties. A lack of facial hair and a general smoothness of the skin would make him look younger, but the eyes tell a different story. They are bright green, and gentle, but they are also old. Perhaps as old as mine. He has a thin, slightly haughty nose. Upon it he wears a pair of round glasses.

"What did? What are you looking for?"

A cat, I think he's going to say, or a dog. A parrot, even. Did I not once meet, one evening as I was walking across Brompton, a man with two blue macaws on his arms? But I forget we are in Edinburgh, in Greyfriars Kirkyard, well past midnight, where and when there's no such thing as a straightforward answer.

"The spunkie," the man says, looking at me as though this is the most reasonable explanation. He switches on an electric torch and the sudden light, when it flashes into my eyes, brings back a memory which is not a memory.

I know this man. The same round glasses, the same nose.

I visited him in a dream, and saw him again in the operating theatre, when I was drifting through the ever-chancing currents of time. I saw Regina as a small child, and her grandfather, and then I saw *him*. He's the man who took the ash I left behind after I was burned.

I shouldn't be surprised that he appears now that I've just parlayed one last time with Regina—the two visions were connected. I saw him once after I found her in my room, tampering with my wings, dooming me to fall. Then a second

240

time when I had a stake through my heart. Now my loose ends are tied and he appears a third time. Agata would have seen this coming. But I know nothing of fate or fortune, and stand there, gaping at the man as he flashes his torch around, behind a gravestone, under a gorse bush.

"I've been chasing it for hours," he says.

"I know," I say, shaking my head to clear it. "I heard you. I thought you were the spirit, not the one chasing it. Why are you trying to catch it?"

A distant horn sounds through the mist. A cab rushing past on Candlemaker Row, or a siren blaring from the sea on the eastern wind. Or something stranger still—a possibility.

The air is immobile, there's no sprite in sight.

"It makes the best ash in the world if you convince it to burn on a bilberry, which is rich in potassium," the man says, then senses my incredulity, and adds:

"I need it for my tomatoes."

MIKOŁAJ

IN THE CITY OF FIRES

His name is Mikołaj. We find the spunkie on the church's eastern window, disguised as starlight upon the stained glass, and catch it in a glass jar with a silver lid. Since I don't know where to go, after Mikołaj bags the spunkie I follow him to Warsaw, where he's from.

When he asks me what I was doing in Greyfriars Kirkyard so late at night, I tell him the truth. He was already with me in the theatre, I see no point in lying. I tell him about the second-mouther and Regina, about the moon and the Royal Diurnal Society, about Martin in London and Agata in Frankenstein. I tell him about the scar on my chest and the colour of my blood. He's not scared, not even surprised. He tells me that I'm going to like his country, if I like castles so much that I was ready to fly to the moon to find one.

"And we have many dead kings, too," he says, smiling with his whole face.

Warsaw is a flat city. Its rollicking parks and oblong squares give an impression of spaciousness which is not foiled, but reinforced, by the maze-like streets of the old centre, which, for all their winding up and down, always end up opening onto plazas and belvederes. Even the city's castle, though proud in appearance, is no more than two or three storeys high, its turrets somehow shorter than the main body.

This is a result of the war, because afterwards, still reeling from the devastation, the city tried hard not to draw attention upon itself. During my stay, though, I come to understand that the flatness is also a feature of the land Warsaw sits upon, for the vast, limitless plain that extends west of the Vistula is so inviting, so rich and ripe, that you can almost see the city stretching her fingers out to it, grabbing lakes and oxbows, hills and forests, and devising forever new ways to grow around them.

This vocation to horizontality hampers the city's new vertical aspirations, so that its tall modern buildings, lording over their squat neighbourhoods, look lonely and forlorn—none more so than the Palace of Culture and Science, the forbidding tower left behind by Stalin, rising eight hundred feet above the city. It looks white and noble when the sky is clear, but when the weather turns grim, it takes on the appearance of a relic, the sole remnant from a long-forgotten civilisation which left behind a language no one understands any longer. All is rustling silence under its shadow.

We arrive at the central station late at night, and from there we make our way to the other side of the Vistula, stopping in front of a run-down red-brick factory, surrounded by a rather desolate parking lot, the concrete cracked by stubborn weeds. Washed-out ribbons from some neighbourhood festivity hang from a wire stretched between two lamp-posts. An old neon sign is thrown against the factory wall, its three-foot-high letters rusty and blackened at the edges.

MUZEUM, the sign says.

Mikołaj fishes a heavy bundle of keys out of his pocket and opens the door, letting us inside. "Welcome," he says, "to the Ash Conservatory."

❧

As we travelled east from Edinburgh, Mikołaj told me something about the Ash Conservatory. Always in riddles I could not fully solve, which hinted at a vast enterprise operating worldwide and devoted to the restoration of what is lost.

It was important for him to stress this point.

"Don't let the name fool you. We are not in the business of preserving what *is*; we recreate what *was*, but not out of archival considerations—we are not interested in the past as such. We want to reinvent it, to give it a second chance, a better chance, to last."

"Who is this 'we'?"

As far as I understood it from Mikołaj's clues, unlike the Royal Diurnal Society, with its codified rules and rigid formality, the Conservatory seemed to be a loosely organised network of like-minded individuals, who seldom met for communal occasions. They called themselves growers, each grower being in charge—though I doubt this is the proper way to express it—of something they referred to as an ashery, or sometimes a cluster.

"But what it is that you do in these clusters?" I asked him while our plane was flying above the great black expanse of the North Sea, indistinguishable from the night sky above our heads. If you squinted, it looked like the plane was floating in space, the strands of cloud rushing past the window as evanescent as distant nebulas.

Mikołaj looked at me. Sometimes, when the light was right,

244

his skin had the sheen of stone, a blue-grey marble. Other times he seemed fashioned out of clay, or out of glass—the glass the artisans of Murano have been blowing for centuries, both dense and light, earthy and ethereal.

He shrugged, the movement as slow and resolute as a mountain's shuddering. "You have to see it," he said.

Now I was about to.

෨

I FIND MYSELF on the threshold of a cavernous space, plunged into a deep, odorous darkness—silty, metallic. Then Mikołaj flicks a switch, and the Conservatory comes alive.

My first impression of it is that of a pyrotechnic brightness, with reds and blues and greens and yellows exploding in bursts all around. It takes me a little time to understand what I'm seeing.

Rows of plants, shrubs and flowers line the floor, while oddly shaped polyhedrons made of mirrors hang from the glass ceiling on sturdy silver cables. They reflect the flame-like leaves of the Saint George's swords, the fire crotons' red veins—so much like a man's—giving the impression that the plants grow not only from the soil strewn across the floor, but from the air too. And it's not just an impression.

At regular intervals along the ceiling, I spot simple glass spheres filled with fat, brown loam and tiny white stones, capped by delicate juniper trees as big as a grown man's little finger. Some spheres are full of a black bark through which run the pale, muscle-like roots of orchids of any shape and colour. Some others have nothing in them save for moist air shot through with the fleshy blades of a cardinal air plant.

Mikołaj takes my hand, leads me inside the Conservatory.

On the ground, scattered among the plants, there are cases of reinforced glass, some so tall that they could house the equestrian statue of a medieval king. Instead, they are filled with strange, opalescent architectures. The one nearest to us houses what looks like a cathedral suspended in the air. The shape of it is familiar. I take one step closer.

In a brief span, I realise two things. The first is that I'm looking at Notre Dame, its needle-like spire soaring high as it used to. The second is that everything—the spire, the flying buttresses, the rose window—is made of gossamer, spun before my eyes by a colony of black-and-white funnel weavers.

Mikołaj directs my face away from the case and to the flower bed that sits in front of it. The orange woolflowers that grow there have the proud look of domed towers, each daring its neighbour to stand higher.

"They feed on the cinders of Notre Dame," Mikołaj says. "I went there the day after the fire, bribed a guard to let me take a handful of ash. The flowers suck something out of it, and in turn the spiders see something in the flowers, in the proportions of the filaments. The petals sing to them a song that's lost to our ears, and they react to it, spinning back into reality that which passed away from it."

"But how?"

He shrugs again, as if to say—I'm content not to know, isn't it better this way? "Spiders are not the most talkative of animals," he says.

We keep walking, venturing deeper inside the Conservatory. I see a Swiss cheese plant, a golden Ceylon creeper, a bed of blue minks, and in front of them a steamboat with smokestacks and a paddlewheel; a palace with slender columns supporting an arched loggia; an entire city of noble-looking buildings and winding streets, the figures walking them made of pearly globules. The spiders mirror leaves and flowers, roots, but it comes to a point where the plants themselves take on the rhythm of the animals' movements, their poses, their colours even.

"Oh, look!" Mikołaj says.

We're near the centre of the Conservatory. He's pointing at a plant with small pike-like leaves, as tall as we are. It sits in the shade offered by the imposing bronze bust of a blindfolded god, which seems positioned there precisely to give the plant some respite from the light that, during the day, streams in from above.

"My tuftroot has grown so much while I was away—and my tomatoes! Look at how round and red they became while I was chasing the spunkie. Now that we've got it, they will grow as big as your head. I'm sorry, but you do have a rather big head."

He pulls me along, laughing, eager to show me his plants and his spiders, all the lost things they are growing back to life. His keenness is infectious, because it doesn't stem from the desire to show off an accomplishment, but from the sheer delight he takes in the mysterious workings of the Conservatory around us. His eyes beam with it.

"Sometimes I recognise what the spiders are spinning," he says as we pass in front of a vivarium standing in the shadow of a sprawling fiddle-leaf fig. "That's a wood-and-glass pavilion which burned down some years ago in the grounds of Ujazdów Castle. And that one is the old La Fenice theatre in Venice, with curtains of silk and lamps made of hoar frost. If you squeeze your eyes, the spiders seem to be dancing a Balanchine ballet, *Theme and Variations*. Other times, though, I have no idea what I'm looking at. Perhaps I see an arch and think I'm seeing the Library of Alexandria; or I spot what looks like a gabled roof and hope I'm the first one to lay eyes on London before the Great Fire."

In a case near the back of the Conservatory, two spiders

are building something for which I have no name, a twinkling architecture of impossible stairways and landings and soda straws and helictites. Beside it, a lonely speckled pear-shaped leucauge spins an empyreal structure of spiralling discs connected by what looks like capsule pipelines.

"It looks like a cave on the moon might," I say, pressing my nose against the glass.

"Perhaps. Often I think this is what spiders see when they sleep; that some ashes, some flowers remind them of something that never existed, save in their dreams. I save all of them, wherever I find them, because you never know. No two people dream the same dream, and with spiders it's the same."

I close my eyes. "I dreamt of you," I say. "Twice I dreamt of burning, though one was not really a dream. It doesn't matter what it was. Both times you were there, at the end. Saving me."

"I know," he says. "I recognised you, even though when I saw you in my garden you had feathers. You were bleeding."

I turn away from the case and look around me, at the glass spheres and the plants, the rich black soil, the flowering buds, and the man in front of me, smiling as though this—being here with me, showing me his work—is the single most precious moment of his life.

The tears come, the first I've cried since the operating theatre. Warm, silent tears. I blink them away.

Above us the sky is coming alive with the first pink of dawn.

"We all fight the same battle," Mikołaj says, stepping close, taking my hand. "Me and the spiders I save. This city is a city of fires, but each time we rebuild. I'm carrying on with the tradition of my people, because what we lose in the fire must not be lost forever. Everything—and everyone—is worth salvaging."

AMBROSE

IN FRONT OF A SHADOW

I DECIDE TO stay with Mikołaj. Sometime after my first visit to his ashery, he takes me to the little town of Wysowa-Zdrój, at the foot of the Carpathians. An old church burned down. He shows me a picture.

It's a squat timber building with slanted roofs, the body of which is made up of three towers of different heights, each one standing up against the others and capped by a black wooden dome. Their style calls to my mind an Asian pagoda. It's called a *tserkva*, Mikołaj tells me as we drive south, and my general impression of it is that of a mighty flight of stairs, climbing towards the sky.

It's late when we arrive. Just off the main road cutting through Wysowa-Zdrój, the grass is black where the *tserkva* used to stand, and covered in a fine white ash. Mikołaj jumps past the drystone wall enclosing the churchyard, and as I wait by the car, an eerie feeling of familiarity makes my nape prickle.

The lonely grey road making its way through the low hills,

the white houses nestling on the slopes, the dark needles of the pine trees. I try to picture how the church's shadow would have fallen on the valley, the sound of its bell in the early evening light. If I close my eyes, I can hear a brook rushing past through reeds and rocks.

If I close my eyes, I am in Frankenstein.

I'm climbing the tree in front of Martin's window; I'm coming up to the castle gate. There's a fallen tree in the forest, its roots splayed in the air like helpful fingers. I round the big red boulder. On my left the village lights shine through the mist like so many eyes looking at me—

—I cannot open my eyes, they are sealed shut, and squeezed so hard that my head hurts. I search my chest in a panic, because my legs won't move, and I know that Waldemar has driven a new stake through my heart—

—the eyes keep looking at me. I'm in the bailey, where we lit the candles and buried Petrus with a wreath of hair around his wrist. The ground shakes under my feet, the willow shudders, the gravestone jolts, but when I fall down, I look up and see that the sky too is shaking, the stars are falling and a cold snow starts to fall too—

—I can't move, I'm a painted statuette in a ceramic courtyard inside a snow globe. The glass above my head starts to crack—

"Ambrose, wake up!"

Mikołaj holds my shoulders, catches me when I fall, sobbing.

He is warm with the effort of salvaging the *tserkva* ashes; with his confidence in the possibility of a do-over. He is solid under my fingers; he's made of the earth and its elements, fire breathed through rock, water sprayed in the summer evening air. He is *here*.

I cannot stop myself. I push him against the church drystone, and circle him with my arms, and kiss him, and press myself so tight against him it feels like we share a single trunk, like we're joined in flesh, or I want us to be.

Mikołaj pulls away. "Not now, not so soon," he says, and with gentle movements takes me back to the car, my legs limp, my neck weak. He has to help me into my seat.

As we drive away, he fills the shaky silence inside with a story. He has many of them. He tells me that he was born not too far from here, in Krynica, where there are more health resorts than houses because of the springs. His family owned a small business there, selling mineral water that tasted like rotten eggs. He smiles, then becomes serious again. "We are deep into Lemko territory here," he says.

"What does it mean, *Lemko*?"

Lemkos were the people living in this region of the Carpathians, Mikołaj tells me. Like all people everywhere, they had a language, a religion. They had music and poetry, and art and architecture, like the *tserkva* that burned down, like the many other wooden *tserkvas* with their onion domes that still cling to this land. They had rituals, traditions. They lost everything after the war.

"Everyone lost everything *during* the war," Mikołaj says. "But the Lemkos lost everything *after*, when they should have been safe. Our government forced them away, relocated them in the north and in the west, gave this land to people with Polish blood. Operation Vistula, it was called. The Lemkos were uprooted, lost land and customs; they lost their churches. Other prayers started being sung inside. The gold-and-silver saints must have been so confused. If you have one, a faith is a terrible thing to lose, like a home. The Lemkos lost both in a day."

Outside the window, the first hint of dawn over the hills'

crest gives the valley a lithographic quality, broad black lines silhouetting roofs, barns, bridges, stands of yews. I think of Regina and the Baron, I think of Ludwig—they too have lost everything. I think of Martin and Mr Shorey. Then I think of myself, and think that perhaps I should count myself as the lucky one, because I still have something to lose.

☙

WE'VE STOPPED IN a *chata* to rest. I still have trouble travelling when the sun's out, and Mikołaj goes along with it. He's told me already that it will take practice, but he's sure that I can learn to appreciate the light in my own way, if I choose.

He shuts the blinds. His bed creaks when he gets in.

My mattress is too hard, the pillow too soft. I'm afraid of closing my eyes, afraid I'll be back inside the snow globe. Sleep doesn't come.

"Are you still awake?"

"Yes," Mikołaj says.

"Tell me another story."

There's a long silence in the room, broken only by the squeaking planks. A warm wind blows from the south, and the air inside the *chata* is muggy. When I think that Mikołaj has fallen asleep, he starts talking.

"Up in the north, not far from the Baltic Sea, there was a tower of red bricks. It was good friends with the Vistula, and since the river flows all the way through Poland, from Kraków in the south to Gdańsk in the far north, it always had something to tell the tower: gossip from the merchants who sailed its water, tales of knights and wars, news of discoveries. The tower loved to hear the river's stories and always asked for more, so the river started flowing closer to the tower, because it had many stories to tell. Closer and closer it flowed, until it started eroding the tower's foundations, and the tower started to lean towards the water. 'Stop, stop it,' said the tower. 'If you go on like this, I'll fall.' 'Fall, then,' the river said. *To ruń*, 'fall then'. That's what we still call the city with the tower, Toruń."

Mikołaj is standing above me. I didn't hear him get up, cross the room.

"Can I come closer?"

"Will I fall like the tower?"

"It did not fall in the end, the river wouldn't hurt his friend. I wouldn't either," he says, and comes into my bed.

He offers me his red blood. I offer him my pink one. When I slide between his legs, the room is dark, but he is bright. We burn, then are reborn.

∾

We are back in Warsaw. We are in Mikołaj's house in Saska Kępa, a quiet neighbourhood close to the ashery. The first time Mikołaj shows me the garden, I go and stand where I stood when I was a pelican and flew here from a burning ruin. I can feel the invisible trace my old self left on the grass, can catch the spoor of my old life, the dovecote in the tower, Agata's chewing tobacco. Memories can linger, persist. Prophesies even more so.

In Saska Kępa the streets are winding, uneven. They are lined with old villas spared by the war, their façades—brick, stucco, wood—often hidden by broadleaf lilacs, pink tamarisks, beeches. You can't hear the city from Saska Kępa, but sometimes you can hear the river, the distant cheers of people drinking *wódka* on the glass veranda of a bar somewhere along the water. The air always smells like autumn, even when it snows, as it does in the winter, perfectly formed crystal flakes falling from the blank sky like a shower of minuscule meteors.

Mikołaj is often away on Conservatory business. Sometimes I accompany him, but I've taken up my diaries again. I'm chronicling everything that has happened in the past year, and further back still, though I often hesitate narrating a particular event and leave the diary unattended for weeks on end. I've also started drawing new maps, though they are labyrinthine affairs: irregular, twisting geometries folding upon themselves; spirals that lead nowhere, resolve into tricks of perspective.

I feel the two are connected, the hesitation to write about certain things—my defective wings, my time on the operating table—and the warped geography of my maps. I'm a warren, my brain playing its old spider-and-hornet trick on me. But now I know spiders are not to be feared; I know they can build something beautiful. It takes time, and I try to allow myself just that, even though some days are harder than others.

On one such day, Mikołaj senses my restlessness. He gets up from the sofa where we're both sitting—he reading, I writing—and disappears into the kitchen. When he comes back, he is carrying a small saucepan and a pitcher of water.

"What is this?"

"A tradition of my people," he says. "It shows you the way."

He often talks about *his people*, and when he does, I'm never sure if he's talking about his country, his own family, or the Ash Conservatory. Sometimes the three seem indistinguishable to him, traditions handed down from his mother's line layering upon the myths of the land he grew up on and the peculiar tenets of his occupation at the Conservatory. A less intelligent person than he would be suspicious of these traditions, but he knows how to scalpel away the false encrustations of hearsay and superstition to get at the true kernel of these legends, these incantations that come from the earth—as he does. I keep thinking of him in these terms, as if he is a physical manifestation of land and river, of tree and hearth, of rock, of root.

Mikołaj puts the saucepan on the table in front of the sofa, pours the cold water inside, then stirs it with his finger. I can see a pale black shadow under the fingernail, where the soil of the Conservatory has resisted the soap. He nods at the water, then starts rummaging around the living room until, after some struggle inside a cupboard, he finds a tall, round candle.

"Your *pierdolety* are everywhere," he says. "I can't find anything."

"You couldn't find anything even before I moved in."

"That's true," he says.

His hands make a flourish in the air—like a magician's—and there's a key on his palm. A big, ancient, rusty key, with the shank as long as his outstretched hand, the bow so large you could fit an egg inside.

He switches off all the lights in the living room, save for the small black lamp sitting on the cupboard, which he moves until only the white wall behind him is lit. The corner where I'm sitting is dark now, and I feel like I'm in a magic parlour, watching a conjurer at his craft; or perhaps at the movies, when the screen is about to flick on, and you have no idea what it's going to show.

Mikołaj crouches down in front of the table, lights the candle.

"This ritual is called *lanie wosku*: candlemancy," he says. "It's officiated on the twenty-ninth of November, Saint Andrew's Eve, but I'm sure the forces that preside over it won't mind us doing it tonight."

"What do I do?"

"You look for your future in the shape the wax draws in the

water. Many claim you see the face of whom you love, but that's because nowadays the ritual is performed with this in mind, as if it's a game of spin the bottle. No, what you really see is a turn in the road ahead. It's different for everyone, but it is powerful—water and wax playing together, conjuring up a solid shape where there was just liquid. It's the fire's doing, it transforms."

"Like with ash," I say, and he nods.

When a pool of hot wax forms around the candle's flame, Mikołaj holds the key in his left hand, tilting the candle with the right one until wax starts to drip through the key's bow, down into the water.

There's a sizzle, and a clumpy flower blossoms at the centre of the saucepan, white tendrils like a squid's fanning out, then retracting towards the centre. The flower twirls around, as if moved by a secret current, but that's just the temperature, adjusting, regaining its balance. The petals are jagged, the anthers delicate like corals.

"I often wonder about the key," Mikołaj says, his voice low, far. "What does the fire see in the bow's empty O? Does it just feel the void, or is it something else, the absence of something that was, or should have been?" He takes the wax flower out of the water, looks at it. "Without fire," he says, "we would all be blind."

He raises the flower in the air between us, puts the candle in front of it, so its shadow falls on the wall behind, awash in the ghost-white light from the lamp.

"What do you see?"

At first, I don't see anything other than the flower's strange lumps projected onto the wall, its indented petals, the filaments, the stigma that almost looks like a tower, a single tower jutting out from the mass below. If I cock my head to the side, it calls to my mind a mountain—no, a hill, its side bristly with larches.

There's a road leading up the mountain, and a large stone boulder at the top of it, detached from it and yet still part of it. Leaning on the boulder, there is a castle, its windows arched and empty, and the tower stands out from it—

The tower crumbles away; the wax wasn't hard enough, or perhaps Mikołaj's fingers were warming it, making it soft like putty. The castle walls fall down, then the boulder, the trees, the road, until Mikołaj is holding a much smaller piece of wax, a polished piece shaped like a square, with something that resembles a lopsided triangle on top of it. Its shadow on the wall is clear enough.

I don't have to squint. I don't have to cock my head.

I know what I'm looking at.

"What do you see?" Mikołaj repeats.

I've found my castle after all, though it's not Castle Frankenstein, and it's not Ludwig's castle on the moon; it's not a castle at all.

"Home," I say.

LUDWIG

IN A MEMORY

THE DAY AFTER the King died, his ministers opened up Neuschwanstein to the public. They had to pay the debts somehow. They placed a cross in the lake where he died; every year someone puts a wreath upon it. There's a procession, but when it's over, the cross stands alone in the water until the flowers wilt, their petals falling into the lake. You can buy a Neuschwanstein snow globe cheap, these days.

AGATA

IN FRANKENSTEIN

I WRITE TO Agata. I tell her about Mikołaj, the Ash Conservatory. I tell her we will soon move south, where it's warmer, close to the sea. Mikołaj loves it. She writes back:

My dearest Father of Cups,

I knew about this, I saw it in the cards. I often pull one thinking of you, and it shows me where you are, what you are doing. I try to do this only once in a long while, because it would pain me if you thought I was prying, but I miss you, Ambrose, and sometimes curiosity and longing are too hard to resist, and I pick a tarot.

I saw you talking with ghosts. I saw you stumbling in the mist.

I saw you finding your Mother of Cups—we talked about this, remember? The last night you spent in Frankenstein.

Now I see the two of you searching for your river, and the water leads you south.

Will you stop by to say goodbye to your old friend?

I destroyed my old portrait. I cut it to pieces with Regina's greatsword, then burned it. I am sorry for the tiger cub. I remember holding her, feeling the strength of her muscles even though she was young, like I myself was. The paws were bigger than my hands. I couldn't look at the picture anymore.

My family never understood why I hated it so, and when I disappeared, I'm sure they were more puzzled by the portrait's absence than by mine. I hated it because the dress they had put me in was too tight, the jewels too heavy, because I knew it wasn't me they wanted the painter to immortalise—it was the daughter they would have wanted instead of me, the one they were forcing me to grow into. I took it with me when I left because one thing at least I recognised: the air of desperation that clung above the girl's head. It used to remind me of what I was running from, but when I looked at it now, I could think only of my second unhappy childhood, the one I spent under Regina's thumb.

Stabius is feeling better and better. I told him what happened with Doctor Hunger in London, when you went to visit him. I told him what his friend had done. He told me that Hunger's actions stemmed from a desire to do good, but I could see he didn't believe it anymore. He seldom talks about the Royal Diurnal Society, and never about the days in the operating theatre hidden away in the attic of Waldemar's church. (It was torn down, by the way, I was happy to see it gone.) I respect his silence because I see that he understands now—or is starting to—the spell he was under, the poisoning effect of the beliefs he was fed.

In many ways, our story is the same. It took me flying to the moon and back, almost dying while doing it, to see the madness of our conceit, thinking that paradise is a place you can storm. It took Stabius being humiliated by his peers, and almost dying because of it, to recognise the false axioms the men in his family had taught him, the violence they did to him by inducting him into the Society when he was still a little boy. Regina and Waldemar too, I've come to think, are not that different.

I see her, you know? Sometimes she's a shadow in a corridor, a rustling in the courtyard. Sometimes her white face floats in the darkness under the ceiling, looking at me as I play, or teach Stabius how to. I don't think she's looking for me, though. She searches only for you, and doesn't disturb us—unlike the Baron. He doesn't know his way inside the castle anymore. He's lost, but he often comes back, even three or four nights a week.

I'll tell you about the last one, yesterday.

We were walking in the bailey, looking at the Gallic roses we planted—they've grown, and are refulgent and odorous when the night is clear, and fretful when the wind comes in from the east.

A knocking came from the gate, and I could see that Stabius was scared.

He doesn't tell me, but I know he fears that one day what remains of the Royal Diurnal Society will find him, accuse him of treason, lock him up; or worse. He doesn't know that, even if they do, I wouldn't let them. I've faced them once, and I can do that again, with happiness in my heart, if it means protecting him.

Stabius approached the gate. "Who is it?" he asked.

261

"Let me in, I live in this castle! With her gone, I'm its lawful lord."

I let my voice be heard. "The crowing cock soon dispels you, shadow! Murderer!"

"Agata, that's you! Open the door! I've brought something for you, a peace offering. It's those flowers you like, the thornapples. They grow by the armful down here."

We didn't open it, and after knocking one more time, he was gone.

Today we've gone out, and on our doorstep found not flowers, but a bouquet of iron spikes, each one piercing a brown toad. I asked Stabius to burn them in the bailey—but far from Petrus' grave, because I didn't want their fetor to disturb his sleep.

He's going to try again, the Baron, whether it's his ghost or just a nightmare.

There are only nightmares left in Castle Frankenstein. And one hope.

It's been years since I've seen the sea. Would you have me and Stabius with you, when you move south? It is a lot to ask, with the tragic history between the two of you, but I cannot stay here any longer, and I cannot go back home—I doubt it even exists anymore.

My home now is with you, my friend, my Ambrose.

Yours, Agata

After I've finish reading her letter to Mikołaj, he says simply: "I've always wanted to see the castle."

ᠵᠤ

"So this is it," Mikołaj says.

We are standing behind the church, at the foot of the hill. On the top, Castle Frankenstein seems small—as small as a model castle. I know that its curtain walls are impressive, the sheer width of them, but the purple August sky dwarfs it, its imposing arched windows reduced to slits by the waning sunset light. The red boulder against which the castle stands has the opaque sheen of a round carnelian.

A gusty breeze makes the grass whistle. The whole hill trembles as if from the first autumn chill. A grove of alders just below the castle gate gather close together, sharing secrets with each other. I know their names, their leaves, their roots in the earth. Frankenstein hasn't changed; the Castle hasn't either.

We start up the hill.

"Did you like living here?" Mikołaj asks. He takes my hand.

It's a simple, straightforward question, that calls for a simple, straightforward answer, but I can't find it.

I think of my dovecote, Agata's room, the cards strewn on the carpet, the hidden gramophone. I think of all the hopes I cherished between the castle's walls, the warmth I found in the company of others like me when I had given up ever finding a true friend. I think of all that was good, and find I cannot remember what wasn't.

"I did," I say. "It was a good place to live—for a while."

"Do you regret going away?"

This is easy. I know this answer.

"No," I say, and even though sadness strangles my voice, it's true. "I had to go. I will always live in the castle, in some way, but I know the walls and the tower, the undercroft. Its geography is a map I've drawn many times already. It's time for me to draw something else."

A late chiffchaff warbles an old song as it flies above our heads, hurrying back to its nest. From deep within the forest that grows behind the castle a lonely nightingale sings his love lament. I think of Ludwig, on the lakeshore, listening for the sound of boats coming to his rescue.

A lump chokes my throat. I squeeze Mikołaj's hand tighter.

We are halfway up the hill when a figure emerges from the castle gate. Behind it, I can see chests and crates in the bailey, ready to be shipped south.

Agata waves at us, and I wave back.

AMBROSE

AT HOME

ONE EVENING A couple of months later, I am standing in front of the Bösendorfer.

Agata has placed it by the large window that looks onto the garden and, beyond that, the canal. Beside the music rack, there's the broken snow globe I gave her—the first one I found sitting before our gate, the first one Waldemar left us.

I visit her often—she and Tanner live just down the road from us—but this is the first time I've seen the broken globe, the miniature castle dusted over with black soot, the fake snowflakes grey and fewer than I remember. I wonder if it always sat there, on the piano, and it was I who didn't notice, or if it's a more recent addition; if Agata found it while unpacking an old box and decided to put it there.

"Why are you keeping it?" I say when I feel her presence behind me.

She still ties up her hair in a ponytail, though her nursing days are behind her. Her skin has the luminous, silky gloss of an

265

apple. She doesn't wear a ruff—I haven't seen her in one since we left Frankenstein together, the Bösendorfer loaded on a truck and our eyes clear and dry, because there was nothing left there for us to miss, save for Petrus' grave. But we have other ways of celebrating him.

"I don't want to forget," Agata says.

"Is there a chance you will?"

"I don't want to risk it. One does well to remember, even the bad. And—"

I hear the front door opening, two sets of steps coming in.

Mikołaj doesn't like Tanner, doesn't trust him yet, because of the role he played in my captivity at the hands of the Royal Diurnal Society. When we are all together, he never talks with him if he can do without. Sometimes I catch him rolling his eyes at something the other says. But he is making an effort, and I think Tanner would like to know more about the Conservatory. He often asks Mikołaj if he can accompany him when he goes on one of his retrieval missions, or out to search for new spiders to rebuild what was once lost. The Warsaw cluster passed on to another grower, Mikołaj is planting the seeds of a new one. The sun is warm here; the air salty. The spiders smell secrets sweeping in from far-away places, weave strange new marvels.

They stop in the kitchen before coming in. I hear the water running in the sink.

Agata's voice drops to a whisper. "Sometimes I think it wards him off, because he doesn't like the look of it any more than we do."

I know she's talking about the Baron. "Does his spirit still visit you?"

"Sometimes I dream I can hear him knocking, demanding to be let in, demanding to know where I've gone, because he can't find me on the moon, and he can't find me in the castle." She fingers the necklace that shines on her collarbone. She has taken one disc from her new wings and set it there, then destroyed the rest.

"Do you see Regina?" she says, her voice lower still.

"Sometimes," I say. "A flicker of red where there shouldn't be any."

I don't know if it's her ghost, or the shade of an old fear. Perhaps it's just her memory I see, but that can be an even more gruesome haunting.

Agata and I don't talk about it any more that day, but during the night I confide in Mikołaj. He comes home a week later with two bags, one filled with twigs he has fetched from the forest around the canal, and the other with swatches of coloured fabric, balls of cotton, ribbons.

That afternoon, we all meet in my study, and he explains what we have to do. It's another tradition, another ritual. Another one of the stories he tells me. I lean in to listen, like the old tower, but I don't fall. He always props me up. His stories are different from those I was used to, the ones Regina told us in the castle. They don't teach the illusion of perfection, they are not inert recreations. They allow for the possibility of change.

Marzanna, this story's called, and it has to do with seasons, their cycle; with winter thawing and spring shooting through the cold hard earth.

"Children would gather," Mikołaj says, emptying the contents of the two bags onto the carpet. "They would build effigies of Marzanna, dress them with strips of cloth, put ribbons on them, and dyed cotton to make the hair of the goddess that must be killed. They would sing as they did, then went out and walked through the streets chanting the name of Marzanna, dipping her in every puddle they crossed. The puppets could be as small as a toy, or as big as the real thing. It's time you do your Marzanna."

I've learned not to question these rites that I didn't know about before him, as I've learned not to question the spiders as they weave their lost architectures. Mikołaj is made of mysteries, as life is, and some things exist even if we don't have names for them, or reasons to explain them away. "You can ask about the *why*," Mikołaj is fond of saying, "as long as you don't forget to ask about the *how*." He always smiles when he says this. He is as sure of who he is as a birch is of its roots.

Agata and I sit down and start building our puppets: the twigs for the bodies, the scraps of fabric for the rest. She puts a swatch of black silk around the shoulders of hers—a cape—then glues some gold sequins onto the ball of cotton that stands for the Baron's face: his mask. I use black cotton for Regina's frock, and a bit of red gauze for her hair.

Mikołaj is somewhere around the house, I can hear his unhurried steps as he tends to his business, but Tanner is still in the room. He's thinner, his beard has grown. Listlessness often gives his face a curious look, as if he's trying too hard to remember something that slipped his mind.

I don't dislike him as Mikołaj does, nor do I distrust him, though Agata is always cautious not to leave the two of us alone in a room, because she knows I have questions, and she knows he's not ready to answer them. "Next week," she always tells me, when she catches me looking at him so. Weeks have turned into months, and sometimes I realise I've forgotten a question I had.

Now I gesture at the twigs, at the many ribbons we have left unused.

"Do you want to make a puppet too? You could make a Waldemar," I say, and sense Agata's fingers freezing in the air, as they did when Regina walked in on her playing Chopin at the Bösendorfer.

Tanner shakes his head. "I don't need to," he says. He looks at Agata, and there's something in his eyes as they find her across the room that dispels the shadows creeping above us. "She took care of him for me, and he's too scared to visit."

When we're done, Mikołaj leads us outside. The cobbled street in front of our house runs westwards towards town, but if you turn east it cuts through an open meadow until it reaches an old stone bridge. After that point, the road sheds its cobblestones, becomes a yellow track following the green-and-blue tongue of the canal as it winds through the countryside. The evening is alive with insects buzzing, the distant quacks of a mallard tending to her ducklings.

Mikołaj stops above the bridge's keystone.

"We are here," he says.

Agata looks around. "Are we going to light the bonfire here? Everyone will see us."

"We are not going to light the puppets on fire," Mikołaj says, shaking his head. "Fire would just change them, and we don't need it. We will drown Marzanna, she can't swim."

I lean over the parapet. The water of the canal is shallow, long dark weeds stretch in the direction the water is flowing, shielding the bottom from view. I look at my Regina of wood and cotton. The red gauze looks silly.

I throw the puppet down, and for a fleeting, fearful instant after it disappears below the lip of the bridge, I think she is going to rise up, fly away towards the moon. But I didn't give my puppet wings, and it sinks fast into the canal. The current tears the puppet away from the weeds, away from me.

The Baron follows Regina into the water, a little behind her, as the real one often was. He still hasn't caught up when the canal makes a sudden turn, and the two puppets disappear from our view.

I lean my head on Agata's shoulder, wrap my fingers around hers.

We keep looking at the water, forever flowing, forever pushing away the bad dreams.

We are still looking on when the last light drains out of the sky, the black fingers of night stretching above our heads. Tanner takes Agata's hand, leads her away—it's time for their practice at the Bösendorfer—but I stay a little longer, and Mikołaj stays with me, his arm around me. The tall pines that line the canal keep watch, so I don't have to anymore.

I don't realise I've closed my eyes until Mikołaj gives my arm a soft tug.

There are a couple of black swans swimming in the canal just below us, their necks regal and sinuous, their beaks red like small flames in the greying air. We can see their webbed feet paddling just below the surface. They are coming towards us from the curve in the canal, and soon they are near the bridge.

The swans don't look up at us as they pass under the stone arch, they keep on swimming, gliding on the water with the lightness of a vision. I wonder if they met Regina and the Baron on their way here, if they recognised their faces in the Marzannas the river is carrying away with it. The swans emerge from the other side of the bridge. It almost looks as if one of them is turning to greet us, before the flowing branches of a willow close around them.

They say that to encounter a black swan is a rarity.

Mikołaj and I saw two that night.

The Father of Cups. The Mother of Cups. Swimming together, away from swords.

❧

I DON'T KNOW if this is what you came to hear from me.

Perhaps you were only interested in the proceedings of the Royal Diurnal Society, of which I've been an unwilling participant; or you just wanted to know what came of them, whether they survived that fateful night in Frankenstein and continue to operate, and in what shape or form. Sometimes I think of writing to Mr Shorey, but I haven't got around to it just yet. I'm busy with the maps I draw. Maps of the Earth and the stars, forever shifting, forever changing, like a body does—like I do.

Perhaps it was my time under Regina's wing—no pun intended—that had you all ears, and eager to know more; or perhaps you are a scholar of the King, and thought I could provide a definitive answer as to what happened on the Starnberger See the night he died.

I don't know, but Ludwig's story is a sad story, and when I think of him in the water, I think that what happened matters less than the fact that he was there, under the pelting rain, alone. I like to think the boats were coming, they were just a moment too late.

It could also be that you wanted to know if there really is a castle on the moon, waiting for those of us with pink blood in our veins. I don't think there is, but I do not have any final evidence that can prove its existence, or dismantle the myth. What I can offer is this:

Why live your life as if there is a castle up there, when there's so much down here?

❧

THE LATE-AFTERNOON LIGHT is yellow and grainy, soft with the first hint of dusk. It streams in from the glass door leading to the garden, which I left ajar for the crêpe myrtle to breathe its fragrance in, mixed as it is with that of soil freshly disturbed.

Every night, before going to sleep, I leave a chicken heart outside this door. Manfred comes and goes as he pleases, as he did in Frankenstein, but in the morning I always find the heart gone. I think Manfred likes it here, and no mouse dares enter our garden.

The light draws an oblong rectangle on the carpet, and I stretch my feet across it to take in the last heat of the day. On the table beside my green armchair, a rose-painted calathea is closing her leaves against the incoming dark. I always smile at her fretfulness, kindred to mine, though of the opposite sign. We both struggle. I'm learning to tolerate the sunlight because Mikołaj loves it, to appreciate it even, but I'll always favour the night, just as the calathea favours the day. There is no derision in my smile, only brotherly understanding. We are in on the same joke.

I get up from my armchair, reach the desk, and lay down the map I've been drawing as of late: the map of all the canals which criss-cross the valley we live in. Mikołaj and I would like to see the black swans again—defy the odds. It wouldn't be the first time for us.

On the desk, between my rulers, the rolls of parchments, the bottles of coloured ink, I keep an orchid, purplish black, with pale yellow veins and a green heart. *Dracula vampira*—though it looks more like a monkey than a vampire.

It reminds me that it's not the chemistry of my brain, nor the biology of my pink moon blood, that counts; and it isn't what others make of them. It's what I do, the meaning I assign them, the meaning I assign to myself.

Like the maps I draw, like the *Dracula vampira*, like the silky sculptures of the Ash Conservatory, like the firmaments above our heads, meaning can—and will—change. And this is good.

I move the fine cotton drape aside and step outside into the garden.

Mikołaj is working on his yellowing tomatoes, his knees planted deep in the earth, his linen shirt billowing in the wind.

The sound of the Bösendorfer comes up from the house down the road.

I look in front of me.

The wall of the garden shed is gessoed white, the olive tree in front of it a faded grey and green—an old printing of a tree. There's the bright, clear blue of a pond, the pink of Mikołaj's shirt. The parrot tulips, our favourites, are finally opening.

ACKNOWLEDGEMENTS

I FIRST ENCOUNTERED King Ludwig II in *The Beast Within: A Gabriel Knight Mystery*, an adventure game masterfully written by Jane Jensen and published by Sierra On-Line in 1995. I still count it among the greatest videogames of all time, if not the very best, and it was the start of a life-long obsession with Ludwig.

This is a speculative novel, so of course the Ludwig who appears in these pages is a highly fictionalised version of the real king. However, in drawing him, I've relied both on the information I've amassed during my visits to Bavaria and on two biographies: *The Mad King* by Greg King (Aurum Press, London 1996) and especially *The Swan King* by Christopher McIntosh (Bloomsbury Academic, London 2019). It goes without saying that all inconsistencies, errors and liberties are entirely my own, though I hope I managed to do Ludwig's spirit and his memory some justice.

Three books were of great help to me when I was fleshing

out my vam-pires—though they do not like being called that: *Vampires, Burial & Death* by Paul Barber (Yale University Press, New Haven 2010); *The Penguin Book of the Undead*, edited by Scott G. Bruce (Penguin Classics, New York 2016); and *With Stake and Spade: Vampiric Diversity in Poland* by Łukasz Kozak (Adam Mickiewicz Institute, Warsaw 2020). The secret language spoken by the moon-kin is drawn from the old thieves' cant and especially from Polari, and for this I'm thankful to *Fabulosa!: The Story of Polari, Britain's Secret Gay Language* by Paul Baker (Reaktion Books, London 2019).

There's really a castle atop a hill in Frankenstein, in the Rhine region, but it only bears a superficial resemblance to the one I imagined here.

ℯ

I WILL ALWAYS owe a huge debt of gratitude to my brilliant agent Sandra Pareja, who fought for this book with teeth and nails. She is fierce, a powerhouse.

Daniel Carpenter is a dream editor to work with, ingenious and kind. He has a knack for finding the best secret pubs in London, and he got all the *Doctor Who* references I snuck into the novel, cherishing them all.

The rest of the team at Titan is equally stellar: thanks to Bahar Kutluk (another fellow *Whovian*), Katharine Carroll, Rachel Vincent, Isabelle Sinnott and Charlotte Kelly. Thank you also to Dan Coxon for his keen eye during the copyediting, and to Andy Ryan for the care he put into proofreading.

Thank you to all the authors who found the time and space to read this novel and decided, on top of that, to say something nice about it. It means a lot. I'm so lucky to be part of this community.

Over the years (and different drafts), some very dear friends read the novel, and I'm grateful to all of them for providing their insight and (more often than not) for reassuring and guiding me: Cristina Cecchi, Camilla Dubini and Claudia Durastanti. Thank you especially to Pier Vittorio Mannucci, who sat down with me one afternoon and helped me wrangle the savage beast that was Part II. And thank you to Pier Vittorio, Gledis Cinque, Martina Perotti and Alessandro Boggiani for taking me on a "Dracula Tour" of Transylvania in July 2023.

Thank you to my friend Kelly Farber, fellow Libra, fellow Vampire Weekend addict and clairvoyant nonpareil. Kelly's tarot readings—and the tarot deck she uses, *The Wild Unknown*—changed the character of Agata, and the book, for the better.

My husband, Bartosz Krawczyk, is funny, frankly handsome, and freakishly perceptive. He is also the most patient person I know. In the summer of 2022, I dragged him all around Germany in search of castles, ruins and graves, and he only *mildly* complained. He gave me the strength to cross the Marienbrücke—a very tall mountain bridge in front of Neueschwanstein—and held my hand, that day on the bridge and many other times, before and after. This book is for you, with love. Thank you.

ABOUT THE AUTHOR

ANDREA MORSTABILINI was born in Lodi, in the misty middle of the Po Valley, in Northern Italy. He studied Modern Literature at the University of Milan with a thesis on the Fantastic in late 19th century Italian literature. He (predictably) loves Gothic novels and architecture, the theatre, cats, and cemeteries. *A Blood as Bright as the Moon* is his English language debut. He also works as an editor. He lives in Milan, and sometimes Kraków, with his husband.

Andrea can be found at andreamortstabilini.com as well as on Instagram and BlueSky.

For more fantastic fiction, author events,
exclusive excerpts, competitions, limited editions and more

VISIT OUR WEBSITE
titanbooks.com

LIKE US ON FACEBOOK
facebook.com/titanbooks

FOLLOW US ON TWITTER AND INSTAGRAM
@TitanBooks

EMAIL US
readerfeedback@titanemail.com